W9-BNC-735

The Black Arrow

ROBERT LOUIS STEVENSON

DOVER PUBLICATIONS, INC.
Mineola, New York

At Dover Publications we're committed to producing books in an earth-friendly manner and to helping our customers make greener choices.

GREEN EDITION ®

Manufacturing books in the United States ensures compliance with strict environmental laws and eliminates the need for international freight shipping, a major contributor to global air pollution. And printing on recycled paper helps minimize our consumption of trees, water and fossil fuels.

The text of this book was printed on paper made with 10% post-consumer waste and the cover was printed on paper made with 10% post-consumer waste. At Dover, we use Environmental Paper Network's Paper Calculator to measure the benefits of these choices, including: the number of trees saved, gallons of water conserved, as well as air emissions and solid waste eliminated.

Courier Corporation, the manufacturer of this book, owns the Green Edition Trademark.

Please visit the product page for *The Black Arrow* at www.doverpublications.com to see a detailed account of the environmental savings we've achieved over the life of this book.

Editor's Note: When a footnote is preceded by an asterisk (*) or by a dagger (†), it was added to the Dover edition (2001), usually to define a word that would not be familiar to most modern readers, when the meaning of the word was not indicated specifically by the remainder of the sentence or paragraph. When a footnote is preceded by a number (¹), it was added by the author before the book was published originally in 1888 in England.

Bibliographical Note

This Dover edition, first published in 2001, is an unabridged, unaltered republication of a standard edition of the work originally published in 1888 by Cassell & Company Ltd., London.

Library of Congress Cataloging-in-Publication Data

Stevenson, Robert Louis, 1850–1894.
    The black arrow / Robert Louis Stevenson.
        p. cm.
    ISBN-13: 978-0-486-41820-9
    ISBN-10: 0-486-41820-0 (pbk.)
    1. Great Britain—History—Wars of the Roses, 1455–1485—Fiction. I. Title.

PR5484 .B3 2001
823'.8—dc21

2001033005

Manufactured in the United States by Courier Corporation
41820003
www.doverpublications.com

Contents

The Black Arrow

A Tale of the Two Roses

PROLOGUE

John Amend-All

ON A CERTAIN afternoon, in the late spring time, the bell upon Tunstall Moat House was heard ringing at an unaccustomed hour. Far and near, in the forest and in the fields along the river, people began to desert their labors and hurry toward the sound; and in Tunstall hamlet a group of poor country-folk stood wondering at the summons.

Tunstall hamlet at that period, in the reign of old King Henry VI, wore much the same appearance that it wears today. A score or so of houses, heavily framed with oak, stood scattered in a long green valley ascending from the river. At the foot, the road crossed a bridge, and mounting on the other side, disappeared into the fringes of the forest on its way to the Moat House, and farther forth to Holywood Abbey. Half-way up the village the church stood among yews. On every side the slopes were crowned and the view bounded by the green elms and greening oak-trees of the forest.

Hard by the bridge there was a stone cross upon a knoll, and here the group had collected—half a dozen women and one tall fellow in a russet smock—discussing what the bell betided. An express had gone through the hamlet half an hour before, and drunk a pot of ale in the saddle, not daring to dismount for the hurry of his errand; but he had been ignorant himself of what was forward, and only bore sealed letters from Sir Daniel Brackley to Sir

3

Oliver Oates, the parson, who kept the Moat House in the master's absence.

But now there was the noise of a horse; and soon, out of the edge of the wood and over the echoing bridge, there rode up young Master Richard Shelton, Sir Daniel's ward. He, at the least, would know, and they hailed him and begged him to explain. He drew bridle willingly enough—a young fellow not yet eighteen, sun-browned and gray-eyed, in a jacket of deer's leather, with a black velvet collar, a green hood upon his head, and a steel cross-bow at his back. The express, it appeared, had brought great news. A battle was impending. Sir Daniel had sent for every man who could draw a bow or carry a bill* to go post-haste to Kettley, under pain of his severe displeasure; but for whom they were to fight, or of where the battle was expected, Dick knew nothing. Sir Oliver would come shortly himself, and Bennet Hatch was arming at that moment, for he it was who should lead the party.

"It is the ruin of this kind land," a woman said. "If the barons live at war, plowfolk must eat roots."

"Nay," said Dick, "every man that follows shall have sixpence a day and archers twelve."

"If they live," returned the woman, "that may very well be; but how if they die, my master?"

"They cannot better die than for their natural lord," said Dick.

"No natural lord of mine," said the man in the smock. "I followed the Walsinghams; so we all did down Brierly way, till two years ago come Candlemas. And now I must side with Brackley! It was the law that did it; call ye that natural? But now, what with Sir Daniel and what with Sir Oliver—that knows more of law than honesty—I have no natural lord but poor King Harry the Sixt, God bless

---

*A weapon, based on a farm tool, with a metal spike and a double-edged hooked blade mounted on a pole.

him!—the poor innocent that cannot tell his right hand from his left."

"Ye speak with an ill tongue, friend," answered Dick, "to miscall your good master and my lord the king in the same libel. But King Harry—praise be the saints!—has come again into his right mind, and will have all things peaceably ordained. And as for Sir Daniel, y'are very brave behind his back. But I will be no tale-bearer; and let that suffice."

"I say no harm of you, Master Richard," returned the peasant. "Y'are a lad; but when ye come to a man's inches ye will find ye have an empty pocket. I say no more: the saints help Sir Daniel's neighbors, and the Blessed Maid protect his wards!"

"Clipsby," said Richard, "you speak what I cannot hear with honor. Sir Daniel is my good master and my guardian."

"Come, now, will ye read me a riddle?" returned Clipsby. "On whose side is Sir Daniel?"

"I know not," said Dick, coloring a little; for his guardian had changed sides continually in the troubles of that period, and every change had brought him some increase of fortune.

"Aye," returned Clipsby, "you, nor no man. For, indeed, he is one that goes to bed Lancaster and gets up York."

Just then the bridge rang under horse-shoe iron, and the party turned and saw Bennet Hatch come galloping—a brown-faced, grizzled fellow, heavy of hand and grim of mien, armed with sword and spear, a steel salet* on his head, a leather jack upon his body. He was a great man in these parts; Sir Daniel's right hand in peace and war, and at that time, by his master's interest, bailiff of the hundred.

"Clipsby," he shouted, "off to the Moat House, and send all other laggards the same gate. Bowyer will give you jack

---

*A rounded one-piece iron helmet that protected only the head and upper face, unless a visor was attached.

and salet. We must ride before curfew. Look to it: he that is last at the lych gate* Sir Daniel shall reward. Look to it right well! I know you for a man of naught. Nance," he added, to one of the women, "is old Appleyard up town?"

"I'll warrant you," replied the woman. "In his field for sure."

So the group dispersed, and while Clipsby walked leisurely over the bridge, Bennet and young Shelton rode up the road together, through the village and past the church.

"Ye will see the old shrew," said Bennet. "He will waste more time grumbling and prating of Harry the Fift than would serve a man to shoe a horse. And all because he has been to the French wars!"

The house to which they were bound was the last in the village, standing alone among lilacs; and beyond it, on three sides, there was open meadow rising toward the borders of the wood.

Hatch dismounted, threw his rein over the fence, and walked down the field, Dick keeping close at his elbow, to where the old soldier was digging, knee-deep in his cabbages, and now and again, in a cracked voice, singing a snatch of song. He was all dressed in leather, only his hood and tippet were of black frieze, and tied with scarlet; his face was like a walnut-shell, both for color and wrinkles; but his old gray eye was still clear enough, and his sight unabated. Perhaps he was deaf; perhaps he thought it unworthy of an old archer of Agincourt to pay any heed to such disturbances; but neither the surly notes of the alarm-bell, nor the near approach of Bennet and the lad, appeared at all to move him; and he continued obstinately digging, and piped up, very thin and shaky:

"Now, dear lady, if thy will be
I pray you that you will rue on me."

---

*A roofed churchyard gate under which the coffin was left at the start of a burial service.

"Nick Appleyard," said Hatch, "Sir Oliver commends him to you, and bids that ye shall come within this hour to the Moat House, there to take command."

The old fellow looked up.

"Save you, my masters!" he said, grinning. "And where goeth Master Hatch?"

"Master Hatch is off to Kettley, with every man that we can horse," returned Bennet. "There is a fight toward, it seems, and my lord stays a reënforcement."

"Aye, verily," returned Appleyard. "And what will ye leave me to garrison withal?"

"I leave you six good men, and Sir Oliver to boot," answered Hatch.

"It'll not hold the place," said Appleyard; "the number sufficeth not. It would take two score to make it good."

"Why, it's for that we came to you, old shrew!" replied the other. "Who else is there but you that could do aught in such a house with such a garrison?"

"Aye, when the pinch comes, ye remember the old shoe," returned Nick. "There is not a man of you can back a horse or hold a bill; and as for archery—Saint Michael! if old Harry the Fift were back again, he would stand and let ye shoot at him for a farthing a shoot!"

"Nay, Nick, there's some can draw a good bow yet," said Bennet.

"Draw a good bow!" cried Appleyard. "Yes! But who'll shoot me a good shoot? It's there the eye comes in, and the head between your shoulders. Now, what might you call a long shoot, Bennet Hatch?"

"Well," said Bennet, looking about him, "it would be a long shoot from here into the forest."

"Aye, it would be a longish shoot," said the old fellow, turning to look over his shoulder; and then he put up his hand over his eyes, and stood staring.

"Why, what are you looking at?" asked Bennet, with a chuckle. "Do you see Harry the Fift?"

The veteran continued looking up the hill in silence. The sun shone broadly over the shelving meadows; a few white sheep wandered browsing; all was still but the distant jangle of the bell.

"What is it, Appleyard?" asked Dick.

"Why, the birds," said Appleyard.

And, sure enough, over the top of the forest, where it ran down in a tongue among the meadows and ended in a pair of goodly green elms, about a bowshot from the field where they were standing, a flight of birds was skimming to and fro in evident disorder.

"What of the birds?" said Bennet.

"Aye!" returned Appleyard, "y'are a wise man to go to war, Master Bennet. Birds are a good sentry; in forest places they be the first line of battle. Look you, now, if we lay here in camp, there might be archers skulking down to get the wind of us; and here would you be, none the wiser!"

"Why, old shrew," said Hatch, "there be no men nearer us than Sir Daniel's, at Kettley; y'are as safe as in London Tower; and ye raise scares upon a man for a few chaffinches and sparrows!"

"Hear him!" grinned Appleyard. "How many a rogue would give his two crop ears to have a shoot at either of us! Saint Michael, man! they hate us like two polecats!"

"Well, sooth it is, they hate Sir Daniel," answered Hatch, a little sobered.

"Aye, they hate Sir Daniel, and they hate every man that serves with him," said Appleyard; "and in the first order of hating, they hate Bennet Hatch and old Nicholas the bowman. See ye here: if there was a stout fellow yonder in the wood-edge, and you and I stood fair for him—as, by Saint George, we stand!—which, think ye, would he choose?"

"You, for a good wager," answered Hatch.

"My surcoat to a leather belt, it would be you!" cried the old archer. "You burned Grimstone, Bennet—they'll ne'er forgive you that, my master. And as for me, I'll soon be in a good place, God grant, and out of bow-shoot—aye, and cannon-shoot—of all their malices. I am an old man, and draw fast to homeward, where the bed is ready. But for you, Bennet, y'are to remain behind here at your own peril, and if ye come to my years unhanged, the old true-blue English spirit will be dead."

"Y'are the shrewishest old bolt in Tunstall Forest," returned Hatch, visibly ruffled by these threats. "Get ye to your arms before Sir Oliver come, and leave prating for one good while. An ye had talked so much with Harry the Fift, his ears would ha' been richer than his pocket."

An arrow sang in the air, like a huge hornet; it struck old Appleyard between the shoulder-blades, and pierced him clean through, and he fell forward on his face among the cabbages. Hatch, with a broken cry, leaped into the air; then, stooping double, he ran for the cover of the house. And in the meanwhile Dick Shelton had dropped behind a lilac, and had his cross-bow bent and shouldered, covering the point of the forest.

Not a leaf stirred. The sheep were patiently browsing; the birds had settled. But there lay the old man, with a clothyard* arrow standing in his back; and there were Hatch holding to the gable, and Dick crouching and ready behind the lilac bush.

"D'ye see aught?" cried Hatch.

"Not a twig stirs," cried Dick.

"I think shame to leave him lying," said Bennet, coming forward once more with hesitating steps and a very pale countenance. "Keep a good eye on the wood, Master Shelton—keep a clear eye on the wood. The saints assoil us! here was a good shoot!"

Bennet raised the old archer on his knee. He was not yet dead; his face worked, and his eyes shut and opened like machinery, and he had a most horrible, ugly look of one in pain.

"Can ye hear, old Nick?" asked Hatch. "Have ye a last wish before ye wend, old brother?"

---

*The length of 37 inches, the Scottish "ell" measurement.

"Pluck out the shaft, and let me pass, a-Mary's name!" gasped Appleyard. "I be done with old England. Pluck it out!"

"Master Dick," said Bennet, "come hither, and pull me a good pull upon the arrow. He would fain pass, the poor sinner."

Dick laid down his cross-bow, and pulling hard upon the arrow, drew it forth. A gush of blood followed; the old archer scrambled half upon his feet, called once more upon the name of God, and then fell dead. Hatch, upon his knees among the cabbages, prayed fervently for the welfare of the passing spirit. But even as he prayed, it was plain that his mind was still divided, and he kept ever an eye upon the corner of the wood from which the shot had come. When he had done, he got to his feet again, drew off one of his mailed gauntlets, and wiped his pale face, which was all wet with terror.

"Aye," he said, "it'll be my turn next."

"Who hath done this, Bennet?" Richard asked, still holding the arrow in his hand.

"Nay, the saints know," said Hatch. "Here are a good two score Christian souls that we have hunted out of house and holding, he and I. He has paid his shot, poor shrew, nor will it be long, mayhap, ere I pay mine. Sir Daniel driveth overhard."

"This is a strange shaft," said the lad, looking at the arrow in his hand.

"Aye, by my faith!" cried Bennet. "Black, and black-feathered. Here is an ill-favored shaft, by my sooth! for black, they say, bodes burial. And here be words written. Wipe the blood away. What read ye?"

"'*Appulyaird fro Jon Amend-All,*'" read Shelton. "What should this betoken?"

"Nay, I like it not," returned the retainer, shaking his head. "John Amend-All! Here is a rogue's name for those that be up in the world! But why stand here to make a mark? Take him by the knees, good Master Shelton, while

I lift him by the shoulders, and let us lay him in his house. This will be a rare shog to poor Sir Oliver; he will turn paper-color; he will pray like a windmill."

They took up the old archer and carried him between them into his house, where he had dwelt alone. And there they laid him on the floor, out of regard for the mattress, and sought as best they might to straighten and compose his limbs.

Appleyard's house was clean and bare. There was a bed with a blue cover, a cupboard, a great chest, a pair of joint-stools, a hinged table in the chimney-corner, and hung upon the wall the old soldier's armory of bows and defensive armor. Hatch began to look about him curiously.

"Nick had money," he said. "He may have had three score pounds put by. I would I could light upon't! When ye lose an old friend, Master Richard, the best consolation is to heir him. See, now, this chest. I would go a mighty wager there is a bushel of gold therein. He had a strong hand to get, and a hard hand to keep withal, had Apple-yard the archer. Now may God rest his spirit! Near eighty years he was afoot and about, and ever getting; but now he's on the broad of his back, poor shrew, and no more lacketh; and if his chattels came to a good friend, he would be merrier, methinks, in heaven."

"Come, Hatch," said Dick, "respect his stone-blind eyes. Would ye rob the man before his body? Nay, he would walk!"

Hatch made several signs of the cross; but by this time his natural complexion had returned, and he was not easily to be dashed from any purpose. It would have gone hard with the chest had not the gate sounded, and presently after the door of the house opened and admitted a tall, portly, ruddy, black-eyed man of near fifty, in a surplice and black robe.

"Appleyard," the newcomer was saying, as he entered, but he stopped dead. "Ave Maria!" he cried. "Saints be our shield! What cheer is his?"

"Cold cheer with Appleyard, sir parson," answered Hatch, with perfect cheerfulness. "Shot at his own door, and alighteth even now at purgatory gates. Aye! there, if tales be true, he shall lack neither coal nor candle."

Sir Oliver groped his way to a joint-stool, and sat down upon it, sick and white.

"This is a judgment! Oh, a great stroke!" he sobbed and rattled off a leash of prayers.

Hatch meanwhile reverently doffed his salet and knelt down.

"Aye, Bennet," said the priest, somewhat recovering, "and what may this be? What enemy hath done this?"

"Here, Sir Oliver, is the arrow. See, it is written upon with words," said Dick.

"Nay," cried the priest, "this is a foul hearing! John Amend-All! A right Lollardy word. And black of hue, as for an omen! Sirs, this knave arrow likes me not. But it importeth rather to take counsel. Who should this be? Bethink you, Bennet. Of so many black ill-willers, which should he be that doth so hardly outface us? Simnel? I do much question it. The Walsinghams? Nay, they are not yet so broken; they still think to have the law over us, when times change. There was Simon Malmesbury, too. How think ye, Bennet?"

"What think ye, sir," returned Hatch, "of Ellis Duckworth?"

"Nay, Bennet, never. Nay, not he," said the priest. "There cometh never any rising, Bennet, from below—so all judicious chroniclers concord in their opinion; but rebellion traveleth ever downward from above; and when Dick, Tom, and Harry take them to their bills, look ever narrowly to see what lord is profited thereby. Now, Sir Daniel, having once more joined him to the Queen's party, is in ill odor with the Yorkist lords. Thence, Bennet, comes the blow—by what procuring, I yet seek; but therein lies the nerve of this discomfiture."

"An't please you, Sir Oliver," said Bennet, "the axles are

so hot in this country that I have long been smelling fire. So did this poor sinner, Appleyard. And, by your leave, men's spirits are so foully inclined to all of us, that it needs neither York nor Lancaster to spur them on. Hear my plain thoughts: You, that are a clerk, and Sir Daniel, that sails on any wind, ye have taken many men's goods, and beaten and hanged not a few. Y'are called to count for this; in the end, I wot not how, ye have ever the uppermost at law, and ye think all patched. But give me leave, Sir Oliver: the man that ye have dispossessed and beaten is but the angrier, and some day, when the black devil is by, he will up with his bow and clout me a yard of arrow through your inwards."

"Nay, Bennet, y'are in the wrong. Bennet, ye should be glad to be corrected," said Sir Oliver. "Y'are a prater, Bennet, a talker, a babbler, your mouth is wider than your two ears. Mend it, Bennet, mend it."

"Nay, I say no more. Have it as ye list," said the retainer.

The priest now rose from the stool, and from the writing-case that hung about his neck took forth wax and a taper, and a flint and steel. With these he sealed up the chest and the cupboard with Sir Daniel's arms, Hatch looking on disconsolate; and then the whole party proceeded, somewhat timorously, to sally from the house and get to horse.

"'Tis time we were on the road, Sir Oliver," said Hatch, as he held the priest's stirrup while he mounted.

"Aye; but, Bennet, things are changed," returned the parson. "There is now no Appleyard—rest his soul!—to keep the garrison. I shall keep you, Bennet. I must have a good man to rest me on in this day of black arrows. 'The arrow that flieth by day,' saith the evangel; I have no mind of the context; nay, I am a sluggard priest, I am too deep in men's affairs. Well, let us ride forth, Master Hatch. The jackmen should be at the church by now."

So they rode forward down the road, with the wind after them, blowing the tails of the parson's cloak; and behind them, as they went, clouds began to arise and blot out the sinking sun. They had passed three of the scattered houses that make up Tunstall hamlet, when, coming to a turn, they saw the church before them. Ten or a dozen houses clustered immediately round it; but to the back the churchyard was next the meadows. At the lych gate, near a score of men were gathered, some in the saddle, some standing by their horses' heads. They were variously armed and mounted; some with spears, some with bills, some with bows, and some bestriding plow-horses, still splashed with the mire of the furrow; for these were the very dregs of the country, and all the better men and the fair equipments were already with Sir Daniel in the field.

"We have not done amiss, praised be the cross of Holywood! Sir Daniel will be right well content," observed the priest, inwardly numbering the troop.

"Who goes? Stand! if ye be true!" shouted Bennet.

A man was seen slipping through the churchyard among the yews; and at the sound of this summons he discarded all concealment, and fairly took to his heels for the forest. The men at the gate, who had been hitherto unaware of the stranger's presence, woke and scattered. Those who had dismounted began scrambling into the saddle: the rest rode in pursuit; but they had to make the circuit of the consecrated ground, and it was plain their quarry would escape them. Hatch, roaring an oath, put his horse at the hedge, to head him off; but the beast refused, and sent his rider sprawling in the dust. And though he was up again in a moment, and had caught the bridle, the time had gone by, and the fugitive had gained too great a lead for any hope of capture.

The wisest of all had been Dick Shelton. Instead of starting in a vain pursuit, he had whipped his cross-bow from his back, bent it, and set a quarrel to the string; and now, when the others had desisted, he turned to Bennet, and asked if he should shoot.

"Shoot! shoot!" cried the priest, with sanguinary violence.

"Cover him, Master Dick," said Bennet. "Bring me him down like a ripe apple."

The fugitive was now within but a few leaps of safety; but this last part of the meadow ran very steeply up hill, and the man ran slower in proportion. What with the grayness of the falling night, and the uneven movements of the runner, it was no easy aim; and as Dick leveled his bow, he felt a kind of pity, and a half desire that he might miss. The quarrel sped.

The man stumbled and fell, and a great cheer arose from Hatch and the pursuers. But they were counting their corn before the harvest. The man fell lightly; he was lightly afoot again, turned and waved his cap in a bravado, and was out of sight next moment in the margin of the wood.

"And the plague go with him!" cried Bennet. "He has thieves' heels: he can run, by Saint Banbury! But you touched him, Master Shelton; he has stolen your quarrel, may he never have good I grudge him less!"

"Nay, but what made he by the church?" asked Sir Oliver. "I am shrewdly afeared there has been mischief here. Clipsby, good fellow, get ye down from your horse, and search thoroughly among the yews."

Clipsby was gone but a little while ere he returned, carrying a paper.

"This writing was pinned to the church door," he said, handing it to the parson. "I found naught else, sir parson."

"Now, by the power of Mother Church," cried Sir Oliver, "but this runs hard on sacrilege! For the king's good pleasure, or the lord of the manor—well! But that every run-the-hedge in a green jerkin should fasten papers to the chancel door—nay, it runs hard on sacrilege, hard; and men have burned for matters of less weight! But what have we here? The light falls apace. Good Master Richard, y'have young eyes. Read me, I pray, this libel."

Dick Shelton took the paper in his hand and read it aloud. It contained some lines of a very rugged doggerel, hardly ever riming, written in a gross character, and most uncouthly spelled. With the spelling somewhat bettered, this is how they ran:

I had four black arrows under my belt,
Four for the greefs that I have felt,

Four for the nomber of ill menne
That have oppressid me now and then.

One is gone; one is wele sped;
Old Apulyaird is ded.

One is for Maister Bennet Hatch,
That burned Grimstone, walls and thatch.

One for Sir Oliver Oates,
That cut Sir Harry Shelton's throat.

Sir Daniel, ye shull have the fourt;
We shull think it fair sport.
    Ye shull each have your own part,
    A blak arrow in each blak heart.
    Get ye to your knees for to pray:
    Ye are ded theeves, by yea and nay.

                JON AMEND-ALL,
                  of the Green Wood,
                  And his jolly fellaweship.

Item, we have mo arrowes and goode hempen cord for otheres of your following.

"Now, well-a-day for charity and the Christian graces!" cried Sir Oliver, lamentably. "Sirs, this is an ill world, and groweth daily worse. I will swear upon the cross of Holywood I am as innocent of that good knight's hurt, whether in act or purpose, as the babe unchristened. Neither was his throat cut; for therein they are again in error, as there still live credible witnesses to show."

"It boots not, sir parson," said Bennet. "Here is unseasonable talk."

"Nay, Master Bennet, not so. Keep ye in your due place, good Bennet," answered the priest. "I shall make my innocence appear. I will upon no consideration lose my poor life in error. I take all men to witness that I am clear of this matter. I was not even in the Moat House. I was sent of an errand before nine upon the clock——"

"Sir Oliver," said Hatch, interrupting, "since it please you not to stop this sermon, I will take other means. Goffe, sound to horse."

And while the tucket was sounding, Bennet moved close to the bewildered parson and whispered violently in his ear.

Dick Shelton saw the priest's eye turned upon him for an instant in a startled glance. He had some cause for thought; for this Sir Harry Shelton was his own natural father. But he said never a word and kept his countenance unmoved.

Hatch and Sir Oliver discussed together for a while their altered situation; ten men, it was decided between them, should be reserved, not only to garrison the Moat House but to escort the priest across the wood. In the meantime, as Bennet was to remain behind, the command of the reënforcement was given to Master Shelton. Indeed, there was no choice; the men were loutish fellows, dull and unskilled in war, while Dick was not only popular, but resolute and grave beyond his age. Although his youth had been spent in these rough country places, the lad had been well taught in letters by Sir Oliver, and Hatch himself had shown him the management of arms and the first principles of command. Bennet had always been kind and helpful; he was one of those who are cruel as the grave to those they call their enemies, but ruggedly faithful and well-willing to their friends; and now, while Sir Oliver entered the next house to write, in his swift, exquisite penmanship, a memorandum of the last occurrences to his master, Sir Daniel Brackley, Bennet came up to his pupil to wish him God-speed upon his enterprise.

"Ye must go the long way about, Master Shelton," he said; "round by the bridge, for your life! Keep a sure man fifty paces afore you, to draw shots; and go softly till y'are past the wood. If the rogues fall upon you, ride for't; ye will do naught by standing. And keep ever forward, Master Shelton; turn me not back again, an ye love your life; there is no help in Tunstall, mind ye that. And now, since ye go to the great wars about the king, and I continue to dwell here in extreme jeopardy of my life, and the saints alone can certify if we shall meet again below, I give you my last counsels now at your riding. Keep an eye on Sir Daniel; he is unsure. Put not your trust in the jack-priest; he intendeth not amiss, but doth the will of others; it is a hand-gun for Sir Daniel! Get you good lordship where ye go; make you strong friends; look to it. And think ever a paternoster-while on Bennet Hatch. There are worse rogues afoot than Bennet. So, God-speed!"

"And Heaven be with you, Bennet!" returned Dick. "Ye were a good friend to me-ward, and so I shall say ever."

"And, look ye, master," added Hatch, with a certain embarrassment, "if this Amend-All should get a shaft into me, ye might, mayhap, lay out a gold mark or mayhap a pound for my poor soul; for it is like to go stiff with me in purgatory."

"Ye shall have your will of it, Bennet," answered Dick. "But, what cheer, man! We shall meet again, where ye shall have more need of ale than masses."

"The saints so grant it, Master Dick!" returned the other. "But here comes Sir Oliver. An he were as quick with the long-bow as with the pen, he would be a brave man-at-arms."

Sir Oliver gave Dick a sealed packet, with this super-scription: "To my ryght worchypful master, Sir Daniel Brackley, knyght, be thys delyvered in haste."

And Dick, putting it in the bosom of his jacket, gave the word and set forth westward up the village.

BOOK I: THE TWO LADS

At the Sign of the Sun in Kettley

SIR DANIEL and his men lay in and about Kettley that night, warmly quartered and well patrolled. But the Knight of Tunstall was one who never rested from money-getting; and even now, when he was on the brink of an adventure which should make or mar him, he was up an hour after midnight to squeeze poor neighbors. He was one who trafficked greatly in disputed inheritances; it was his way to buy out the most unlikely claimant, and then, by the favor he curried with great lords about the king, procure unjust decisions in his favor; or, if that was too roundabout, to seize the disputed manor by force of arms and rely on his influence and Sir Oliver's cunning in the law to hold what he had snatched. Kettley was one such place; it had come very lately into his clutches; he still met with opposition from the tenants; and it was to overawe discontent that he had led his troops that way.

By two in the morning, Sir Daniel sat in the inn room, close by the fire-side, for it was cold at that hour among the fens of Kettley. By his elbow stood a pottle of spiced ale. He had taken off his visored headpiece and sat with his bald head and thin, dark visage resting on one hand, wrapped warmly in a sanguine-colored cloak. At the lower end of the room about a dozen of his men stood sentry over the door or lay asleep on benches; and, somewhat nearer hand, a young lad, apparently of twelve or thirteen, was stretched in a mantle on the floor. The host of the Sun stood before the great man.

"Now, mark me, mine host," Sir Daniel said, "follow but mine orders, and I shall be your good lord ever. I must have good men for head boroughs, and I will have Adam-a-More high constable; see to it narrowly. If other men be chosen, it shall avail you nothing; rather it shall be found to your sore cost. For those that have paid rent to Walsingham I shall take good measure—you among the rest, mine host."

"Good knight," said the host, "I will swear upon the cross of Holywood I did but pay to Walsingham under compulsion. Nay, bully knight, I love not the rogue Walsinghams; they were as poor as thieves, bully knight. Give me a great lord like you. Nay; ask me among the neighbors, I am stout for Brackley."

"It may be," said Sir Daniel, dryly. "Ye shall then pay twice."

The innkeeper made a horrid grimace; but this was a piece of bad luck that might readily befall a tenant in these unruly times, and he was perhaps glad to make his peace so easily.

"Bring up yon fellow, Selden!" cried the knight.

And one of his retainers led up a poor, cringing old man, as pale as a candle, and all shaking with the fen fever.

"Sirrah," said Sir Daniel, "your name?"

"An't please your worship," replied the man, "my name is Condall—Condall of Shoreby, at your good worship's pleasure."

"I have heard you ill reported on," returned the knight. "Ye deal in treason, rogue; ye trudge the country leasing; ye are heavily suspicioned of the death of severals. How, fellow, are ye so bold? But I will bring you down."

"Right honorable and my reverend lord," the man cried, "here is some hodge-podge, saving your good presence. I am but a poor private man and have hurt none."

"The under-sheriff did report of you most vilely," said the knight. "'Seize me,' saith he, 'that Tyndal of Shoreby.'"

"Condall, my good lord; Condall is my poor name," said the unfortunate.

"Condall or Tyndal, it is all one," replied Sir Daniel, coolly. "For, by my sooth, y'are here, and I do mightily suspect your honesty. If you would save your neck, write me swiftly an obligation for twenty pound."

"For twenty pound, my good lord!" cried Condall. "Here is midsummer madness! My whole estate amounteth not to seventy shillings."

"Condall or Tyndal," returned Sir Daniel, grinning, "I will run my peril of that loss. Write me down twenty, and when I have recovered all I may, I will be good lord to you and pardon you the rest."

"Alas! my good lord, it may not be; I have no skill to write," said Condall.

"Well-a-day!" returned the knight. "Here, then, is no remedy. Yet I would fain have spared you, Tyndal, had my conscience suffered. Selden, take me this old shrew softly to the nearest elm, and hang me him tenderly by the neck, where I may see him at my riding. Fare ye well, good Master Condall, dear Master Tyndal; y'are posthaste for Paradise; fare ye then well!"

"Nay, my right pleasant lord," replied Condall, forcing an obsequious smile, "an ye be so masterful, as doth right well become you, I will even, with all my poor skill, do your bidding."

"Friend," quoth Sir Daniel, "ye will now write two score. Go to! y'are too cunning for a livelihood of seventy shillings. Selden, see him write me this in good form, and have it duly witnessed."

And Sir Daniel, who was a very merry knight, none merrier in England, took a drink of his mulled ale and lay back smiling.

Meanwhile, the boy upon the floor began to stir and presently sat up and looked about him with a scare.

"Hither," said Sir Daniel; and as the other rose at his command and came slowly toward him, he leaned back and laughed outright. "By the rood!"* he cried, "a sturdy boy!"

---

*Cross or crucifix.

The lad flushed crimson with anger and darted a look of
hate out of his dark eyes. Now that he was on his legs, it
was more difficult to make certain of his age. His face
looked somewhat older in expression, but it was as
smooth as a young child's; and in bone and body he was
unusually slender and somewhat awkward of gait.

"Ye have called me, Sir Daniel," he said. "Was it to laugh
at my poor plight?"

"Nay, now, let laugh," said the knight. "Good shrew, let
laugh, I pray you. An ye could see yourself, I warrant ye
would laugh the first."

"Well," cried the lad, flushing, "ye shall answer this
when ye answer for the other. Laugh while yet ye may!"

"Nay, now, good cousin," replied Sir Daniel, with some
earnestness, "think not that I mock at you, except in
mirth, as between kinsfolk and singular friends. I will
make you a marriage of a thousand pounds, go to! and
cherish you exceedingly. I took you, indeed, roughly, as
the time demanded; but from henceforth I shall ungrudg-
ingly maintain and cheerfully serve you. Ye shall be Mrs.
Shelton—Lady Shelton, by my troth! for the lad promiseth
bravely. Tut! ye will not shy for honest laughter; it purgeth
melancholy. They are no rogues who laugh, good cousin.
Good mine host, lay me a meal now for my cousin, Master
John. Sit ye down, sweetheart, and eat."

"Nay," said Master John, "I will break no bread. Since ye
force me to this sin, I will fast for my soul's interest. But,
good mine host, I pray you of courtesy give me a cup of
fair water; I shall be much beholden to your courtesy
indeed."

"Ye shall have a dispensation, go to!" cried the knight.
"Shalt be well shriven, by my faith! Content you, then, and
eat."

But the lad was obstinate, drank a cup of water, and
once more wrapping himself closely in his mantle, sat in a
far corner brooding.

In an hour or two there rose a stir in the village, of sentries challenging and the clatter of arms and horses; and

then a troop drew up by the inn door, and Richard Shelton, splashed with mud, presented himself upon the threshold.

"Save you, Sir Daniel," he said.

"How! Dickie Shelton!" cried the knight; and at the mention of Dick's name the other lad looked curiously across. "What maketh Bennet Hatch?"

"Please you, sir knight, to take cognizance of this packet from Sir Oliver, wherein are all things fully stated," answered Richard, presenting the priest's letter. "And please you further, ye were best make all speed to Risingham; for on the way hither we encountered one riding furiously with letters, and by his report, my Lord of Risingham was sore bested, and lacked exceedingly your presence."

"How say you? Sore bested?" returned the knight. "Nay, then, we will make speed sitting down, good Richard. As the world goes in this poor realm of England, he that rides softliest rides surest. Delay, they say, begetteth peril; but it is rather this itch of doing that undoes men; mark it, Dick. But let me see, first, what cattle ye have brought. Selden, a link here at the door!"

And Sir Daniel strode forth into the village street, and by the red glow of a torch inspected his new troops. He was an unpopular neighbor and an unpopular master; but as a leader in war he was well beloved by those who rode behind his pennant. His dash, his proved courage, his forethought for the soldiers' comfort, even his rough gibes, were all to the taste of the bold blades in jack and salet.

"Nay, by the rood!" he cried, "what poor dogs are these? Here be some as crooked as a bow and some as lean as a spear. Friends, ye shall ride in the front of the battle; I can spare you, friends. Mark me this old villain on the piebald! A two-year mutton riding on a hog would look more soldierly! Ha! Clipsby, are ye there, old rat? Y'are a man I could lose with a good heart; ye shall go in front of all, with a bull's-eye painted on your jack, to be the better butt for archery; sirrah, ye shall show me the way."

"I will show you any way, Sir Daniel, but the way to change sides," returned Clipsby, sturdily.

Sir Daniel laughed a guffaw.

"Why, well said," he cried. "Hast a shrewd tongue in thy mouth, go to! I will forgive you for that merry word. Selden, see them fed, both man and brute."

The knight reëntered the inn.

"Now, friend Dick," he said, "fall to. Here is good ale and bacon. Eat, while that I read."

Sir Daniel opened the packet, and as he read his brow darkened. When he had done he sat a little, musing. Then he looked sharply at his ward.

"Dick," said he, "y'have seen this penny rime?"

The lad replied in the affirmative.

"It bears your father's name," continued the knight; "and our poor shrew of a parson is, by some mad soul, accused of slaying him."

"He did most eagerly deny it," answered Dick.

"He did?" cried the knight, very sharply. "Heed him not. He has a loose tongue; he babbles like a jack-sparrow. Some day, when I may find the leisure, Dick, I will myself more fully inform you of these matters. There was one Duckworth shrewdly blamed for it; but the times were troubled, and there was no justice to be got."

"It befell at the Moat House?" Dick ventured, with a beating at his heart.

"It befell between the Moat House and Holywood," replied Sir Daniel, calmly; but he shot a covert glance, black with suspicion, at Dick's face. "And now," added the knight, "speed you with your meal; ye shall return to Tunstall with a line from me."

Dick's face fell sorely.

"Prithee, Sir Daniel," he cried, "send one of the villains!*

---

*A villager or peasant of a specific feudal class (villein). The term, which comes from the Middle English and Middle French languages, does not mean a bad person or evildoer.

I beseech you let me to the battle. I can strike a stroke, I promise you."

"I misdoubt it not," replied Sir Daniel, sitting down to write. "But here, Dick, is no honor to be won. I lie in Kettley till I have sure tidings of the war, and then ride to join me with the conqueror. Cry not on cowardice; it is but wisdom, Dick; for this poor realm so tosseth with rebellion, and the king's name and custody so changeth hands, that no man may be certain of the morrow. Toss-pot and Shuttle-wit run in, but my Lord Good-Counsel sits o' one side, waiting."

With that, Sir Daniel, turning his back to Dick, and quite at the farther end of the long table, began to write his letter with his mouth on one side, for this business of the Black Arrow stuck sorely in his throat.

Meanwhile, young Shelton was going on heartily enough with his breakfast, when he felt a touch upon his arm, and a very soft voice whispering in his ear.

"Make not a sign, I do beseech you," said the voice, "but of your charity teach me the straight way to Holywood. Beseech you, now, good boy, comfort a poor soul in peril and extreme distress, and set me so far forth upon the way to my repose."

"Take the path by the windmill," answered Dick, in the same tone; "it will bring you to Till Ferry; there inquire again."

And without turning his head, he fell again to eating. But with the tail of his eye he caught a glimpse of the young lad called Master John stealthily creeping from the room.

"Why," thought Dick, "he is as young as I. 'Good boy' doth he call me? An I had known, I should have seen the varlet hanged ere I had told him. Well, if he goes through the fen, I may come up with him and pull his ears."

Half an hour later, Sir Daniel gave Dick the letter, and bade him speed to the Moat House. And again, some half an hour after Dick's departure, a messenger came in hot haste from my Lord Risingham.

"Sir Daniel," the messenger said, "ye lose great honor, by my sooth! The fight began again this morning ere the dawn, and we have beaten their van and scattered their right wing. Only the main battle standeth fast. An we had your fresh men, we should tilt them all into the river. What, sir knight! Will ye be the last? It stands not with your good credit."

"Nay," cried the knight, "I was but now upon the march. Selden, sound me the tucket. Sir, I am with you on the instant. It is not two hours since the more part of my command came in, sir messenger. What would ye have? Spurring is good meat, but yet it killed the charger. Bustle, boys!"

By this time the tucket was sounding cheerily in the morning, and from all sides Sir Daniel's men poured into the main street and formed before the inn. They had slept upon their arms, with chargers saddled, and in ten minutes five-score men-at-arms and archers, cleanly equipped and briskly disciplined, stood ranked and ready. The chief part were in Sir Daniel's livery, murrey* and blue, which gave the greater show to their array. The best armed rode first; and away out of sight, at the tail of the column, came the sorry reënforcement of the night before. Sir Daniel looked with pride along the line.

"Here be the lads to serve you in a pinch," he said.

"They are pretty men, indeed," replied the messenger. "It but augments my sorrow that ye had not marched the earlier."

"Well," said the knight, "what would ye? The beginning of a feast and the end of a fray, sir messenger"; and he mounted into his saddle. "Why! how now!" he cried. "John! Joanna! Nay, by the sacred rood! where is she? Host, where is that girl?"

"Girl, Sir Daniel?" cried the landlord. "Nay, sir, I saw no girl."

---

*Mulberry; that is, a purplish black.

"Boy, then, dotard!" cried the knight. "Could ye not see it was a wench? She in the murrey-colored mantle—she that broke her fast with water, rogue—where is she?"

"Nay, the saints bless us! Master John, ye called him," said the host. "Well, I thought none evil. He is gone. I saw him—her—I saw her in the stable a good hour agone; 'a was saddling a gray horse."

"Now, by the rood!" cried Sir Daniel, "the wench was worth five hundred pound to me and more."

"Sir knight," observed the messenger, with bitterness, "while that ye are here, roaring for five hundred pounds, the realm of England is elsewhere being lost and won."

"It is well said," replied Sir Daniel. "Selden, fall me out with six cross-bowmen; hunt me her down. I care not what it cost; but at my returning, let me find her at the Moat House. Be it upon your head. And now, sir messenger, we march."

And the troop broke into a good trot, and Selden and his six men were left behind upon the street of Kettley, with the staring villagers.

In the Fen

It was near six in the May morning when Dick began to ride down into the fen upon his homeward way. The sky was all blue; the jolly wind blew loud and steady; the windmill-sails were spinning; and the willows over all the fen rippling and whitening like a field of corn. He had been all night in the saddle, but his heart was good and his body sound, and he rode right merrily.

The path went down and down into the marsh, till he lost sight of all the neighboring landmarks but Kettley windmill on the knoll behind him and the extreme top of Tunstall Forest far before. On either hand there were great fields of blowing reeds and willows, pools of water shaking in the wind, and treacherous bogs as green as emerald to tempt and to betray the traveler. The path lay almost straight through the morass. It was already very ancient; its foundation had been laid by Roman soldiery; in the lapse of ages much of it had sunk, and every here and there, for a few hundred yards, it lay submerged below the stagnant waters of the fen.

About a mile from Kettley, Dick came to one such break in the plain line of causeway, where the reeds and willows grew dispersedly like little islands and confused the eye. The gap, besides, was more than usually long; it was a place where any stranger might come readily to mischief; and Dick bethought him, with something like a pang, of the lad whom he had so imperfectly directed. As for himself, one look backward to where the windmill-sails were turning black against the blue of heaven—one look forward to the high ground of Tunstall Forest, and he was sufficiently directed and held straight on, the water washing to his horse's knees, as safe as on a highway.

Half-way across, and when he had already sighted the path rising high and dry upon the farther side, he was aware of a great splashing on his right, and saw a gray horse, sunk to its belly in the mud, and still spasmodically struggling. Instantly, as though it had divined the neighborhood of help, the poor beast began to neigh most piercingly. It rolled, meanwhile, a blood-shot eye, insane with terror; and as it sprawled wallowing in the quag, clouds of stinging insects rose and buzzed about it in the air.

"Alack!" thought Dick, "can the poor lad have perished? There is his horse, for certain—a brave gray! Nay, comrade, if thou criest to me so piteously, I will do all man can to help thee. Shalt not lie there to drown by inches!"

And he made ready his cross-bow and put a quarrel through the creature's head.

Dick rode on after this act of rugged mercy, somewhat sobered in spirit and looking closely about him for any sign of his less happy predecessor in the way.

"I would I had dared to tell him further," he thought; "for I fear he has miscarried in the slough."

And just as he was so thinking, a voice cried upon his name from the causeway side, and looking over his shoulder, he saw the lad's face peering from a clump of reeds.

"Are ye there?" he said, reining in. "Ye lay so close among the reeds that I had passed you by. I saw your horse bemired and put him from his agony; which, by my sooth! an ye had been a more merciful rider, ye had done yourself. But come forth out of your hiding. Here be none to trouble you."

"Nay, good boy, I have no arms, nor skill to use them if I had," replied the other, stepping forth upon the pathway.

"Why call me 'boy'?" cried Dick. "Y'are not, I trow, the elder of us twain."

"Good Master Shelton," said the other, "prithee forgive me. I have none the least intention to offend. Rather I would in every way beseech your gentleness and favor, for I am now worse bested than ever, having lost my way, my cloak, and my poor horse. To have a riding-rod and spurs, and never a horse to sit upon! And before all," he added, looking ruefully upon his clothes—"before all, to be so sorrily besmirched!"

"Tut!" cried Dick. "Would ye mind a ducking? Blood of wound or dust of travel—that's a man's adornment."

"Nay, then, I like him better plain," observed the lad. "But, prithee, how shall I do? Prithee, good Master Richard, help me with your good counsel. If I come not safe to Holywood, I am undone."

"Nay," said Dick, dismounting, "I will give more than counsel. Take my horse, and I will run awhile, and when I am weary we shall change again, that so, riding and running, both may go the speedier."

So the change was made, and they went forward as briskly as they durst on the uneven causeway, Dick with his hand upon the other's knee.

"How call ye your name?" asked Dick.

"Call me John Matcham," replied the lad.

"And what make ye to Holywood?" Dick continued.

"I seek sanctuary from a man that would oppress me,"

was the answer. "The good Abbot of Holywood is a strong pillar to the weak."

"And how came ye with Sir Daniel, Master Matcham?" pursued Dick.

"Nay," cried the other, "by the abuse of force! He hath taken me by violence from my own place; dressed me in these weeds; ridden with me till my heart was sick; gibed me till I could 'a wept; and when certain of my friends pursued, thinking to have me back, claps me in the rear to stand their shot! I was even grazed in the right foot and walk but lamely. Nay, there shall come a day between us; he shall smart for all!"

"Would ye shoot at the moon with a hand-gun?" said Dick. "'Tis a valiant knight and hath a hand of iron. An he guessed I had made or meddled with your flight, it would go sore with me."

"Aye, poor boy," returned the other, "y'are his ward, I know it. By the same token, so am I, or so he saith; or else he hath bought my marriage—I wot not rightly which; but it is some handle to oppress me by."

"Boy again!" said Dick.

"Nay, then, shall I call you girl, good Richard?" asked Matcham.

"Never a girl for me," returned Dick. "I do abjure the crew of them!"

"Ye speak boyishly," said the other. "Ye think more of them than ye pretend."

"Not I," said Dick, stoutly. "They come not in my mind. A plague of them, say I! Give me to hunt and to fight and to feast, and to live with jolly foresters. I never heard of a maid yet that was for any service, save one only; and she, poor shrew, was burned for a witch and the wearing of men's clothes in spite of nature."

Master Matcham crossed himself with fervor and appeared to pray.

"What make ye?" Dick inquired.

"I pray for her spirit," answered the other with a somewhat troubled voice.

"For a witch's spirit?" Dick cried. "But pray for her, an ye list; she was the best wench in Europe, was this Joan of Arc. Old Appleyard the archer ran from her, he said, as if she had been Mahoun. Nay, she was a brave wench."

"Well, but, good Master Richard," resumed Matcham, "an ye like maids so little, y'are no true natural man; for God made them twain by intention, and brought true love into the world to be man's hope and woman's comfort."

"Faugh!" said Dick. "Y'are a milk-sopping baby, so to harp on women. An ye think I be no true man, get down upon the path, and whether at fists, backsword, or bow and arrow, I will prove my manhood on your body."

"Nay, I am no fighter," said Matcham, eagerly. "I meant no tittle of offence. I meant but pleasantry. And if I talk of women, it is because I heard ye were to marry."

"I to marry!" Dick exclaimed. "Well, it is the first I hear of it. And with whom was I to marry?"

"One Joan Sedley," replied Matcham, coloring. "It was Sir Daniel's doing; he hath money to gain upon both sides; and, indeed, I have heard the poor wench bemoaning herself pitifully of the match. It seems she is of your mind or else distasted to the bridegroom."

"Well! marriage is like death, it comes to all," said Dick, with resignation. "And she bemoaned herself? I pray ye now, see there how shuttle-witted are these girls: to bemoan herself before that she had seen me? Do I bemoan myself? Not I. An I be to marry, I will marry dry-eyed! but if ye know her, prithee, of what favor is she? fair or foul? And is she shrewish or pleasant?"

"Nay, what matters it?" said Matcham. "An y'are to marry, ye can but marry. What matters foul or fair? These be but toys. Y'are no milksop, Master Richard; ye will wed with dry eyes, anyhow."

"It is well said," replied Shelton. "Little I reck."

"Your lady wife is like to have a pleasant lord," said Matcham.

"She shall have the lord Heaven made her for," returned Dick. "I trow there be worse as well as better."

"Aye, the poor wench!" cried the other.

"And why so poor?" asked Dick.

"To wed a man of wood," replied his companion. "O me, for a wooden husband!"

"I think I be a man of wood, indeed," said Dick, "to trudge afoot the while you ride my horse; but it is good wood, I trow."

"Good Dick, forgive me," cried the other. "Nay, y'are the best heart in England; I but laughed. Forgive me now, sweet Dick."

"Nay, no fool words," returned Dick, a little embarrassed by his companion's warmth. "No harm is done. I am not touchy, praise the saints."

And at that moment the wind, which was blowing straight behind them as they went, brought them the rough flourish of Sir Daniel's trumpeter.

"Hark!" said Dick, "the tucket soundeth."

"Aye," said Matcham, "they have found my flight, and now I am unhorsed!" and he became pale as death.

"Nay, what cheer!" returned Dick. "Y'have a long start, and we are near the ferry. And it is I, methinks, that am unhorsed."

"Alack, I shall be taken!" cried the fugitive. "Dick, kind Dick, beseech ye help me but a little!"

"Why, now what aileth thee?" said Dick. "Methinks I help you very patently. But my heart is sorry for so spiritless a fellow! And see ye here, John Matcham—sith John Matcham is your name—I, Richard Shelton, tide that betideth, come what may, will see you safe in Holywood. The saints so do to me again if I default you. Come, pick me up a good heart, Sir Whiteface. The way betters here; spur me the horse. Go faster! faster! Nay, mind not for me; I can run like a deer."

So, with the horse trotting hard, and Dick running easily alongside, they crossed the remainder of the fen and came out upon the banks of the river by the ferryman's hut.

The Fen Ferry

The river Till was a wide, sluggish, clayey water, oozing out of fens, and in this part of its course it strained among some score of willow-covered, marshy islets.

It was a dingy stream: but upon this bright, spirited morning everything was become beautiful. The wind and the martins broke it up into innumerable dimples; and the reflection of the sky was scattered over all the surface in crumbs of smiling blue.

A creek ran up to meet the path, and close under the bank the ferryman's hut lay snugly. It was of wattle and clay, and the grass grew green upon the roof.

Dick went to the door and opened it. Within, upon a foul old russet cloak, the ferryman lay stretched and shivering; a great hulk of a man but lean and shaken by the country fever.

"Hey, Master Shelton," he said, "be ye for the ferry? Ill times, ill times! Look to yourself. There is a fellowship abroad. Ye were better turn round on your two heels and try the bridge."

"Nay; time's in the saddle," answered Dick. "Time will ride, Hugh Ferryman. I am hot in haste."

"A willful man!" returned the ferryman, rising. "An ye win safe to the Moat House, y'have done lucky; but I say no more." And then catching sight of Matcham, "Who be this?" he asked, as he paused, blinking, on the threshold of his cabin.

"It is my kinsman, Master Matcham," answered Dick.

"Give ye good day, good ferryman," said Matcham, who had dismounted and now came forward leading the horse. "Launch me your boat, I prithee; we are sore in haste."

The gaunt ferryman continued staring.

"By the mass!" he cried at length and laughed with open throat.

Matcham colored to his neck and winced; and Dick,

with an angry countenance, put his hand on the lout's shoulder.

"How now, churl!" he cried. "Fall to thy business, and leave mocking thy betters."

Hugh Ferryman grumblingly undid his boat, and shoved it a little forth into the deep water. Then Dick led in the horse, and Matcham followed.

"Ye be mortal small made, master," said Hugh, with a wide grin; "something o' the wrong model, belike. Nay, Master Shelton, I am for you," he added, getting to his oars. "A cat may look at a king. I did but take a shot of the eye at Master Matcham."

"Sirrah, no more words," said Dick. "Bend me your back."

They were by that time at the mouth of the creek, and the view opened up and down the river. Everywhere it was inclosed with islands. Clay banks were falling in, willows nodding, reeds waving, martins dipping and piping. There was no sign of man in the labyrinth of waters.

"My master," said the ferryman, keeping the boat steady with one oar, "I have a shrewd guess that John-a-Fenne is on the island. He bears me a black grudge to all Sir Daniel's. How if I turned me up stream and landed you an arrow-flight above the path? Ye were best not meddle with John Fenne."

"How, then? is he of this company?" asked Dick.

"Nay, mum is the word," said Hugh. "But I would go up water, Dick. How if Master Matcham came by an arrow?" and he laughed again.

"Be it so, Hugh," answered Dick.

"Look ye, then," pursued Hugh. "Sith it shall so be, unsling me your cross-bow—so; now make it ready—good; place me a quarrel. Aye, keep it so, and look upon me grimly."

"What meaneth this?" asked Dick.

"Why, my master, if I steal you across, it must be under force or fear," replied the ferryman; "for else, if John

Fenne got wind of it, he were like to prove my most distressful neighbor."

"Do these churls ride so roughly?" Dick inquired. "Do they command Sir Daniel's own ferry?"

"Nay," whispered the ferryman, winking. "Mark me! Sir Daniel shall down. His time is out. He shall down. Mum!" And he bent over his oars.

They pulled a long way up the river, turned the tail of an island, and came softly down a narrow channel next the opposite bank. Then Hugh held water in midstream.

"I must land here among the willows," he said.

"Here is no path but willow swamps and quagmires," answered Dick.

"Master Shelton," replied Hugh, "I dare not take ye nearer down, for your own sake now. He watcheth me the ferry, lying on his bow. All that go by and owe Sir Daniel good will, he shooteth down like rabbits. I heard him swear it by the rood. An I had not known you of old days—aye, and from so high upward—I would 'a' let you go on; but for old days' remembrance, and because ye had this toy with you that's not fit for wounds or warfare, I did risk my two poor ears to have you over whole. Content you; I can no more, on my salvation!"

Hugh was still speaking, lying on his oars, when there came a great shout from among the willows on the island, and sounds followed as of a strong man breasting roughly through the wood.

"A murrain!" cried Hugh. "He was on the upper island all the while!" He pulled straight for the shore. "Threat me with your bow, good Dick; threat me with it plain," he added. "I have tried to save your skins, save you mine!"

The boat ran into a tough thicket of willows with a crash. Matcham, pale, but steady and alert, at a sign from Dick, ran along the thwarts and leaped ashore; Dick, taking the horse by the bridle, sought to follow, but what with the animal's bulk, and what with the closeness of the thicket, both stuck fast. The horse neighed and trampled;

and the boat, which was swinging in an eddy, came on and off and pitched with violence.

"It may not be, Hugh; here is no landing," cried Dick; but he still struggled valiantly with the obstinate thicket and the startled animal.

A tall man appeared upon the shore of the island, a long-bow in his hand. Dick saw him for an instant, with the corner of his eye, bending the bow with a great effort, his face crimson with hurry.

"Who goes?" he shouted. "Hugh, who goes?"

"'Tis Master Shelton, John," replied the ferryman.

"Stand, Dick Shelton!" bawled the man upon the island. "Ye shall have no hurt, upon the rood! Stand! Back out, Hugh Ferryman."

Dick cried a taunting answer.

"Nay, then, ye shall go afoot," returned the man; and he let drive an arrow.

The horse, struck by the shaft, lashed out in agony and terror; the boat capsized, and next moment all were struggling in the eddies of the river.

When Dick came up, he was within a yard of the bank; and before his eyes were clear, his hand had closed on something firm and strong that instantly began to drag him forward. It was the riding-rod, that Matcham, crawling forth upon an overhanging willow, had opportunely thrust into his grasp.

"By the mass!" cried Dick as he was helped ashore, "that makes a life I owe you. I swim like a cannon ball." And he turned instantly toward the island.

Midway over, Hugh Ferryman was swimming with his upturned boat, while John-a-Fenne, furious at the ill-fortune of his shot, bawled at him to hurry.

"Come, Jack," said Shelton, "run for it! Ere Hugh can hale his barge across, or the pair of 'em can get it righted, we may be out of cry."

And adding example to his words, he began to run, dodging among the willows, and in marshy places leaping from tussock to tussock. He had no time to look for his direction; all he could do was to turn his back upon the river and put all his heart to running.

Presently, however, the ground began to rise, which showed him he was still in the right way, and soon after they came forth upon a slope of solid turf, where elms began to mingle with the willows.

But here Matcham, who had been dragging far into the rear, threw himself fairly down.

"Leave me, Dick!" he cried, pantingly; "I can no more."

Dick turned, and came back to where his companion lay.

"Nay, Jack, leave thee!" he cried. "That were a knave's trick, to be sure, when ye risked a shot and a ducking, aye, and a drowning too, to save my life. Drowning, in sooth; for why I did not pull you in along with me, the saints alone can tell!"

"Nay," said Matcham, "I would 'a' saved us both, good Dick, for I can swim."

"Can ye so?" cried Dick, with open eyes. It was the one manly accomplishment of which he was himself incapable. In the order of the things that he admired, next to having killed a man in single fight came swimming. "Well," he said, "here is a lesson to despise no man. I promised to care for you as far as Holywood, and, by the rood, Jack, y'are more capable to care for me."

"Well, Dick, we're friends now," said Matcham.

"Nay, I never was unfriends," answered Dick. "Y'are a brave lad in your way, albeit something of a milksop, too. I never met your like before this day. But, prithee, fetch back your breath, and let us on. Here is no place for chatter."

"My foot hurts shrewdly," said Matcham.

"Nay, I had forgot your foot," returned Dick. "Well, we must go the gentlier. I would I knew rightly where we were. I have clean lost the path; yet that may be for the better, too. An they watch the ferry, they watch the path, belike, as well. I would Sir Daniel were back with two-score men; he would sweep me these rascals as the wind sweeps leaves. Come, Jack, lean ye on my shoulder, ye poor shrew. Nay, y'are not tall enough. What age are ye, for a wager?—twelve?"

"Nay, I am sixteen," said Matcham.

"Y'are poorly grown to height then," answered Dick. "But take my hand. We shall go softly, never fear. I owe you a life; I am a good repayer, Jack, of good or evil."

They began to go forward up the slope.

"We must hit the road, early or late," continued Dick; "and then for a fresh start. By the mass! but y'ave a rickety hand, Jack. If I had a hand like that, I would think shame. I tell you," he went on, with a sudden chuckle, "I swear by the mass I believe Hugh Ferryman took you for a maid."

"Nay, never!" cried the other, coloring high.

"'A did, though, for a wager!" Dick exclaimed. "Small blame to him. Ye look liker maid than man; and I tell ye more—y'are a strange-looking rogue for a boy; but for a hussy, Jack, ye would be right fair—ye would. Ye would be well-favored for a wench."

"Well," said Matcham; "ye know right well that I am none."

"Nay, I know that; I do but jest," said Dick. "Ye'll be a man before your mother, Jack. What cheer, my bully! Ye shall strike shrewd strokes. Now, which, I marvel, of you or me, shall be first knighted, Jack? for knighted I shall be, or die for't. 'Sir Richard Shelton, Knight': it soundeth bravely. But 'Sir John Matcham' soundeth not amiss."

"Prithee, Dick, stop till I drink," said the other, pausing where a little clear spring welled out of the slope into a graveled basin no bigger than a pocket. "And O Dick, if I might come by anything to eat!—my very heart aches with hunger."

"Why, fool, did ye not eat at Kettley?" said Dick.

"I made a vow—it was a sin I had been led into," stammered Matcham; "but now, if it were but dry bread, I would eat it greedily."

"Sit ye, then, and eat," said Dick, "while that I scout a

little forward for the road." And he took a wallet from his girdle, wherein were bread and pieces of dry bacon, and, while Matcham fell heartily to, struck farther forth among the trees.

A little beyond there was a dip in the ground, where a streamlet soaked among dead leaves; and beyond that again the trees were better grown and stood wider, and oak and beech began to take the place of willow and elm. The continued tossing and pouring of the wind among the leaves sufficiently concealed the sounds of his footsteps on the mast; it was for the ear what a moonless night is to the eye; but for all that Dick went cautiously, slipping from one big trunk to another and looking sharply about him as he went. Suddenly a doe passed like a shadow through the underwood in front of him and he paused, disgusted at the chance. This part of the wood had been certainly deserted, but now that the poor deer had run, she was like a messenger he should have sent before him to announce his coming; and instead of pushing farther, he turned him to the nearest well-grown tree and rapidly began to climb.

Luck had served him well. The oak on which he had mounted was one of the tallest in that quarter of the wood and easily outtopped its neighbors by a fathom and a half; and when Dick had clambered into the topmost fork and clung there, swinging dizzily in the great wind, he saw behind him the whole fenny plain as far as Kettley, and the Till wandering among woody islets, and in front of him the white line of high-road winding through the forest. The boat had been righted—it was even now midway on the ferry. Beyond that there was no sign of man nor aught moving but the wind. He was about to descend, when, taking a last view, his eye lit upon a string of moving points about the middle of the fen. Plainly a small troop was threading the causeway, and that at a good pace; and this gave him some concern as he shinned vigorously down the trunk and returned across the wood for his companion.

A Greenwood Company

Matcham was well rested and revived; and the two lads, winged by what Dick had seen, hurried through the remainder of the outwood, crossed the road in safety, and began to mount into the high ground of Tunstall Forest. The trees grew more and more in groves with heathy places in between, sandy, gorsy, and dotted with old yews. The ground became more and more uneven, full of pits and hillocks. And with every step of the ascent the wind still blew the shriller, and the trees bent before the gusts like fishing-rods.

They had just entered one of the clearings when Dick suddenly clapped down upon his face among the brambles and began to crawl slowly backward toward the shelter of the grove. Matcham, in great bewilderment, for he could see no reason for this flight, still imitated his companion's course; and it was not until they had gained the harbor of a thicket that he turned and begged him to explain.

For all reply, Dick pointed with his finger.

At the far end of the clearing, a fir grew high above the neighboring wood and planted its black shock of foliage clear against the sky. For about fifty feet above the ground the trunk grew straight and solid like a column. At that level it split into two massive boughs; and in the fork, like a mast-headed seaman, there stood a man in a green tabard, spying far and wide. The sun glistened upon his hair; with one hand he shaded his eyes to look abroad, and he kept slowly rolling his head from side to side with the regularity of a machine.

The lads exchanged glances.

"Let us try to the left," said Dick. "We had near fallen foully, Jack."

Ten minutes afterwards they struck into a beaten path.

"Here is a piece of forest that I know not," Dick remarked. "Where goeth me this track?"

"Let us even try," said Matcham.

A few yards farther the path came to the top of a ridge

and began to go down abruptly into a cup-shaped hollow. At the foot, out of a thick wood of flowering hawthorn, two or three roofless gables, blackened as if by fire, and a single tall chimney marked the ruins of a house.

"What may this be?" whispered Matcham.

"Nay, by the mass, I know not," answered Dick. "I am all at sea. Let us go warily."

With beating hearts, they descended through the hawthorns. Here and there they passed signs of recent cultivation; fruit-trees and pot-herbs ran wild among the thicket; a sun-dial had fallen in the grass; it seemed they were treading what once had been a garden. Yet a little farther and they came forth before the ruins of the house.

It had been a pleasant mansion and a strong. A dry ditch was dug deep about it; but it was now choked with masonry and bridged by a fallen rafter. The two farther walls still stood, the sun shining through their empty windows; but the remainder of the building had collapsed and now lay in a great cairn of ruin, grimed with fire. Already in the interior a few plants were springing green among the chinks.

"Now I bethink me," whispered Dick, "this must be Grimstone. It was a hold of one Simon Malmesbury; Sir Daniel was his bane! 'Twas Bennet Hatch that burned it, now five years agone. In sooth, 'twas pity, for it was a fair house."

Down in the hollow where no wind blew it was both warm and still, and Matcham, laying one hand upon Dick's arm, held up a warning finger.

"Hist!" he said.

Then came a strange sound breaking on the quiet. It was twice repeated ere they recognized its nature. It was the sound of a big man clearing his throat; and just then a hoarse, untuneful voice broke into singing:

"Then up and spake the master, the king of the outlaws:
 'What make ye here, my merry men, among the greenwood
   shaws?'
And Gamelyn made answer—he looked never adown:
 'Oh, they must need to walk in wood that may not walk in
   town!'"

The singer paused, a faint click of iron followed and then silence.

The two lads stood looking at each other. Whoever he might be, their invisible neighbor was just beyond the ruin. And suddenly the color came into Matcham's face, and next moment he had crossed the fallen rafter and was climbing cautiously on the huge pile of lumber that filled the interior of the roofless house. Dick would have withheld him, had he been in time; as it was, he was fain to follow.

Right in the corner of the ruin, two rafters had fallen crosswise and protected a clear space no larger than a pew in church. Into this the lads silently lowered themselves. There they were perfectly concealed and through an arrow loophole commanded a view upon the farther side.

Peering through this, they were struck stiff with terror at their predicament. To retreat was impossible; they scarce dared to breathe. Upon the very margin of the ditch, not thirty feet from where they crouched, an iron caldron bubbled and steamed above a glowing fire; and close by, in an attitude of listening, as though he had caught some sound of their clambering among the ruins, a tall, red-faced, battered-looking man stood poised, an iron spoon in his right hand, a horn and a formidable dagger at his belt. Plainly this was the singer; plainly he had been stirring the caldron when some incautious step among the lumber had fallen upon his ear. A little farther off another man lay slumbering, rolled in a brown cloak, with a butterfly hovering above his face. All this was in a clearing white with daisies; and at the extreme verge a bow, a sheaf of arrows, and a part of a deer's carcass hung upon a flowering hawthorn.

Presently the fellow relaxed from his attitude of attention, raised the spoon to his mouth, tasted its contents, nodded, and then fell again to stirring and singing.

"'Oh, they must need to walk in wood that may not walk in town!'"

he croaked, taking up his song where he had left it.

"'O sir, we walk not here at all an evil thing to do,
But if we meet with the good king's deer to shoot a shaft into.'"

Still as he sang, he took from time to time another spoonful of the broth, blew upon it, and tasted it with all the airs of an experienced cook. At length, apparently, he judged the mess was ready, for taking the horn from his girdle he blew three modulated calls.

The other fellow awoke, rolled over, brushed away the butterfly, and looked about him.

"How now, brother?" he said. "Dinner?"

"Aye, sot," replied the cook, "dinner it is, and a dry dinner, too, with neither ale nor bread. But there is little pleasure in the greenwood now; time was when a good fellow could live here like a mitered abbot, set aside the rain and white frosts; he had his heart's desire both of ale and wine. But now are men's spirits dead, and this John Amend-All, save us and guard us! but a stuffed booby to scare crows withal."

"Nay," returned the other, "y'are too set on meat and drinking, Lawless. Bide ye a bit; the good time cometh."

"Look ye," returned the cook, "I have even waited for this good time sith that I was so high. I have been a gray friar; I have been a king's archer; I have been a shipman and sailed the salt seas; and I have been in greenwood before this, forsooth! and shot the king's deer. What cometh of it? Naught! I were better to have bided in the cloister. John Abbot availeth more than Amend-All. By'r Lady! here they come."

One after another, tall likely fellows began to stroll into the lawn. Each as he came produced a knife and a horn cup, helped himself from the caldron, and sat down upon the grass to eat. They were very variously equipped and armed; some in rusty smocks and with nothing but a knife and an old bow; others in the height of forest gallantry, all in Lincoln green, both hood and jerkin, with dainty peacock arrows in their belts, a horn upon a baldric, and a sword and dagger at their sides. They came in the silence of hunger and scarce growled a salutation but fell instantly to meat.

There were, perhaps, a score of them already gathered, when a sound of suppressed cheering arose close by among the hawthorns, and immediately after five or six woodmen carrying a stretcher debouched upon the lawn. A tall, lusty fellow, somewhat grizzled and as brown as a smoked ham, walked before them with an air of some authority, his bow at his back, a bright boar-spear in his hand.

"Lads!" he cried, "good fellows all and my right merry friends, y'have sung this while on a dry whistle and lived at little ease. But what said I ever? Abide Fortune constantly; she turneth, turneth swift. And lo! here is her firstling—even that good creature, ale!"

There was a murmur of applause as the bearers set down the stretcher and displayed a goodly cask.

"And now haste, ye boys," the man continued. "There is work toward. A handful of archers are but now come to the ferry; murrey and blue is their wear; they are our butts—they shall all taste arrows—no man of them shall struggle through this wood. For, lads, we are here some fifty strong, each man of us most foully wronged; for some they have lost lands, and some friends; and some have been outlawed—all oppressed! Who, then, hath done this evil? Sir Daniel, by the rood! Shall he then profit? shall he sit snug in our houses? shall he till our fields? shall he suck the bone he robbed us of? I trow not. He getteth him strength at law; he gaineth cases; nay, there is one case he shall not gain—I have a writ here at my belt that, please the saints, shall conquer him."

Lawless the cook was by this time already at his second horn of ale. He raised it as if to pledge the speaker.

"Master Ellis," he said, "y'are for vengeance—well it becometh you!—but your poor brother o' the greenwood, that had never lands to lose nor friends to think upon, looketh rather, for his poor part, to the profit of the thing.

He had liever a gold noble and a pottle of canary wine than all the vengeances in purgatory."

"Lawless," replied the other, "to reach the Moat House, Sir Daniel must pass the forest. We shall make that passage dearer, pardy, than any battle. Then, when he has got to earth with such ragged handful as escapeth us—all his great friends fallen and fled away, and none to give him aid—we shall beleaguer that old fox about, and great shall be the fall of him. 'Tis a fat buck; he will make a dinner for us all."

"Aye," returned Lawless, "I have eaten many of these dinners beforehand; but the cooking of them is hot work, good Master Ellis. And meanwhile what do we? We make black arrows, we write rimes, and we drink fair cold water, that discomfortable drink."

"Y'are untrue, Will Lawless. Ye still smell of the Gray Friars' buttery; greed is your undoing," answered Ellis. "We took twenty pounds from Appleyard. We took seven marks from the messenger last night. A day ago we had fifty from the merchant."

"And today," said one of the men, "I stopped a fat pardoner riding apace for Holywood. Here is his purse."

Ellis counted the contents.

"Five-score shillings!" he grumbled. "Fool, he had more in his sandal or stitched into the tippet. Y'are but a child, Tom Cuckow; ye have lost the fish."

But for all that Ellis pocketed the purse with nonchalance. He stood leaning on his boar-spear and looked round upon the rest. They, in various attitudes, took greedily of the venison pottage and liberally washed it down with ale. This was a good day; they were in luck; but business pressed, and they were speedy in their eating. The first comers had by this time even dispatched their dinner. Some lay down upon the grass and fell instantly asleep, like boa-constrictors; others talked together, or overhauled their weapons; and one, whose humor was particularly gay, holding forth an ale-horn, began to sing:

"Here is no law in good green shaw,
　　Here is no lack of meat;
'Tis merry and quiet, with deer for our diet,
　　In summer, when all is sweet.

"Come winter again, with wind and rain—
　　Come winter, with snow and sleet,
Get home to your places, with hoods on your faces,
　　And sit by the fire and eat."

All this while the two lads had listened and lain close;
only Richard had unslung his cross-bow and held ready in
one hand the windac, or grappling-iron, that he used to
bend it. Otherwise they had not dared to stir; and this
scene of forest life had gone on before their eyes like a
scene upon a theater. But now there came a strange interruption. The tall chimney which overtopped the remainder of the ruins rose right above their hiding place. There
came a whistle in the air and then a sounding smack, and
the fragments of a broken arrow fell about their ears.
Someone from the upper quarters of the wood, perhaps
the very sentinel they saw posted in the fir, had shot an
arrow at the chimney-top.

Matcham could not restrain a little cry, which he
instantly stifled, and even Dick started with surprise, and
dropped the windac from his fingers. But to the fellows on
the lawn this shaft was an expected signal. They were all
afoot together, tightening their belts, testing their bow-
strings, loosening sword and dagger in the sheath. Ellis
held up his hand; his face had suddenly assumed a look of
savage energy; the white of his eyes shone in his sun-
brown face.

"Lads," he said, "ye know your places. Let not one man's
soul escape you. Appleyard was a whet before a meal; but
now we go to table. I have three men whom I will bitterly
avenge—Harry Shelton, Simon Malmesbury, and"—striking his broad bosom—"and Ellis Duckworth, by the mass!"

Another man came, red with hurry, through the thorns.

"'Tis not Sir Daniel!" he replied. "They are but seven. Is the arrow gone?"

"It struck but now," replied Ellis.

"A murrain!" cried the messenger. "Methought I heard it whistle. And I go dinnerless!"

In the space of a minute, some running, some walking sharply, according as their stations were nearer or farther away, the men of the Black Arrow had all disappeared from the neighborhood of the ruined house; and the caldron, and the fire, which was now burning low, and the dead deer's carcass on the hawthorn, remained alone to testify they had been there.

"Bloody as the Hunter"

The lads lay quiet till the last footstep had melted on the wind. Then they arose, and with many an ache, for they were weary with constraint, clambered through the ruins and recrossed the ditch upon the rafter. Matcham had picked up the windac and went first, Dick following stiffly with his cross-bow on his arm.

"And now," said Matcham, "forth to Holywood."

"To Holywood!" cried Dick, "when good fellows stand shot? Not I! I would see you hanged first, Jack!"

"Ye would leave me, would ye?" Matcham asked.

"Aye, by my sooth!" returned Dick. "An I be not in time to warn these lads, I will go die with them. What! would ye have me leave my own men that I have lived among? I trow not! Give me my windac."

But there was nothing farther from Matcham's mind.

"Dick," he said, "ye sware before the saints that ye would see me safe to Holywood. Would ye be forsworn? Would you desert me—a perjurer?"

"Nay, I sware for the best," returned Dick. "I meant it too; but now! But look ye, Jack, turn again with me. Let me but warn these men, and, if needs must, stand shot with them; then shall all be clear, and I will on again to Holy-wood and purge mine oath."

"Ye but deride me," answered Matcham. "These men ye go to succor are the same that hunt me to my ruin."

Dick scratched his head.

"I cannot help it, Jack," he said. "Here is no remedy. What would ye? Ye run no great peril, man; and these are in the way of death. Death!" he added. "Think of it! What a murrain do ye keep me here for? Give me the windac. Saint George! shall they all die?"

"Richard Shelton," said Matcham, looking him squarely in the face, "would ye, then, join party with Sir Daniel? Have ye not ears? Heard ye not this Ellis, what he said? or have ye no heart for your own kindly blood and the father that men slew? 'Harry Shelton,' he said; and Sir Harry Shelton was your father, as the sun shines in heaven."

"What would ye?" Dick cried again. "Would ye have me credit thieves?"

"Nay, I have heard it before now," returned Matcham. "The fame goeth currently, it was Sir Daniel slew him. He slew him under oath; in his own house he shed the innocent blood. Heaven wearies for the avenging on't; and you—the man's son—ye go about to comfort and defend the murderer!"

"Jack," cried the lad, "I know not. It may be; what know I? But, see here: This man has bred me up and fostered me, and his men I have hunted with and played among; and to leave them in the hour of peril—O man, if I did that, I were stark dead to honor! Nay, Jack, ye would not ask it; ye would not wish me to be base."

"But your father, Dick?" said Matcham, somewhat wavering. "Your father? and your oath to me? Ye took the saints to witness."

"My father?" cried Shelton. "Nay, he would have me go! If Sir Daniel slew him, when the hour comes this hand shall slay Sir Daniel; but neither him nor his will I desert in peril. And for mine oath, good Jack, ye shall absolve me of it here. For the lives' sake of many men that hurt you not, and for mine honor, ye shall set me free."

"I, Dick? never!" returned Matcham. "An ye leave me, y'are forsworn, and so I shall declare it."

"My blood beats," said Dick. "Give me the windac! Give it me!"

"I'll not," said Matcham. "I'll save you in your teeth."

"Not?" cried Dick. "I'll make you!"

"Try it," said the other.

They stood, looking in each other's eyes, each ready for a spring. Then Dick leaped; and though Matcham turned instantly and fled, in two bounds he was overtaken, the windac was twisted from his grasp, he was thrown roughly to the ground, and Dick stood across him, flushed and menacing, with doubled fist. Matcham lay where he had fallen, with his face in the grass, not thinking of resistance.

Dick bent his bow.

"I'll teach you!" he cried fiercely. "Oath or no oath, ye may go hang for me."

And he turned and began to run. Matcham was on his feet at once and began running after him.

"What d'ye want?" cried Dick, stopping. "What make ye after me? Stand off!"

"I will follow an I please," said Matcham. "This wood is free to me."

"Stand back, by'r Lady!" retorted Dick, raising his bow.

"Ah, y'are a brave boy!" retorted Matcham. "Shoot!"

Dick lowered his weapon in some confusion.

"See here," he said. "Y'have done me ill enough. Go, then. Go your own way in fair wise; or, whether I will or not, I must even drive you to it."

"Well," said Matcham, doggedly, "y'are the stronger. Do your worst. I shall not leave to follow thee, Dick, unless thou makest me," he added.

Dick was almost beside himself. It went against his heart to beat a creature so defenseless; and, for the life of him, he knew no other way to rid himself of this unwelcome and, as he began to think, perhaps untrue companion.

"Y'are mad, I think," he cried. "Fool-fellow, I am hastening to your foes; as fast as foot can carry me, go I thither."

"I care not, Dick," replied the lad. "If y'are bound to die,

Dick, I'll die too. I would liever go with you to prison than to go free without you."

"Well," returned the other, "I may stand no longer prating. Follow me, if ye must; but if ye play me false, it shall but little advance you, mark ye that. Shalt have a quarrel in thine inwards, boy."

So saying, Dick took once more to his heels, keeping in the margin of the thicket and looking briskly about him as he went. At a good pace he rattled out of the dell and came again into the more open quarters of the wood. To the left a little eminence appeared, spotted with golden gorse and crowned with a black tuft of firs.

"I shall see from there," he thought, and struck for it across a heathy clearing.

He had gone but a few yards, when Matcham touched him on the arm and pointed. To the eastward of the summit there was a dip, and, as it were, a valley passing to the other side; the heath was not yet out; all the ground was rusty like an unscoured buckler, and dotted sparingly with yews; and there, one following another, Dick saw half a score green jerkins mounting the ascent, and marching at their head, conspicuous by his boar-spear, Ellis Duckworth in person. One after another gained the top, showed for a moment against the sky, and then dipped upon the farther side, until the last was gone.

Dick looked at Matcham with a kindlier eye.

"So y'are to be true to me, Jack?" he asked. "I thought ye were of the other party?"

Matcham began to sob.

"What cheer!" cried Dick. "Now the saints behold us! would ye snivel for a word?"

"Ye hurt me," sobbed Matcham. "Ye hurt me when ye threw me down. Y'are a coward to abuse your strength."

"Nay, that is fool's talk," said Dick, roughly. "Y'had no title to my windac, Master John. I would 'a' done right to have well basted you. If ye go with me, ye must obey me; and so, come."

Matcham had half a thought to stay behind; but, seeing

that Dick continued to scour full-tilt toward the eminence, and not so much as looking across his shoulder, he soon thought better of that, and began to run in turn. But the ground was very difficult and steep; Dick had already a long start, and had at any rate the lighter heels, and he had long since come to the summit, crawled forward through the firs, and ensconced himself in a thick tuft of gorse before Matcham, panting like a deer, rejoined him and lay down in silence by his side.

Below, in the bottom of a considerable valley, the short cut from Tunstall hamlet wound downward to the ferry. It was well beaten, and the eye followed it easily from point to point. Here it was bordered by open glades; there the forest closed upon it; every hundred yards it ran beside an ambush. Far down the path, the sun shone on seven steel salets, and from time to time, as the trees opened, Selden and his men could be seen riding briskly, still bent upon Sir Daniel's mission. The wind had somewhat fallen, but still tussled merrily with the trees, and, perhaps, had Appleyard been there, he would have drawn a warning from the troubled conduct of the birds.

"Now, mark," Dick whispered. "They be already well advanced into the wood; their safety lieth rather in continuing forward. But see ye where this wide glade runneth down before us, and in the midst of it, these two-score trees make like an island? There were their safety. An they but come sound as far as that, I will make shift to warn them. But my heart misgiveth me; they are but seven against so many, and they but carry cross-bows. The long-bow, Jack, will have the uppermost ever."

Meanwhile, Selden and his men still wound up the path, ignorant of their danger, and momently drew nearer hand. Once, indeed, they paused, drew into a group, and seemed to point and listen. But it was something from far away across the plain that had arrested their attention— a hollow growl of cannon that came from time to time upon the wind and told of the great battle. It was worth a thought, to be sure; for if the voice of the big guns were thus become audible in Tunstall Forest, the fight must have rolled ever eastward, and the day, by consequence, gone sore against Sir Daniel and the lords of the dark rose.

But presently the little troop began again to move forward, and came next to a very open, heathy portion of the way, where but a single tongue of forest ran down to join the road. They were but just abreast of this, when an arrow shone flying. One of the men threw up his arms, his horse reared, and both fell and struggled together in a mass. Even from where the boys lay they could hear the rumor of the men's voices crying out; they could see the startled horses prancing, and, presently, as the troop began to recover from their first surprise, one fellow beginning to dismount. A second arrow from somewhat farther glanced in a wide arch; a second rider bit the dust. The man who was dismounting lost hold upon the rein, and his horse fled galloping, and dragged him by the foot along the road, bumping from stone to stone, and battered by the fleeing hoofs. The four who still kept the saddle instantly broke and scattered; one wheeled and rode, shrieking, toward the ferry; the other three with loose rein and flying raiment came galloping up the road from Tunstall. From every clump they passed an arrow sped. Soon a horse fell, but the rider found his feet and continued to pursue his comrades till a second shot dispatched him. Another man fell; then another horse; out of the whole troop there was but one fellow left, and he on foot; only, in different directions, the noise of the galloping of three riderless horses was dying fast into the distance.

All this time not one of the assailants had for a moment shown himself. Here and there along the path, horse or man rolled, undispatched, in his agony; but no merciful enemy broke cover to put them from their pain.

The solitary survivor stood bewildered in the road beside his fallen charger. He had come the length of that broad glade, with the island of timber, pointed out by Dick. He was not, perhaps, five hundred yards from where the boys lay hidden; and they could see him plainly, looking to and fro in deadly expectation. But nothing came; and the man began to pluck up his courage and suddenly unslung and bent his bow. At the same time, by something in his action, Dick recognized Selden.

At this offer of resistance, from all about him in the covert of the woods there went up the sound of laughter. A score of men, at least, for this was the very thickest of the ambush, joined in this cruel and untimely mirth. Then an arrow glanced over Selden's shoulder; and he leaped and ran a little back. Another dart struck quivering at his heel. He made for the cover. A third shaft leaped out right in his face and fell short in front of him. And then the laughter was repeated loudly, rising and reëchoing from different thickets.

It was plain that his assailants were but baiting him, as men in those days baited the poor bull, or as the cat still trifles with the mouse. The skirmish was well over; farther down the road a fellow in green was already calmly gathering the arrows; and now, in the evil pleasure of their hearts, they gave themselves the spectacle of their poor fellow-sinner in his torture.

Selden began to understand; he uttered a roar of anger, shouldered his cross-bow and sent a quarrel at a venture into the wood. Chance favored him, for a slight cry responded. Then, throwing down his weapon, Selden began to run before him up the glade and almost in a straight line for Dick and Matcham.

The companions of the Black Arrow now began to shoot in earnest. But they were properly served; their chance had passed; most of them had now to shoot against the sun; and Selden, as he ran, bounded from side to side to baffle and deceive their aim. Best of all, by turning up the glade he had defeated their preparations; there were no marksmen posted higher up than the one whom he had just killed or wounded; and the confusion of the foresters' counsels soon became apparent. A whistle sounded thrice and then again twice. It was repeated from another quarter. The woods on either side became full of the sound of people bursting through the underwood; and a bewildered deer ran out into the open, stood for a second on three feet with nose in air and then plunged again into the thicket.

Selden still ran, bounding; ever and again an arrow followed him but still would miss. It began to appear as if he might escape. Dick had his bow armed, ready to support him; even Matcham, forgetful of his interest, took sides at heart for the poor fugitive; and both lads glowed and trembled in the ardor of their hearts.

He was within fifty yards of them, when an arrow struck him and he fell. He was up again, indeed, upon the instant; but now he ran staggering, and like a blind man turned aside from his direction.

Dick leaped to his feet and waved to him.

"Here!" he cried. "This way! here is help! Nay, run, fellow—run!"

But just then a second arrow struck Selden in the shoulder between the plates of his brigandine, and piercing through his jack brought him like a stone to earth.

"Oh, the poor heart!" cried Matcham, with clasped hands.

And Dick stood petrified upon the hill, a mark for archery.

Ten to one he had speedily been shot—for the foresters were furious with themselves, and taken unawares by Dick's appearance in the rear of their position—but instantly out of a quarter of the wood surprisingly near to the two lads, a stentorian voice arose, the voice of Ellis Duckworth.

"Hold!" it roared. "Shoot not! Take him alive! It is young Shelton—Harry's son."

And immediately after a shrill whistle sounded several times and was again taken up and repeated farther off. The whistle, it appeared, was John Amend-All's battle trumpet, by which he published his directions.

"Ah, foul fortune!" cried Dick. "We are undone. Swiftly, Jack, come swiftly!"

And the pair turned and ran back through the open pine clump that covered the summit of the hill.

To the Day's End

It was, indeed, high time for them to run. On every side the company of the Black Arrow was making for the hill. Some, being better runners or having open ground to run upon, had far outstripped the others and were already close upon the goal; some, following valleys, had spread out to right and left and outflanked the lads on either side.

Dick plunged into the nearest cover. It was a tall grove of oaks, firm under foot and clear of underbrush, and as it lay down hill, they made good speed. There followed next a piece of open, which Dick avoided, holding to his left. Two minutes after, and the same obstacle arising, the lads followed the same course. Thus it followed that, while the lads, bending continually to the left, drew nearer and nearer to the high-road and the river which they had crossed an hour or two before, the great bulk of their pursuers were leaning to the other hand and running toward Tunstall.

The lads paused to breathe. There was no sound of pursuit. Dick put his ear to the ground, and still there was nothing; but the wind, to be sure, still made a turmoil in the trees, and it was hard to make certain.

"On again!" said Dick; and tired as they were, Matcham limping with his injured foot, they pulled themselves together and once more pelted down the hill.

Three minutes later, they were breasting through a low thicket of evergreen. High overhead the tall trees made a continuous roof of foliage. It was a pillared grove as high as a cathedral, and except for the hollies among which the lads were struggling, open and smoothly swarded.

On the other side, pushing through the last fringe of evergreen, they blundered forth again into the open twilight of the grove.

"Stand!" cried a voice.

And there, between the huge stems, not fifty feet before them, they beheld a stout fellow in green, sore blown with running, who instantly drew an arrow to the head and covered them. Matcham stopped with a cry; but Dick, without a pause, ran straight upon the forester, drawing his dagger as he went on. The other, whether he was startled by the daring of the onslaught, or whether he was hampered by his orders, did not shoot: he stood wavering; and before he had time to come to himself, Dick bounded at his throat and sent him sprawling backward on the turf. The arrow went one way and the bow another with a sounding twang. The disarmed forester grappled his assailant; but the dagger shone and descended twice. Then came a couple of groans, and then Dick rose to his feet again, and the man lay motionless, stabbed to the heart.

"On!" said Dick; and he once more pelted forward, Matcham trailing in the rear. To say truth, they made but poor speed of it by now, laboring dismally as they ran and catching for their breath like fish. Matcham had a cruel stitch, and his head swam; and as for Dick, his knees were like lead. But they kept up the form of running with undiminished courage.

Presently they came to the end of the grove. It stopped abruptly; and there, a few yards before them, was the high-road from Risingham to Shoreby, lying at this point between two even walls of forest.

At the sight Dick paused; and as soon as he stopped running, he became aware of a confused noise which rapidly grew louder. It was at first like the rush of a very high gust of wind, but it soon became more definite and resolved itself into the galloping of horses; and then, in a flash, a whole company of men-at-arms came driving round the corner, swept before the lads, and were gone again upon the instant. They rode as for their lives, in complete disorder; some of them were wounded; riderless horses galloped at their side with bloody saddles. They were plainly fugitives from the great battle.

The noise of their passage had scarce begun to die away toward Shoreby before fresh hoofs came echoing in their wake, and another deserter clattered down the road; this time a single rider, and by his splendid armor a man of high degree. Close after him there followed several baggage-wagons, fleeing at an ungainly canter, the drivers flailing at the horses as if for life. These must have run early in the day; but their cowardice was not to save them. For just before they came abreast of where the lads stood wondering, a man in hacked armor and seemingly beside himself with fury overtook the wagons and with the truncheon of a sword began to cut the drivers down. Some leaped from their places and plunged into the wood; the others he sabered as they sat, cursing them the while for cowards in a voice that was scarce human.

All this time the noise in the distance had continued to increase; the rumble of carts, the clatter of horses, and cries of men, a great, confused rumor came swelling on the wind; and it was plain that the rout of a whole army was pouring like an inundation down the road.

Dick stood somber. He had meant to follow the highway till the turn for Holywood, and now he had to change his plan. But above all, he had recognized the colors of Earl Risingham, and he knew that the battle had gone finally against the rose of Lancaster. Had Sir Daniel joined, and was he now a fugitive and ruined? or had he deserted to the side of York, and was he forfeit to honor? It was an ugly choice.

"Come," he said, sternly; and, turning on his heel, he began to walk forward through the grove with Matcham limping in his rear.

For some time they continued to thread the forest in silence. It was now growing late; the sun was setting in the plain beyond Kettley; the tree-tops overhead glowed golden; but the shadows had begun to grow darker and the chill of the night to fall.

"If there was anything to eat!" cried Dick, suddenly, pausing as he spoke.

Matcham sat down and began to weep.

"Ye can weep for your own supper, but when it was to save men's lives, your heart was hard enough," said Dick, contemptuously. "Y'ave seven deaths upon your conscience, Master John; I'll ne'er forgive you that."

"Conscience!" cried Matcham, looking fiercely up. "Mine! And ye have the man's red blood upon your dagger! And wherefore did ye slay him, the poor soul? he drew his arrow, but he let not fly; he held you in his hand and spared you! 'Tis as brave to kill a kitten as a man that not defends himself."

Dick was struck dumb.

"I slew him fair. I ran me in upon his bow," he cried.

"It was a coward blow," returned Matcham. "Y'are but a lout and bully, Master Dick; ye but abuse advantages; let there come a stronger, we will see you truckle at his boot! Ye care not for vengeance, neither—for your father's death that goes unpaid, and his poor ghost that clamoreth for justice. But if there come but a poor creature in your hands that lacketh skill and strength and would befriend you, down she shall go!"

Dick was too furious to observe that "she."

"Marry!" he cried, "and here is news! Of any two the one will still be stronger. The better man throweth the worse, and the worse is well served. Ye deserve a belting, Master Matcham, for your ill-guidance and unthankfulness to meward; and what ye deserve ye shall have."

And Dick, who even in his angriest temper still preserved the appearance of composure, began to unbuckle his belt.

"Here shall be your supper," he said, grimly.

Matcham had stopped his tears; he was as white as a sheet, but he looked Dick steadily in the face and never moved. Dick took a step, swinging the belt. Then he

clumps of yew. And here they paused and looked upon each other.

"Y'are weary?" Dick said.

"Nay, I am so weary," answered Matcham, "that methinks I could lie down and die."

"I hear the chiding of a river," returned Dick. "Let us go so far forth, for I am sore athirst."

The ground sloped down gently, and sure enough, in the bottom they found a little murmuring river running among willows. Here they threw themselves down together by the brink; and putting their mouths to the level of a starry pool, they drank their fill.

"Dick," said Matcham, "it may not be. I can no more."

"I saw a pit as we came down," said Dick. "Let us lie down therein and sleep."

"Nay, but with all my heart!" cried Matcham.

The pit was sandy and dry; a shock of brambles hung upon one edge and made a partial shelter; and there the two lads lay down, keeping close together for the sake of warmth, their quarrel all forgotten. And soon sleep fell upon them like a cloud, and under the dew and stars they rested peacefully.

The Hooded Face

They awoke in the gray of the morning; the birds were not yet in full song, but twittered here and there among the woods; the sun was not yet up, but the eastern sky was barred with solemn colors. Half-starved and over-weary as they were, they lay without moving, sunk in a delightful lassitude. And as they thus lay, the clang of a bell fell suddenly upon their ears.

"A bell!" said Dick, sitting up. "Can we be, then, so near to Holywood?"

A little after, the bell clanged again, but this time somewhat nearer hand; and from that time forth, and still drawing nearer and nearer, it continued to sound brokenly abroad in the silence of the morning.

"Nay, what should this betoken?" said Dick, who was now broad awake.

"It is someone walking," returned Matcham, "and the bell tolleth ever as he moves."

"I see that well," said Dick. "But wherefore? What maketh he in Tunstall Woods? Jack," he added, "laugh at me an ye will, but I like not the hollow sound of it."

"Nay," said Matcham, with a shiver, "it hath a doleful note. An the day were not come——"

But just then the bell, quickening its pace, began to ring thick and hurried, and then it gave a single hammering jangle and was silent for a space.

"It is as though the bearer had run for a paternoster-while and then leaped the river," Dick observed.

"And now beginneth he again to pace soberly forward," added Matcham.

"Nay," returned Dick, "nay, not so soberly, Jack. 'Tis a man that walketh yon right speedily. 'Tis a man in some fear of his life or about some hurried business. See ye not how swift the beating draweth near?"

"It is now close by," said Matcham.

They were now on the edge of the pit; and as the pit itself was on a certain eminence, they commanded a view over the greater proportion of the clearing up to the thick woods that closed it in.

The daylight, which was very clear and gray, showed them a ribbon of white footpath wandering among the gorse. It passed some hundred yards from the pit and ran by the whole length of the clearing, east and west. By the line of its course, Dick judged it should lead more or less directly to the Moat House.

Upon this path, stepping forth from the margin of the wood, a white figure now appeared. It paused a little and seemed to look about; and then at a slow pace and bent almost double, it began to draw near across the heath. At every step the bell clanked. Face it had none; a white hood, not even pierced with eyeholes, veiled the head; and as the creature moved, it seemed to feel its way with the tapping of a stick. Fear fell upon the lads, as cold as death.

"A leper!" said Dick, hoarsely.

"His touch is death," said Matcham. "Let us run."

"Not so," returned Dick. "See ye not? He is stone-blind. He guideth him with a staff. Let us lie still; the wind bloweth toward the path, and he will go by and hurt us not. Alas, poor soul, and we should rather pity him!"

"I will pity him when he is by," replied Matcham.

The blind leper was now about half-way toward them, and just then the sun rose and shone full on his veiled face. He had been a tall man before he was bowed by his disgusting sickness, and even now he walked with a vigorous step. The dismal beating of his bell, the pattering of the stick, the eyeless screen before his countenance, and the knowledge that he was not only doomed to death and suffering but shut out forever from the touch of his fellowmen filled the lads' bosoms with dismay; and at every step that brought him nearer, their courage and strength seemed to desert them.

As he came about level with the pit, he paused and turned his face full upon the lads.

"Mary be my shield! He sees us!" said Matcham, faintly.

"Hush!" whispered Dick. "He doth but hearken. He is blind, fool!"

The leper looked or listened, whichever he was really doing, for some seconds. Then he began to move on again but presently paused once more and again turned and seemed to gaze upon the lads. Even Dick became dead-white and closed his eyes, as if by the mere sight he might become infected. But soon the bell sounded, and this time, without any further hesitation, the leper crossed the remainder of the little heath and disappeared into the covert of the woods.

"He saw us," said Matcham. "I could swear it!"

"Tut!" returned Dick, recovering some sparks of

courage. "He but heard us. He was in fear, poor soul! An ye were blind and walked in a perpetual night, ye would start yourself, if ever a twig rustled or a bird cried 'Peep.'"

"Dick, good Dick, he saw us," repeated Matcham. "When a man hearkeneth, he doth not as this man; he doth otherwise, Dick. This was seeing; it was not hearing. He means foully. Hark, else, if his bell be not stopped!"

Such was the case. The bell rang no longer.

"Nay," said Dick, "I like not that. Nay," he cried again, "I like that little. What may this betoken? Let us go, by the mass!"

"He hath gone east," added Matcham. "Good Dick, let us go westward straight. I shall not breathe till I have my back turned upon that leper."

"Jack, y'are too cowardly," replied Dick. "We shall go fair for Holywood, or as fair, at least, as I can guide you, and that will be due north."

They were afoot at once, passed the stream upon some stepping-stones, and began to mount on the other side, which was steeper, toward the margin of the wood. The ground became very uneven, full of knolls and hollows; trees grew scattered or in clumps; it became difficult to choose a path, and the lads somewhat wandered. They were weary besides with yesterday's exertions and the lack of food, and they moved but heavily and dragged their feet among the sand.

Presently, coming to the top of a knoll, they were aware of the leper, some hundred feet in front of them, crossing the line of their march by a hollow. His bell was silent, his staff no longer tapped the ground, and he went before him with the swift and assured footsteps of a man who sees. Next moment he had disappeared into a little thicket.

The lads, at the first glimpse, had crouched behind a tuft of gorse; there they lay, horror-struck

"Certain, he pursueth us," said Dick, "certain. He held the clapper of his bell in one hand, saw ye? that it should not sound. Now may the saints aid and guide us, for I have no strength to combat pestilence!"

"What maketh he?" cried Matcham. "What doth he

want? Who ever heard the like, that a leper, out of mere malice, should pursue unfortunates? Hath he not his bell to that very end, that people may avoid him? Dick, there is below this something deeper."

"Nay, I care not," moaned Dick; "the strength is gone out of me; my legs are like water. The saints be mine assistance!"

"Would ye lie there idle?" cried Matcham. "Let us back into the open. We have the better chance; he cannot steal upon us unawares."

"Not I," said Dick. "My time is come; and peradventure he may pass us by."

"Bend me, then, your bow!" cried the other. "What! will ye be a man?"

Dick crossed himself. "Would ye have me shoot upon a leper?" he cried. "The hand would fail me. Nay, now," he added, "nay, now, let be! With sound men I will fight, but not with ghosts and lepers. Which this is, I wot not. One or other, Heaven be our protection!"

"Now," said Matcham, "if this be man's courage, what a poor thing is man! But sith ye will do naught, let us lie close."

Then came a single, broken jangle on the bell.

"He hath missed his hold upon the clapper," whispered Matcham. "Saints! how near he is!"

But Dick answered never a word; his teeth were near chattering.

Soon they saw a piece of the white robe between some bushes; then the leper's head was thrust forth from behind a trunk, and he seemed narrowly to scan the neighborhood before he once again withdrew. To their stretched senses the whole bush appeared alive with rustlings and the creak of twigs; and they heard the beating of each other's heart.

Suddenly, with a cry, the leper sprang into the open close by and ran straight upon the lads. They, shrieking aloud, separated and began to run different ways. But their horrible enemy fastened upon Matcham, ran him swiftly down, and had him almost instantly a prisoner. The lad gave one scream that echoed high and far over the forest, he had one spasm of struggling, and then all his limbs relaxed, and he fell limp into his captor's arms.

Dick heard the cry and turned. He saw Matcham fall; and on the instant his spirit and his strength revived. With a cry of pity and anger, he unslung and bent his arblast. But ere he had time to shoot, the leper held up his hand.

"Hold your shot, Dickon!" cried a familiar voice. "Hold your shot, mad wag! Know ye not a friend?"

And then laying down Matcham on the turf, he undid the hood from off his face and disclosed the features of Sir Daniel Brackley.

"Sir Daniel!" cried Dick.

"Aye, by the mass, Sir Daniel!" returned the knight. "Would ye shoot your guardian, rogue? But here is this ——" And here he broke off, and pointing to Matcham, asked, "How call ye him, Dick?"

"Nay," said Dick, "I call him Master Matcham. Know ye him not? He said ye knew him!"

"Aye," replied Sir Daniel, "I know the lad"; and he chuckled. "But he has fainted; and, by my sooth, he might have had less to faint for. Hey, Dick? Did I put the fear of death upon you?"

"Indeed, Sir Daniel, ye did that," said Dick, and sighed again at the mere recollection. "Nay, sir, saving your respect, I had as lief 'a' met the devil in person; and to speak the truth, I am yet all a-quake. But what made ye, sir, in such a guise?"

Sir Daniel's brow grew suddenly black with anger.

"What made I?" he said. "Ye do well to mind me of it! What? I skulked for my poor life in my own wood of Tunstall, Dick. We were ill sped at the battle; we but got there to be swept among the rout. Where be all my good men-at-arms? Dick, by the mass, I know not! We were swept down; the shot fell thick among us; I have not seen one man in my own colors since I saw three fall. For myself, I came sound to Shoreby, and being mindful of the Black Arrow, got me this gown and bell, and came softly by the path for the Moat House. There is no disguise to be compared with it, the jingle of this bell would scare me the stoutest outlaw in the forest; they would all turn pale to hear it. At length I came by you and Matcham. I could see but evilly through this same hood and was not sure of you, being chiefly, and for many a good cause, astonished at the finding you together. Moreover, in the open, where I had to go slowly and tap with my staff, I feared to disclose myself. But see," he added, "this poor shrew begins a little to revive. A little good canary will comfort the heart of it."

The knight from under his long dress produced a stout bottle and began to rub the temples and wet the lips of the patient, who returned gradually to consciousness and began to roll dim eyes from one to another.

"What cheer, Jack!" said Dick. "It was no leper, after all; it was Sir Daniel! See!"

"Swallow me a good draught of this," said the knight. "This will give you manhood. Thereafter, I will give you both a meal, and we shall all three on to Tunstall. For, Dick," he continued, laying forth bread and meat upon the grass, "I will avow to you, in all good conscience, it irks me sorely to be safe between four walls. Not since I backed a horse have I been pressed so hard; peril of life, jeopardy of land and livelihood, and to sum up, all these losels in the wood to hunt me down. But I be not yet shent. Some of my lads will pick me their way home. Hatch hath ten fellows; Selden, he had six. Nay, we shall soon be strong again; and if I can but buy my peace with my right fortunate and undeserving Lord of York, why, Dick, we'll be a man again and go a-horseback!"

And so saying, the knight filled himself a horn of canary and pledged his ward in dumb show.

"Selden," Dick faltered, "Selden——" And he paused again.

Sir Daniel put down the wine untasted.

"How!" he cried, in a changed voice. "Selden? Speak! What of Selden?"

Dick stammered forth the tale of the ambush and the massacre.

The knight heard in silence; but as he listened his countenance became convulsed with rage and grief.

"Now here," he cried, "on my right hand I swear to avenge it! If that I fail, if that I spill not ten men's souls for each, may this hand wither from my body! I broke this Duckworth like a rush; I beggared him to his door; I burned that thatch above his head; I drove him from this country; and now, cometh he back to beard me? Nay, but, Duckworth, this time it shall go bitter hard!"

He was silent for some time, his face working.

"Eat!" he cried, suddenly. "And you here," he added to Matcham, "swear me an oath to follow straight to the Moat House."

"I will pledge mine honor," replied Matcham.

"What make I with your honor," replied the knight. "Swear me upon your mother's welfare!"

Matcham gave the required oath; and Sir Daniel readjusted the hood over his face and prepared his bell and staff. To see him once more in that appalling travesty somewhat revived the horror of his two companions. But the knight was soon upon his feet.

"Eat with dispatch," he said, "and follow me yarely to mine house."

And with that he set forth again into the woods; and presently after the bell began to sound, numbering his steps, and the two lads sat by their untasted meal and heard it die slowly away up-hill into the distance.

"And so ye go to Tunstall!" Dick inquired.

"Yea, verily," said Matcham, "when needs must! I am braver behind Sir Daniel's back than to his face."

They ate hastily and set forth along the path through the airy upper levels of the forest, where great beeches stood apart among green lawns, and the birds and squir-rels made merry on the boughs. Two hours later, they began to descend upon the other side, and already, among the tree-tops, saw before them the red walls and roofs of Tunstall House.

"Here," said Matcham, pausing, "ye shall take your leave of your friend Jack, whom y'are to see no more. Come, Dick, forgive him what he did amiss, as he, for his part, cheerfully and lovingly forgiveth you."

"And wherefore so?" asked Dick. "An we both go to Tun-stall, I shall see you yet again, I trow, and that right often."

"Ye'll never again see poor Jack Matcham," replied the other, "that was so fearful and burthensome, and yet plucked you from the river; ye'll not see him more, Dick, mine honor!" He held his arms open, and the lads embraced and kissed. "And Dick," continued Matcham, "my spirit bodeth ill. Y'are now to see a new Sir Daniel; for heretofore hath all prospered in his hands exceedingly, and fortune followed him; but now, methinks, when his fate has come upon him, and he runs the adventure of his life, he will prove but a foul lord to both of us. He may be brave in battle, but he hath the liar's eye; there is fear in his eye, Dick, and fear is as cruel as the wolf! We go down into that house, Saint Mary guide us forth again!"

And so they continued their descent in silence and came out at last before Sir Daniel's forest stronghold, where it stood, low and shady, flanked with round towers and stained with moss and lichen, in the lilied waters of the moat. Even as they appeared, the doors were opened, the bridge lowered, and Sir Daniel himself with Hatch and the parson at his side stood ready to receive them.

BOOK II: THE MOAT HOUSE

Dick Asks Questions

THE MOAT House stood not far from the rough forest road. Externally it was a compact rectangle of red stone, flanked at each corner by a round tower, pierced for archery and battlemented at the top. Within, it inclosed a narrow court. The moat was perhaps twelve feet wide, crossed by a single drawbridge. It was supplied with water by a trench leading to a forest pool and commanded through its whole length from the battlements of the two southern towers. Except that one or two tall and thick trees had been suffered to remain within half a bowshot of the walls, the house was in a good posture for defense.

In the court Dick found a part of the garrison busy with preparations for defense and gloomily discussing the chances of a siege. Some were making arrows, some sharpening swords that had long been disused; but even as they worked, they shook their heads.

Twelve of Sir Daniel's party had escaped the battle, run the gauntlet through the wood, and come alive to the Moat House. But out of this dozen, three had been gravely wounded: two at Risingham in the disorder of the rout, one by John Amend-All's marksmen as he crossed the forest. This raised the force of the garrison, counting Hatch, Sir Daniel, and young Shelton, to twenty-two effective men. And more might be continually expected to arrive. The danger lay not, therefore, in the lack of men.

It was the terror of the black arrow that oppressed the spirits of the garrison. For their open foes of the party of York, in these most changing times, they felt but a far-away concern. "The world," as people said in those days, "might change again" before harm came. But for their neighbors in the wood they trembled. It was not Sir Daniel alone who was a mark for hatred. His men, conscious of impunity, had carried themselves cruelly through all the country. Harsh commands had been harshly executed; and of the little band that now sat talking in the court, there was not one but had been guilty of some act of oppression or barbarity. And now, by the fortune of war, Sir Daniel had become powerless to protect his instruments; now, by the issue of some hours of battle, at which many of them had not been present, they had all become punishable traitors to the State, outside the buckler of the law, a shrunken company in a poor fortress that was hardly tenable, and exposed upon all sides to the just resentment of their victims. Nor had there been lacking grisly advertisements of what they might expect.

At different periods of the evening and the night, no fewer than seven riderless horses had come neighing in terror to the gate. Two were from Selden's troop; five belonged to men who had ridden with Sir Daniel to the field. Lastly, a little before dawn, a spearman had come staggering to the moat-side, pierced by three arrows; even as they carried him in, his spirit had departed; but by the words that he uttered in his agony, he must have been the last survivor of a considerable company of men.

Hatch himself showed under his sun-brown the pallor of anxiety; and when he had taken Dick aside and learned the fate of Selden, he fell on a stone bench and fairly wept. The others, from where they sat on stools or doorsteps in the sunny angle of the court, looked at him with wonder and alarm, but none ventured to inquire the cause of his emotion.

"Nay, Master Shelton," said Hatch at last, "nay, but what said I? We shall all go. Selden was a man of his hands; he was like a brother to me. Well, he has gone second; well, we shall all follow! For what said their knave rime?—'A black arrow in each black heart.' Was it not so it went? Appleyard, Selden, Smith, old Humphrey gone; and there lieth poor John Carter, crying, poor sinner, for the priest."

Dick gave ear. Out of a low window hard by where they were talking groans and murmurs came to his ear.

"Lieth he there?" he asked.

"Aye, in the second porter's chamber," answered Hatch. "We could not bear him farther, soul and body were so bitterly at odds. At every step we lifted him, he thought to wend. But now, methinks, it is the soul that suffereth. Ever for the priest he crieth, and Sir Oliver, I wot not why, still cometh not. 'Twill be a long shrift; but poor Appleyard and poor Selden, they had none."

Dick stooped to the window and looked in. The little cell was low and dark, but he could make out the wounded soldier lying moaning on his pallet.

"Carter, poor friend, how goeth it?" he asked.

"Master Shelton," returned the man, in an excited whisper, "for the dear light of heaven, bring the priest. Alack, I am sped: I am brought very low down; my hurt is to the death. Ye may do me no more service; this shall be the last. Now, for my poor soul's interest, and as a loyal gentleman, bestir you; for I have that matter on my conscience that shall drag me deep."

He groaned, and Dick heard the grating of his teeth, whether in pain or terror.

Just then Sir Daniel appeared upon the threshold of the hall. He had a letter in one hand.

"Lads," he said, "we have had a shog, we have had a tumble; wherefore, then, deny it? Rather it imputeth to get speedily again to saddle. This old Harry the Sixt has had the undermost. Wash we, then, our hands of him. I have a good friend that rideth next the Duke, the Lord of Wensleydale. Well, I have writ a letter to my friend, praying his good lordship, and offering large satisfaction for the past and reasonable surety for the future. Doubt not but he will lend a favorable ear. A prayer without gifts is like a song without music; I surfeit him with promises, boys—I spare not to promise. What, then, is lacking? Nay, a great thing—wherefore should I deceive you?—a great thing and a difficult: a messenger to bear it. The woods—y'are not ignorant of that—lie thick with our ill-willers. Haste is most needful; but without sleight and caution all is naught. Which, then, of this company will take me this letter, bear it to my Lord of Wensleydale and bring me the answer back?"

One man instantly arose.

"I will, an't like you," said he. "I will even risk my carcass."

"Nay, Dicky Bowyer, not so," returned the knight. "It likes me not. Y'are sly, indeed, but not speedy. Ye were a laggard ever."

"An't be so, Sir Daniel, here am I," cried another.

"The saints forfend!" said the knight. "Y'are speedy but not sly. Ye would blunder me headforemost into John Amend-All's camp. I thank you both for your good courage; but, in sooth, it may not be."

Then Hatch offered himself, and he also was refused.

"I want you here, good Bennet; y'are my right hand, indeed," returned the knight; and then several coming forward in a group, Sir Daniel at length selected one and gave him the letter.

"Now," he said, "upon your good speed and better discretion we do all depend. Bring me a good answer back, and before three weeks I will have purged my forest of these vagabonds that brave us to our faces. But mark it well, Throgmorton: the matter is not easy. Ye must steal forth under night, and go like a fox; and how ye are to cross the Till I know not, neither by the bridge nor ferry."

"I can swim," returned Throgmorton. "I will come soundly, fear not."

"Well, friend, get ye to the buttery," replied Sir Daniel. "Ye shall swim first of all in nut-brown ale." And with that he turned back into the hall.

"Sir Daniel hath a wise tongue," said Hatch, aside, to

Dick. "See, now, where many a lesser man had glossed the matter over, he speaketh it out plainly to his company. Here is a danger, 'a saith, and here difficulty; and jesteth in the very saying. Nay, by Saint Barbary, he is a born captain! Not a man but he is some deal heartened up! See how they fall again to work."

This praise of Sir Daniel put a thought in the lad's head. "Bennet," he said, "how came my father by his end?"

"Ask me not that," replied Hatch. "I had no hand nor knowledge in it; furthermore, I will even be silent, Master Dick. For look you, in a man's own business, there he may speak; but of hearsay matters and of common talk, not so. Ask me Sir Oliver—aye, or Carter, if ye will; not me."

And Hatch set off to make the rounds, leaving Dick in a muse.

"Wherefore would he not tell me?" thought the lad. "And wherefore named he Carter? Carter—nay, then Carter had a hand in it, perchance."

He entered the house, and passing some little way along a flagged and vaulted passage, came to the door of the cell where the hurt man lay groaning. At his entrance Carter started eagerly.

"Have ye brought the priest?" he cried.

"Not yet awhile," returned Dick. "Y'ave a word to tell me first. How came my father, Harry Shelton, by his death?"

The man's face altered instantly.

"I know not," he replied, doggedly.

"Nay, ye know well," returned Dick. "Seek not to put me by."

"I tell you I know not," repeated Carter.

"Then," said Dick, "ye shall die unshriven. Here am I and here shall stay. There shall no priest come near you, rest assured. For of what avail is penitence, an ye have no mind to right those wrongs ye had a hand in? and without penitence, confession is but mockery."

"Ye say what ye mean not, Master Dick," said Carter composedly. "It is ill threatening the dying, and becometh you (to speak truth) little. And for as little as it commends you, it shall serve you less. Stay, an ye please. Ye will condemn my soul—ye shall learn nothing! There is my last word to you." And the wounded man turned upon the other side.

Now, Dick, to say truth, had spoken hastily and was ashamed of his threat. But he made one more effort.

"Carter," he said, "mistake me not. I know ye were but an instrument in the hands of others; a churl must obey his lord; I would not bear heavily on such an one. But I begin to learn upon many sides that this great duty lieth on my youth and ignorance, to avenge my father. Prithee, then, good Carter, set aside the memory of my threatenings, and in pure good will and honest penitence, give me a word of help."

The wounded man lay silent; nor, say what Dick pleased, could he extract another word from him.

"Well," said Dick, "I will go call the priest to you as ye desired; for howsoever ye be in fault to me or mine, I would not be willingly in fault to any, least of all to one upon the last change."

Again the old soldier heard him without speech or motion; even his groans he had suppressed; and as Dick turned and left the room, he was filled with admiration for that rugged fortitude.

"And yet," he thought, "of what use is courage without wit? Had his hands been clean, he would have spoken; his silence did confess the secret louder than words. Nay, upon all sides, proof floweth on me. Sir Daniel, he or his men, hath done this thing."

Dick paused in the stone passage with a heavy heart. At that hour, in the ebb of Sir Daniel's fortune, when he was beleaguered by the archers of the Black Arrow and proscribed by the victorious Yorkists, was Dick, also, to turn upon the man who had nourished and taught him, who had severely punished indeed, but yet unwearyingly protected his youth? The necessity, if it should prove to be one, was cruel.

"Pray Heaven he be innocent!" he said.

And then steps sounded on the flagging, and Sir Oliver came gravely toward the lad.

"One seeketh you earnestly," said Dick.

"I am upon the way, good Richard," said the priest. "It is this poor Carter. Alack, he is beyond cure."

"And yet his soul is sicker than his body," answered Dick.

"Have ye seen him?" asked Sir Oliver, with a manifest start.

"I do but come from him," replied Dick.

"What said he—what said he?" snapped the priest, with extraordinary eagerness.

"He but cried for you the more piteously, Sir Oliver. It were well done to go the faster, for his hurt is grievous," returned the lad.

"I am straight for him," was the reply. "Well, we have all our sins. We must all come to our latter day, good Richard."

"Aye, sir; and it were well if we came fairly," answered Dick.

The priest dropped his eyes and with an inaudible benediction hurried on.

"He, too!" thought Dick—"he, that taught me in piety! Nay, then, what a world is this, if all that care for me be blood-guilty of my father's death! Vengeance! Alas! what a sore fate is mine, if I must be avenged upon my friends!"

The thought put Matcham in his head. He smiled at the remembrance of his strange companion and then wondered where he was. Ever since they had come together to the doors of the Moat House the younger lad had disappeared, and Dick began to weary for a word with him.

About an hour after, mass being somewhat hastily run through by Sir Oliver, the company gathered in the hall for dinner. It was a long, low apartment, strewn with green rushes and the walls hung with arras* in a design of savage men and questing bloodhounds; here and there hung

---

*A tapestry of Flemish origin.

spears and bows and bucklers; a fire blazed in the big chimney; there were arras-covered benches round the wall, and in the midst the table, fairly spread, awaited the arrival of the diners. Neither Sir Daniel nor his lady made their appearance. Sir Oliver himself was absent, and here again there was no word of Matcham. Dick began to grow alarmed, to recall his companion's melancholy forebodings, and to wonder to himself if any foul play had befallen him in that house.

After dinner he found Goody Hatch, who was hurrying to my lady Brackley.

"Goody," he said, "where is Master Matcham, I prithee? I saw ye go in with him when we arrived."

The old woman laughed aloud.

"Ah, Master Dick," she said, "y'have a famous bright eye in your head, to be sure!" and laughed again.

"Nay, but where is he, indeed?" persisted Dick.

"Ye will never see him more," she returned; "never. It is sure."

"An I do not," returned the lad, "I will know the reason why. He came not hither of his full free will; such as I am, I am his best protector, and I will see him justly used. There be too many mysteries; I do begin to weary of the game!"

But as Dick was speaking, a heavy hand fell on his shoulder. It was Bennet Hatch that had come unperceived behind him. With a jerk of his thumb the retainer dismissed his wife.

"Friend Dick," he said, as soon as they were alone, "are ye a moonstruck natural? An ye leave not certain things in peace, ye were better in the salt sea than here in Tunstall Moat House. Y'have questioned me; y'have baited Carter; y'have frightened the jack-priest with hints. Bear ye more wisely, fool; and even now, when Sir Daniel calleth you, show me a smooth face, for the love of wisdom. Y'are to be sharply questioned. Look to your answers."

"Hatch," returned Dick, "in all this I smell a guilty conscience."

"An ye go not the wiser, ye will soon smell blood," replied Bennet. "I do but warn you. And here cometh one to call you."

And indeed, at that very moment, a messenger came across the court to summon Dick into the presence of Sir Daniel.

The Two Oaths

Sir Daniel was in the hall; there he paced angrily before the fire, awaiting Dick's arrival. None was by except Sir Oliver, and he sat discreetly backward, thumbing and muttering over his breviary.

"Y'have sent for me, Sir Daniel?" said young Shelton.

"I have sent for you, indeed," replied the knight. "For what cometh to mine ears? Have I been to you so heavy a guardian that ye make haste to credit ill of me? Or sith that ye see me, for the nonce, some worsted, do ye think to quit my party? By the mass, your father was not so! Those he was near, those he stood by, come wind or weather. But you, Dick, y'are a fair-day friend, it seemeth, and now seek to clear yourself of your allegiance."

"An't please you, Sir Daniel, not so," returned Dick, firmly. "I am grateful and faithful where gratitude and faith are due. And before more is said, I thank you, and I thank Sir Oliver; y'have great claims upon me, both—none can have more; I were a hound if I forgot them."

"It is well," said Sir Daniel; and then, rising into anger: "Gratitude and faith are words, Dick Shelton," he continued; "but I look to deeds. In this hour of my peril, when my name is attainted, when my lands are forfeit, when this wood is full of men that hunger and thirst for my destruction, what doth gratitude? what doth faith? I have but a little company remaining; is it grateful or faithful to poison me their hearts with your insidious whisperings? Save me from such gratitude! But, come, now, what is it ye wish?

Speak; we are here to answer. If ye have aught against me, stand forth and say it."

"Sir," replied Dick, "my father fell when I was yet a child. It hath come to mine ears that he was foully done by. It hath come to mine ears—for I will not dissemble—that ye had a hand in his undoing. And in all verity, I shall not be at peace of mine own mind, nor very clear to help you, till I have certain resolution of these doubts."

Sir Daniel sat down in a deep settle. He took his chin in his hand and looked at Dick fixedly.

"And ye think I would be guardian to the man's son that I had murdered?" he asked.

"Nay," said Dick, "pardon me if I answer churlishly; but indeed ye know right well a wardship is most profitable. All these years have ye not enjoyed my revenues and led my men? Have ye not still my marriage? I wot not what it may be worth—it is worth something. Pardon me again; but if ye were base enough to slay a man under trust, here were, perhaps, reasons enough to move you to the lesser baseness."

"When I was a lad of your years," returned Sir Daniel, sternly, "my mind had not so turned upon suspicions. And Sir Oliver here," he added, "why should he, a priest, be guilty of this act?"

"Nay, Sir Daniel," said Dick, "but where the master biddeth, there will the dog go. It is well known this priest is but your instrument. I speak very freely; the time is not for courtesies. Even as I speak, so would I be answered. And answer get I none! Ye but put more questions. I rede ye beware, Sir Daniel; for in this way ye will but nourish and not satisfy my doubts."

"I will answer you fairly, Master Richard," said the knight. "Were I to pretend ye have not stirred my wrath, I were no honest man. But I will be just even in anger. Come to me with these words when y'are grown and come to man's estate, and I am no longer your guardian and so helpless to resent them. Come to me then, and I will answer you as ye merit, with a buffet in the mouth. Till then ye have two courses: either swallow me down these insults, keep a silent tongue, and fight in the meanwhile for the man that fed and fought for your infancy; or else—the door standeth open, the woods are full of mine enemies—go."

The spirit with which these words were uttered, the looks with which they were accompanied, staggered Dick; and yet he could not but observe that he had got no answer.

"I desire nothing more earnestly, Sir Daniel, than to believe you," he replied. "Assure me ye are free from this."

"Will ye take my word of honor, Dick?" inquired the knight.

"That would I," answered the lad.

"I give it you," returned Sir Daniel. "Upon my word of honor, upon the eternal welfare of my spirit, and as I shall answer for my deeds hereafter, I had no hand nor portion in your father's death."

He extended his hand, and Dick took it eagerly. Neither of them observed the priest, who, at the pronunciation of that solemn and false oath, had half arisen from his seat in an agony of horror and remorse.

"Ah," cried Dick, "ye must find it in your greatheartedness to pardon me! I was a churl indeed to doubt of you. But ye have my hand upon it; I will doubt no more."

"Nay, Dick," replied Sir Daniel, "y'are forgiven. Ye know not the world and its calumnious nature."

"I was the more to blame," added Dick, "in that the rogues pointed, not directly at yourself, but at Sir Oliver."

As he spoke, he turned toward the priest, and paused in the middle of the last word. This tall, ruddy, corpulent, high-stepping man had fallen, you might say, to pieces; his color was gone, his limbs were relaxed, his lips stammered prayers; and now, when Dick's eyes were fixed upon him suddenly, he cried out aloud, like some wild animal, and buried his face in his hands.

Sir Daniel was by him in two strides and shook him

fiercely by the shoulder. At the same moment Dick's suspicions reawakened.

"Nay," he said, "Sir Oliver may swear also. 'Twas him they accused."

"He shall swear," said the knight.

Sir Oliver speechlessly waved his arms.

"Aye, by the mass! but ye shall swear," cried Sir Daniel, beside himself with fury. "Here upon this book ye shall swear," he continued, picking up the breviary, which had fallen to the ground. "What! Ye make me doubt you! Swear, I say; swear."

But the priest was still incapable of speech. His terror of Sir Daniel, his terror of perjury, risen to about an equal height, strangled him.

And just then, through the high stained-glass window of the hall, a black arrow crashed and struck, and stuck quivering in the midst of the long table.

Sir Oliver, with a loud scream, fell fainting on the rushes; while the knight, followed by Dick, dashed into the court and up the nearest corkscrew stair to the battlements. The sentries were all on the alert. The sun shone quietly on green lawns dotted with trees and on the wooded hills of the forest which inclosed the view. There was no sign of a besieger.

"Whence came that shot?" asked the knight.

"From yonder clump, Sir Daniel," returned a sentinel.

The knight stood a little, musing. Then he turned to Dick. "Dick," he said, "keep me an eye upon these men; I leave you in charge here. As for the priest, he shall clear himself, or I will know the reason why. I do almost begin to share in your suspicions. He shall swear, trust me, or we shall prove him guilty."

Dick answered somewhat coldly, and the knight, giving him a piercing glance, hurriedly returned to the hall. His first glance was for the arrow. It was the first of these missiles he had seen, and as he turned it to and fro, the dark hue of it touched him with some fear. Again there was some writing: one word—"Earthed."

"Aye," he broke out, "they know I am home, then. Earthed! Aye, but there is not a dog among them fit to dig me out."

Sir Oliver had come to himself and now scrambled to his feet.

"Alack, Sir Daniel!" he moaned, "y'ave sworn a dread oath; y'are doomed to the end of time."

"Aye," returned the knight, "I have sworn an oath, indeed, thou chuckle-head; but thyself shalt swear a greater. It shall be on the blessed cross of Holywood. Look to it; get the words ready. It shall be sworn tonight."

"Now, may Heaven lighten you!" replied the priest; "may Heaven incline your heart from this iniquity!"

"Look you, my good father," said Sir Daniel, "if y'are for piety, I say no more; ye begin late, that is all. But if y'are in any sense bent upon wisdom, hear me. This lad beginneth to irk me like a wasp. I have a need for him, for I would sell his marriage. But I tell you, in all plainness, if that he continues to weary me, he shall go join his father. I give orders now to change him to the chamber above the chapel. If that ye can swear your innocency with a good solid oath and an assured countenance, it is well; the lad will be at peace a little, and I will spare him. If that ye stammer, or blench, or anyways boggle at the swearing, he will not believe you; and by the mass, he shall die. There is for your thinking on."

"The chamber above the chapel!" gasped the priest.

"That same," replied the knight. "So if ye desire to save him, save him; and if ye desire not, prithee, go to, and let me be at peace! For an I had been an hasty man, I would already have put my sword through you for your intolerable cowardice and folly. Have ye chosen? Say!"

"I have chosen," said the priest. "Heaven pardon me, I will do evil for good. I will swear for the lad's sake."

"So is it best!" said Sir Daniel. "Send for him then, speedily. Ye shall see him alone. Yet I shall have an eye on you. I shall be here in the panel room."

The knight raised the arras and let it fall again behind

him. There was the sound of a spring opening; then followed the creaking of trod stairs.

Sir Oliver, left alone, cast a timorous glance upward at the arras-covered wall and crossed himself with every appearance of terror and contrition.

"Nay, if he is in the chapel room," the priest murmured, "were it at my soul's cost, I must save him."

Three minutes later, Dick, who had been summoned by another messenger, found Sir Oliver standing by the hall table, resolute and pale.

"Richard Shelton," he said, "ye have required an oath from me. I might complain, I might deny you; but my heart is moved toward you for the past, and I will even content you as ye choose. By the true cross of Holywood, I did not slay your father."

"Sir Oliver," returned Dick, "when first we read John Amend-All's paper, I was convinced of so much. But suffer me to put two questions. Ye did not slay him; granted. But had ye no hand in it?"

"None," said Sir Oliver. And at the same time he began to contort his face and signal with his mouth and eyebrows, like one who desires to convey a warning, yet dared not utter a sound.

Dick regarded him in wonder; then he turned and looked all about him at the empty hall.

"What make ye?" he inquired.

"Why, naught," returned the priest, hastily smoothing his countenance. "I make naught; I do but suffer; I am sick. I—I—prithee, Dick, I must be gone. On the true cross of Holywood, I am clean innocent alike of violence or treachery. Content ye, good lad. Farewell!"

And he made his escape from the apartment with unusual alacrity.

Dick remained rooted to the spot, his eyes wandering about the room, his face a changing picture of various emotions—wonder, doubt, suspicion, and amusement. Gradually, as his mind grew clearer, suspicion took the upper hand, and was succeeded by certainty of the worst.

He raised his head, and, as he did so, violently started. High upon the wall there was the figure of a savage hunter woven in the tapestry. With one hand he held a horn to his mouth; in the other he brandished a stout spear. His face was dark, for he was meant to represent an African.

Now here was what startled Richard Shelton. The sun had moved away from the hall windows, and at the same time the fire had blazed up high on the wide hearth and shed a changeful glow upon the roof and hangings. In this light the figure of the black hunter had winked at him with a white eyelid.

He continued staring at the eye. The light shone upon it like a gem; it was liquid, it was alive. Again the white eyelid closed upon it for a fraction of a second, and the next moment it was gone.

There could be no mistake. The live eye that had been watching him through a hole in the tapestry was gone. The firelight no longer shone on a reflecting surface.

And instantly Dick awoke to the terrors of his position. Hatch's warning, the mute signals of the priest, this eye that had observed him from the wall ran together in his mind. He saw he had been put upon his trial, that he had once more betrayed his suspicions, and that, short of some miracle, he was lost.

"If I cannot get me forth out of this house," he thought, "I am a dead man! And this poor Matcham, too—to what a cockatrice's nest have I not led him!"

He was still so thinking, when there came one in haste, to bid him help in changing his arms, his clothing, and his two or three books to a new chamber.

"A new chamber?" he repeated. "Wherefore so? What chamber?"

"'Tis one above the chapel," answered the messenger.

"It hath stood long empty," said Dick, musing. "What manner of room is it?"

"Nay, a brave room," returned the man. "But yet"—lowering his voice—"they call it haunted."

"Haunted?" repeated Dick, with a chill. "I have not heard of it. Nay, then, and by whom?"

The messenger looked about him; and then, in a low whisper, "By the sacrist of Saint John's," he said. "They had him there to sleep one night, and in the morning—whew!—he was gone. The devil had taken him, they said; the more betoken, he had drunk late the night before."

Dick followed the man with black forebodings.

The Room over the Chapel

From the battlements nothing further was observed. The sun journeyed westward and at last went down; but to the eyes of all these eager sentinels, no living thing appeared in the neighborhood of Tunstall House.

When the night was at length fairly come, Throgmorton was led to a room overlooking an angle of the moat. Thence he was lowered with every precaution; the ripple of his swimming was audible for a brief period; then a black figure was observed to land by the branches of a willow and crawl away among the grass. For some half hour Sir Daniel and Hatch stood eagerly giving ear; but all remained quiet. The messenger had got away in safety.

Sir Daniel's brow grew clearer. He turned to Hatch.

"Bennet," said he, "this John Amend-All is no more than a man, ye see. He sleepeth. We will make a good end of him. Go to!"

All the afternoon and evening Dick had been ordered hither and thither, one command following another, till he was bewildered with the number and the hurry of commissions. All that time he had seen no more of Sir Oliver and nothing of Matcham; and yet both the priest and the young lad ran continually in his mind. It was now his chief purpose to escape from Tunstall Moat House as speedily as might be; and yet, before he went, he desired a word with both of these.

At length with a lamp in one hand he mounted to his new apartment. It was large, low, and somewhat dark. The window looked upon the moat, and although it was so high up, it was heavily barred. The bed was luxurious, with one pillow of down and one of lavender, and a red coverlet worked in a pattern of roses. All about the walls were cupboards, locked and padlocked, and concealed from view by hangings of dark-colored arras. Dick made the round, lifting the arras, sounding the panels, seeking vainly to open the cupboards. He assured himself that the door was strong and the bolt solid; then he set down his lamp upon a bracket and once more looked all around.

For what reason had he been given this chamber? It was larger and finer than his own. Could it conceal a snare? Was there a secret entrance? Was it indeed haunted? His blood ran a little chilly in his veins.

Immediately over him the heavy foot of a sentry trod the leads. Below him, he knew, was the arched roof of the chapel; and next to the chapel was the hall. Certainly there was a secret passage in the hall; the eye that had watched him from the arras gave him proof of that. Was it not more than probable that the passage extended to the chapel, and if so, that it had an opening in his room?

To sleep in such a place, he felt, would be foolhardy. He made his weapons ready and took his position in a corner of the room behind the door. If ill was intended he would sell his life dear.

The sound of many feet, the challenge, and the password sounded overhead along the battlements; the watch was being changed.

And just then there came a scratching at the door of the chamber; it grew a little louder; then a whisper:

"Dick, Dick, it is I!"

Dick ran to the door, drew the bolt, and admitted Matcham. He was very pale and carried a lamp in one hand and a drawn dagger in the other.

"Shut me the door," he whispered. "Swift, Dick! This

house is full of spies; I hear their feet follow me in the corridors; I hear them breathe behind the arras."

"Well, content you," returned Dick, "it is closed. We are safe for this while, if there be safety anywhere within these walls. But my heart is glad to see you. By the mass, lad, I thought ye were sped. Where hid ye?"

"It matters not," returned Matcham. "Since we be met, it matters not. But, Dick, are your eyes open? Have they told ye of tomorrow's doings?"

"Not they," replied Dick. "What make they of tomorrow?"

"Tomorrow or tonight, I know not," said the other; "but one time or other, Dick, they do intend upon your life. I had the proof of it: I have heard them whisper; nay, they as good as told me."

"Aye," returned Dick, "is it so? I had thought as much."

And he told him the day's occurrences at length.

When it was done, Matcham arose and began, in turn, to examine the apartment.

"No," he said, "there is no entrance visible. Yet 'tis a pure certainty there is one. Dick, I will stay by you. An y'are to die, I will die with you. And I can help—look! I have stolen a dagger—I will do my best! And meanwhile, an ye know of any issue, any sally-port we could get opened or any window that we might descend by, I will most joyfully face any jeopardy to flee with you."

"Jack," said Dick, "by the mass, Jack, y'are the best soul, and the truest, and the bravest in all England! Give me your hand, Jack."

And he grasped the other's hand in silence.

"I will tell you," he resumed. "There is a window out of which the messenger descended; the rope should still be in the chamber. 'Tis a hope."

"Hist!" said Matcham.

Both gave ear. There was a sound below the floor; then it paused, and then began again.

"Someone walketh in the room below," whispered Matcham.

"Nay," returned Dick, "there is no room below; we are above the chapel. It is my murderer in the secret passage. Well, let him come: it shall go hard with him!" And he ground his teeth.

"Blow me the lights out," said the other. "Perchance he will betray himself."

They blew out both the lamps and lay still as death. The footfalls underneath were very soft, but they were clearly audible. Several times they came and went; and then there was a loud jar of a key turning in a lock, followed by a considerable silence.

Presently the steps began again, and then, all of a sudden, a chink of light appeared in the planking of the room in a far corner. It widened; a trap-door was being opened, letting in a gush of light. They could see the strong hand pushing it up; and Dick raised his cross-bow, waiting for the head to follow.

But now there came an interruption. From a distant corner of the Moat House shouts began to be heard, and first one voice and then several crying aloud upon a name. This noise had plainly disconcerted the murderer, for the trap-door was silently lowered to its place, and the steps hurriedly returned, passed once more close below the lads and died away in the distance.

Here was a moment's respite. Dick breathed deep, and then and not till then, he gave ear to the disturbance which had interrupted the attack, and which was now rather increasing than diminishing. All about the Moat House feet were running, doors were opening and slamming, and still the voice of Sir Daniel towered above all this bustle, shouting for "Joanna."

"Joanna!" repeated Dick. "Why, who the murrain should this be? Here is no Joanna, nor ever hath been. What meaneth it?"

Matcham was silent. He seemed to have drawn farther away. But only a little faint starlight entered by the window, and at the far end of the apartment, where the pair were, the darkness was complete.

"Jack," said Dick, "I wot not where ye were all day. Saw ye this Joanna?"

"Nay," returned Matcham, "I saw her not."

"Nor heard tell of her?" he pursued.

The steps drew nearer. Sir Daniel was still roaring the name of Joanna from the courtyard.

"Did ye hear of her?" repeated Dick.

"I heard of her," said Matcham.

"How your voice twitters! What aileth you?" said Dick. "'Tis a most excellent good fortune, this Joanna; it will take their minds from us."

"Dick," cried Matcham, "I am lost; we are both lost! Let us flee if there be yet time. They will not rest till they have found me. Or, see; let me go forth; when they have found me, ye may flee. Let me forth, Dick—good Dick, let me away!"

She was groping for the bolt, when Dick at last comprehended.

"By the mass!" he cried, "y'are no Jack; y'are Joanna Sedley; y'are the maid that would not marry me!"

The girl paused and stood silent and motionless. Dick, too, was silent for a little while; then he spoke again.

"Joanna," he said, "y'ave saved my life, and I have saved yours; and we have seen blood flow and been friends and enemies—aye, and I took my belt to thrash you; and all that time I thought ye were a boy. But now death has me, and my time's out, and before I die I must say this: Y'are the best maid and the bravest under heaven, and, if only I could live, I would marry you blithely; and live or die, I love you!"

She answered nothing.

"Come," he said, "speak up, Jack. Come, be a good maid, and say ye love me!"

"Why, Dick," she cried, "would I be here?"

"Well, see ye here," continued Dick, "an we but escape whole, we'll marry, and an we're to die, we die, and there's an end on't. But now that I think, how found ye my chamber?"

"I asked it of Dame Hatch," she answered.

"Well, the dame's staunch," he answered, "she'll not tell upon you. We have time before us."

And just then, as if to contradict his words, feet came down the corridor, and a fist beat roughly on the door.

"Here!" cried a voice. "Open, Master Dick; open!"

Dick neither moved nor answered.

"It is all over," said the girl; and she put her arms about Dick's neck.

One after another, men came trooping to the door. Then Sir Daniel arrived himself, and there was a sudden cessation of the noise.

"Dick," cried the knight, "be not an ass. The Seven Sleepers had been awake ere now. We know she is within there. Open, then, the door, man."

Dick was silent again.

"Down with it," said Sir Daniel. And immediately his followers fell savagely upon the door with foot and fist. Solid as it was and strongly bolted, it would soon have given way, but once more fortune interfered. Over the thunderstorm of blows the cry of a sentinel was heard; it was followed by another; shouts ran along the battlements, shouts answered out of the wood. In the first moment of alarm it sounded as if the foresters were carrying the Moat House by assault. And Sir Daniel and his men, desisting instantly from their attack upon Dick's chamber, hurried to defend the walls.

"Now," cried Dick, "we are saved."

He seized the great old bedstead with both hands and bent himself in vain to move it.

"Help me, Jack. For your life's sake, help me stoutly!" he cried.

Between them, with a huge effort, they dragged the big frame of oak across the room and thrust it endwise to the chamber door.

"Ye do but make things worse," said Joanna, sadly. "He will then enter by the trap."

"Not so," replied Dick. "He durst not tell his secret to so

many. It is by the trap that we shall flee. Hark! The attack is over. Nay, it was none!"

It had, indeed, been no attack; it was the arrival of another party of stragglers from the defeat of Risingham that had disturbed Sir Daniel. They had run the gauntlet under cover of the darkness; they had been admitted by the great gate; and now with a great stamping of hoofs and jingle of accouterments and arms, they were dismounting in the court.

"He will return anon," said Dick. "To the trap!"

He lighted a lamp, and they went together into the corner of the room. The open chink through which some light still glittered was easily discovered, and, taking a stout sword from his small armory, Dick thrust it deep into the seam and weighed strenuously on the hilt. The trap moved, gaped a little, and at length came widely open. Seizing it with their hands, the two young folk threw it back. It disclosed a few steps descending, and at the foot of them, where the would-be murderer had left it, a burning lamp.

"Now," said Dick, "go first and take the lamp. I will follow to close the trap."

So they descended one after the other, and as Dick lowered the trap the blows began once again to thunder on the panels of the door.

The Passage

The passage in which Dick and Joanna now found themselves was narrow, dirty, and short. At the other end of it a door stood partly open; the same door, without doubt, that they had heard the man unlocking. Heavy cobwebs hung from the roof, and the paved flooring echoed hollow under the lightest tread.

Beyond the door there were two branches at right angles. Dick chose one of them at random, and the pair hurried with echoing footsteps along the hollow of the chapel roof. The top of the arched ceiling rose like a whale's back in the dim glimmer of the lamp. Here and there were spy-holes, concealed on the other side by the carving of the cornice; and looking down through one of these, Dick saw the paved floor of the chapel—the altar with its burning tapers—and stretched before it on the steps, the figure of Sir Oliver praying with uplifted hands.

At the other end, they descended a few steps. The passage grew narrower; the wall upon one hand was now of wood; the noise of people talking and a faint flickering of lights came through the interstices; and presently they came to a round hole about the size of a man's eye, and Dick looking down through it beheld the interior of the hall and some half a dozen men sitting in their jacks about the table, drinking deep and demolishing a venison pie. These were certainly some of the late arrivals.

"Here is no help," said Dick. "Let us try back."

"Nay," said Joanna; "maybe the passage goeth farther."

And she pushed on. But a few yards farther the passage ended at the top of a short flight of steps; and it became plain that as long as the soldiers occupied the hall escape was impossible upon that side.

They retraced their steps with all imaginable speed and set forward to explore the other branch. It was exceedingly narrow, scarce wide enough for a large man; and it led them continually up and down by little breakneck stairs until even Dick had lost all notion of his whereabouts.

At length it grew both narrower and lower; the stairs continued to descend; the walls on either hand became damp and slimy to the touch; and far in front of them they heard the squeaking and scuttling of rats.

"We must be in the dungeons," Dick remarked.

"And still there is no outlet," added Joanna.

"Nay, but an outlet there must be!" Dick answered.

Presently, sure enough, they came to a sharp angle, and then the passage ended in a flight of steps. On the top of that was a solid flag of stone by way of trap, and to this they both set their backs. It was immovable.

"Someone holdeth it," suggested Joanna.

"Not so," said Dick, "for were a man as strong as ten he must still yield a little. But this resisteth like dead rock. There is a weight upon the trap. Here is no issue; and, by my sooth, Jack, we are here as fairly prisoners as though the gyves were on our ankle-bones. Sit ye then down and let us talk. After a while we shall return, when perchance they shall be less carefully upon their guard; and who knoweth? we may break out and stand a chance. But in my poor opinion we are as good as shent."

"Dick!" she cried, "alas the day that ever ye should have seen me! For like a most unhappy and unthankful maid, it is I have led you hither."

"What cheer!" returned Dick. "It was all written, and that which is written, willy nilly, cometh still to pass. But tell me a little what manner of maid ye are and how ye came into Sir Daniel's hands; that will do better than to bemoan yourself, whether for your sake or mine."

"I am an orphan, like yourself, of father and mother," said Joanna; "and for my great misfortune, Dick, and hitherto for yours, I am a rich marriage. My Lord Foxham had me to ward; yet it appears Sir Daniel bought the marriage of me from the king, and a right dear price he paid for it. So here was I, poor babe, with two great and rich men fighting which should marry me, and I still at nurse! Well, then the world changed, and there was a new chancellor, and Sir Daniel bought the warding of me over Lord Foxham's head. And then the world changed again, and Lord Foxham bought my marriage over Sir Daniel's; and from then to now it went on ill betwixt the two of them. But still Lord Foxham kept me in his hands, and was a good lord to me. And at last I was to be married—or sold, if ye like it better. Five hundred pounds Lord Foxham was to get for me. Hamley was the groom's name, and tomorrow, Dick, of all days in the year, was I to be betrothed. Had it not come to Sir Daniel, I had been wedded, sure—and never seen thee, Dick—dear Dick!"

And here she took his hand and kissed it with the prettiest grace; and Dick drew her hand to him and did the like.

"Well," she went on, "Sir Daniel took me unawares in the garden, and made me dress in these men's clothes, which is a deadly sin for a woman; and besides they fit me not. He rode with me to Kettley, as ye saw, telling me I was to marry you; but I, in my heart, made sure I would marry Hamley in his teeth."

"Aye!" cried Dick, "and so ye loved this Hamley?"

"Nay," replied Joanna, "not I. I did but hate Sir Daniel. And then, Dick, ye helped me, and ye were right kind and very bold, and my heart turned toward you in my own despite; and now, if we can in any way compass it, I would marry you with right good will. And if by cruel destiny it may not be, still ye'll be dear to me. While my heart beats, it'll be true to you."

"And I," said Dick, "that never cared a straw for any manner of woman until now, I took to you when I thought ye were a boy. I had a pity to you and knew not why. When I would have belted you, my hand failed me. But when ye owned ye were a maid, Jack—for still I will call you Jack— I made sure ye were the maid for me. Hark!" he said, breaking off—"one cometh."

And indeed a heavy tread was now audible in the echoing passage, and the rats again fled in armies.

Dick reconnoitered his position. The sudden turn gave him a post of vantage. He could thus shoot in safety from the cover of the wall. But it was plain the light was too near him, and running some way forward he set down the lamp in the middle of the passage and then returned to watch.

Presently, at the far end of the passage, Bennet hove in sight. He seemed to be alone, and he carried in his hand a burning torch, which made him the better mark.

"Stand, Bennet!" cried Dick. "Another step and y'are dead."

"So here ye are," returned Hatch, peering forward into the darkness. "I see you not. Aha! y'ave done wisely, Dick; y'ave put your lamp before you. By my sooth, but, though it was done to shoot my own knave body, I do rejoice to see ye profit by my lessons! And now, what make ye? what seek ye here? Why would ye shoot upon an old, kind friend? And have ye the young gentlewoman there?"

"Nay, Bennet, it is I should question and you answer," replied Dick. "Why am I in this jeopardy of my life? Why do men come privily to slay me in my bed? Why am I now fleeing in mine own guardian's strong house and from the friends that I have lived among and never injured?"

"Master Dick, Master Dick," said Bennet, "what told I you? Y'are brave, but the most uncrafty lad that I can think upon!"

"Well," returned Dick, "I see ye know all and that I am doomed indeed. It is well. Here, where I am, I stay. Let Sir Daniel get me out if he be able!"

Hatch was silent for a space.

"Hark ye," he began, "I return to Sir Daniel, to tell him where ye are, and how posted; for, in truth, it was to that end he sent me. But you, if ye are no fool, had best be gone ere I return."

"Be gone!" repeated Dick, "I would be gone already an' I wist how. I cannot move the trap."

"Put me your hand into the corner, and see what ye find there," replied Bennet. "Throgmorton's rope is still in the brown chamber. Fare ye well."

And Hatch, turning upon his heel, disappeared again into the windings of the passage.

Dick instantly returned for his lamp and proceeded to act upon the hint. At one corner of the trap there was a deep cavity in the wall. Pushing his arm into the aperture, Dick found an iron bar, which he thrust vigorously upward. There followed a snapping noise, and the slab of stone instantly started in its bed.

They were free of the passage. A little exercise of strength easily raised the trap; and they came forth into a vaulted chamber opening on one hand upon the court, where one or two fellows, with bare arms, were rubbing down the horses of the last arrivals. A torch or two, each stuck in an iron ring against the wall, changefully lit up the scene.

How Dick Changed Sides

Dick, blowing out his lamp lest it should attract attention, led the way upstairs and along the corridor. In the brown chamber the rope had been made fast to the frame of an exceedingly heavy and ancient bed. It had not been detached, and Dick, taking the coil to the window, began to lower it slowly and cautiously into the darkness of the night. Joan stood by; but as the rope lengthened and still Dick continued to pay out, extreme fear began to conquer her resolution.

"Dick," she said, "is it so deep? I may not essay it. I should infallibly fall, good Dick."

It was just at the delicate moment of the operations that she spoke. Dick started; the remainder of the coil slipped from his grasp, and the end fell with a splash into the moat. Instantly, from the battlement above, the voice of a sentinel cried, "Who goes?"

"A murrain!" cried Dick. "We are paid now! Down with you—take the rope."

"I cannot," she cried, recoiling.

"An ye cannot, no more can I," said Shelton. "How can I swim the moat without you? Do ye desert me, then?"

"Dick," she gasped, "I cannot. The strength is gone from me."

"By the mass, then, we are all shent!" he shouted, stamping his foot; and then, hearing steps, he ran to the room door and sought to close it.

Before he could shoot the bolt, strong arms were thrusting it back upon him from the other side. He struggled for a second; then, feeling himself overpowered, ran back to the window. The girl had fallen against the wall in the embrasure of the window; she was more than half insensible; and when he tried to raise her in his arms, her body was limp and unresponsive.

At the same moment the men who had forced the door against him laid hold upon him. The first he poniarded at a blow, and the others falling back for a second in some disorder, he profited by the chance, bestrode the windowsill, seized the cord in both hands and let his body slip.

The cord was knotted, which made it the easier to descend; but so furious was Dick's hurry, and so small his experience of such gymnastics, that he spun round and round in mid-air like a criminal upon a gibbet and now beat his head and now bruised his hands against the rugged stone work of the wall. The air roared in his ears; he saw the stars overhead and the reflected stars below him in the moat, whirling like dead leaves before the tempest. And then he lost his hold and fell and soused head over ears into the icy water.

When he came to the surface his hand encountered the rope, which, newly lightened of his weight, was swinging wildly to and fro. There was a red glow overhead, and looking up he saw by the light of several torches and a cresset full of burning coals the battlements lined with faces. He saw the men's eyes turning hither and thither in quest of him; but he was too far below, the light reached him not, and they looked in vain.

And now he perceived that the rope was considerably too long, and he began to struggle as well as he could toward the other side of the moat, still keeping his head above water. In this way he got much more than halfway over; indeed, the bank was almost within reach before the rope began to draw him back by its own weight. Taking his courage in both hands, he let go and made a leap for the trailing sprays of willow that had already that same evening helped Sir Daniel's messenger to land. He went down, rose again, sank a second time, and then his hand caught a branch, and with the speed of thought he had dragged himself into the thick of the tree and clung there, dripping and panting, and still half uncertain of his escape.

But all this had not been done without a considerable splashing, which had so far indicated his position to the men along the battlements. Arrows and quarrels fell thick around him in the darkness, thick like driving hail; and suddenly a torch was thrown down—flared through the air in its swift passage—stuck for a moment on the edge of the bank, where it burned high and lit up its whole sur-roundings like a bonfire—and then, in a good hour for Dick, slipped off, plumped into the moat, and was instantly extinguished.

It had served its purpose. The marksmen had had time to see the willow, and Dick ensconced among its boughs; and though the lad instantly sprang higher up the bank and ran for his life, he was not yet quick enough to escape a shot. An arrow struck him in the shoulder, another grazed his head.

The pain of his wounds lent him wings; and he had no sooner got upon the level than he took to his heels and ran straight before him in the dark, without a thought for the direction of his flight.

For a few steps missiles followed him, but these soon ceased; and when at length he came to look behind, he was already a good way from the Moat House, though he could still see the torches moving to and fro along its battlements.

He leaned against a tree, streaming with blood and water, bruised, wounded, and alone. For all that, he had saved his life for that bout; and though Joanna remained behind in the power of Sir Daniel, he neither blamed himself for an accident that it had been beyond his power to prevent,

nor did he augur any fatal consequences to the girl herself. Sir Daniel was cruel, but he was not likely to be
cruel to a young gentlewoman who had other protectors,
willing and able to bring him to account. It was more probable he would make haste to marry her to some friend of
his own.

"Well," thought Dick, "between then and now, I will find
the means to bring that traitor under; for I think, by the
mass, that I be now absolved from any gratitude or obligation; and when war is open, there is a fair chance for all."

In the meanwhile, here he was in a sore plight.

For some little way farther he struggled forward
through the forest; but what with the pain of his wounds,
the darkness of the night, and the extreme uneasiness and
confusion of his mind, he soon became equally unable to
guide himself or to continue to push through the close
undergrowth, and he was fain at length to sit down and
lean his back against a tree.

When he awoke from something betwixt sleep and
swooning, the gray of the morning had begun to take the
place of night. A little chilly breeze was bustling among
the trees, and as he sat still staring before him, only half
awake, he became aware of something dark that swung to
and fro among the branches, some hundred yards in front
of him. The progressive brightening of the day and the
return of his own senses at last enabled him to recognize
the object. It was a man hanging from the bough of a tall
oak. His head had fallen forward on his breast; but at
every stronger puff of wind his body spun round and
round, and his legs and arms tossed like some ridiculous
plaything.

Dick clambered to his feet, and, staggering and leaning
on the tree-trunks as he went, drew near to this grim
object.

The bough was perhaps twenty feet above the ground,
and the poor fellow had been drawn up so high by his exe-
cutioners that his boots swung clear above Dick's reach;

and as his hood had been drawn over his face, it was impossible to recognize the man.

Dick looked about him right and left; and at last he perceived that the other end of the cord had been made fast to the trunk of a little hawthorn which grew, thick with blossom, under the lofty arcade of the oak. With his dagger, which alone remained to him of all his arms, young Shelton severed the rope, and instantly with a dead thump the corpse fell in a heap upon the ground.

Dick raised the hood; it was Throgmorton, Sir Daniel's messenger. He had not gone far upon his errand. A paper, which had apparently escaped the notice of the men of the Black Arrow, stuck from the bosom of his doublet, and Dick, pulling it forth, found it was Sir Daniel's letter to Lord Wensleydale.

"Come," thought he, "if the world changes yet again, I may have the wherewithal to shame Sir Daniel—nay, and perchance to bring him to the block."

And he put the paper in his own bosom, said a prayer over the dead man, and set forth again through the woods.

His fatigue and weakness increased; his ears sang, his steps faltered, his mind at intervals failed him, so low had he been brought by loss of blood. Doubtless he made many deviations from his true path, but at last he came out upon the high-road not very far from Tunstall hamlet.

A rough voice bid him stand.

"Stand?" repeated Dick. "By the mass, but I am nearer falling."

And he suited the action to the word and fell all his length upon the road.

Two men came forth out of the thicket, each in green forest jerkin, each with long-bow and quiver and short sword.

"Why, Lawless," said the younger of the two, "it is young Shelton."

"Aye, this will be as good as bread to John Amend-All,"

returned the other. "Though, faith, he hath been to the wars. Here is a tear in his scalp that must 'a' cost him many a good ounce of blood."

"And here," added Greensheve, "is a hole in his shoulder that must have pricked him well. Who hath done this, think ye? If it be one of ours, he may all to prayer; Ellis will give him a short shrift and a long rope."

"Up with the cub," said Lawless. "Clap him on my back."

And then, when Dick had been hoisted to his shoulders, and he had taken the lad's arms about his neck and got a firm hold of him, the ex–Gray Friar added—

"Keep ye the post, brother Greensheve. I will on with him by myself."

So Greensheve returned to his ambush on the wayside, and Lawless trudged down the hill, whistling as he went, with Dick, still in a dead faint, comfortably settled on his shoulders.

The sun rose as he came out of the skirts of the wood and saw Tunstall hamlet straggling up the opposite hill. All seemed quiet, but a strong post of some half a score of archers lay close by the bridge on either side of the road, and, as soon as they perceived Lawless with his burden, began to bestir themselves and set arrow to string like vigilant sentries.

"Who goes?" cried the man in command.

"Will Lawless, by the rood—ye know me as well as your own hand," returned the outlaw contemptuously.

"Give the word, Lawless," returned the other.

"Now, Heaven lighten thee, thou great fool," replied Lawless. "Did I not tell it thee myself? But ye are all mad for this playing at soldiers. When I am in the greenwood, give me greenwood ways; and my word for this tide is, 'A fig for all mock soldiery!'"

"Lawless, ye but show an ill example; give us the word, fool jester," said the commander of the post.

"And if I had forgotten it?" asked the other.

"An ye had forgotten it—as I know y'ave not—by the

mass, I would clap an arrow into your big body," returned the first.

"Nay, an y'are so ill a jester," said Lawless, "ye shall have your word for me. 'Duckworth and Shelton' is the word; and here, to the illustration, is Shelton on my shoulders, and to Duckworth do I carry him."

"Pass, Lawless," said the sentry.

"And where is John?" asked the Gray Friar.

"He holdeth a court, by the mass, and taketh rents as to the manner born!" cried another of the company.

So it proved. When Lawless got as far up the village as the little inn, he found Ellis Duckworth surrounded by Sir Daniel's tenants, and, by the right of his good company of archers, coolly taking rents and giving written receipts in return for them. By the faces of the tenants, it was plain how little this proceeding pleased them; for they argued very rightly that they would simply have to pay them twice.

As soon as he knew what had brought Lawless, Ellis dismissed the remainder of the tenants, and with every mark of interest and apprehension conducted Dick into an inner chamber of the inn. There the lad's hurts were looked to, and he was recalled by simple remedies to consciousness.

"Dear lad," said Ellis, pressing his hand, "y'are in a friend's hands that loved your father and loves you for his sake. Rest ye a little quietly, for ye are somewhat out of case. Then shall ye tell me your story, and betwixt the two of us we shall find a remedy for all."

A little later in the day and after Dick had awakened from a comfortable slumber to find himself still very weak but clearer in mind and easier in body, Ellis returned and sitting down by the bedside, begged him in the name of his father to relate the circumstances of his escape from Tunstall Moat House. There was something in the strength of Duckworth's frame, in the honesty of his brown face, in the clearness and shrewdness of his eyes that moved Dick to obey him; and from first to last the lad told him the story of his two days' adventures.

"Well," said Ellis, when he had done, "see what the kind saints have done for you, Dick Shelton, not alone to save your body in so numerous and deadly perils, but to bring you into my hands that have no dearer wish than to assist your father's son. Be but true to me—and I see y'are true—and betwixt you and me, we shall bring that false-heart traitor to the death."

"Will ye assault the house?" asked Dick.

"I were mad, indeed, to think of it," returned Ellis. "He hath too much power; his men gather to him; those that gave me the slip last night, and, by the mass, came in so handily for you—those have made him safe. Nay, Dick, to the contrary, thou and I and our brave bowmen, we must all slip from this forest speedily and leave Sir Daniel free."

"My mind misgiveth me for Jack," said the lad.

"For Jack!" repeated Duckworth. "Oh, I see, for the wench! Nay, Dick, I promise you if there come talk of any marriage we shall act at once; till then or till the time is ripe we shall all disappear, even like shadows at morning; Sir Daniel shall look east and west and see none enemies; he shall think, by the mass, that he hath dreamed awhile and hath now awakened in his bed. But our four eyes, Dick, shall follow him right close, and our four hands—so help us all the army of the saints!—shall bring that traitor low!"

Two days later Sir Daniel's garrison had grown to such a strength that he ventured on a sally, and at the head of some two score horsemen pushed without opposition as far as Tunstall hamlet. Not an arrow flew, not a man stirred in the thicket; the bridge was no longer guarded but stood open to all comers; and as Sir Daniel crossed it, he saw the villagers looking timidly from their doors.

Presently one of them, taking heart of grace, came forward and with the lowliest salutations presented a letter to the knight.

His face darkened as he read the contents. It ran thus:

To the most untrue and cruel gentylman, Sir Daniel Brackley,
Knyght,
These:

I fynde ye were untrue and unkynd fro the first. Ye have my
father's blood upon your hands; let it be, it will not wasshe.
Some day ye shall perish by my procurement, so much I let you
to wytte; and I let you to wytte farther, that if ye seek to wed to
any other the gentylwoman, Mistress Joan Sedley, whom that I
am bound upon a great oath to wed myself, the blow will be
very swift. The first step thereinne will be thy first step to the
grave.

Ric. Shelton.

BOOK III: MY LORD FOXHAM

The House by the Shore

MONTHS HAD passed away since Richard Shelton made his escape from the hands of his guardian. These months had been eventful for England. The party of Lancaster, which was then in the very article of death, had once more raised its head. The Yorkists defeated and dispersed, their leader butchered on the field, it seemed for a very brief season in the winter following upon the events already recorded as if the House of Lancaster had finally triumphed over its foes.

The small town of Shoreby-on-the-Till was full of Lancastrian nobles of the neighborhood. Earl Risingham was there with three hundred men-at-arms; Lord Shoreby with two hundred; Sir Daniel himself, high in favor and once more growing rich on confiscations, lay in a house of his own on the main street with three score men. The world had changed indeed.

It was a black, bitter cold evening in the first week of January, with a hard frost, a high wind, and every likelihood of snow before the morning.

In an obscure alehouse in a by-street near the harbor three or four men sat drinking ale and eating a hasty mess of eggs. They were all likely, lusty, weather-beaten fellows, hard of hand, bold of eye; and though they wore plain tabards, like country plowmen, even a drunken soldier might have looked twice before he sought a quarrel in such company.

A little apart before the huge fire sat a younger man, almost a boy, dressed in much the same fashion, though it was easy to see by his looks that he was better born, and might have worn a sword, had the time suited.

"Nay," said one of the men at the table, "I like it not. Ill will come of it. This is no place for jolly fellows. A jolly fellow loveth open country, good cover, and scarce foes; but here we are shut in a town, girt about with enemies; and for the bull's-eye of misfortune, see if it snow not ere the morning."

"'Tis for Master Shelton there," said another, nodding his head toward the lad before the fire.

"I will do much for Master Shelton," returned the first; "but to come to the gallows for any man—nay, brothers, not that!"

The door of the inn opened, and another man entered hastily and approached the youth before the fire.

"Master Shelton," he said, "Sir Daniel goeth forth with a pair of links and four archers."

Dick (for this was our young friend) rose instantly to his feet.

"Lawless," he said, "ye will take John Capper's watch. Greensheve, follow with me. Capper, lead forward. We will follow him this time, an he go to York."

The next moment they were outside in the dark street, and Capper, the man who had just come, pointed to where two torches flared in the wind at a little distance.

The town was already sound asleep; no one moved upon the streets, and there was nothing easier than to follow the party without observation. The two link-bearers went first; next followed a single man, whose long cloak blew about him in the wind; and the rear was brought up by the four archers, each with his bow upon his arm. They moved at a brisk walk, threading the intricate lanes and drawing nearer to the shore.

"He hath gone each night in this direction?" asked Dick, in a whisper.

"This is the third night running, Master Shelton,"

returned Capper, "and still at the same hour and with the same small following, as though his end were secret."

Sir Daniel and his six men were now come to the outskirts of the country. Shoreby was an open town, and though the Lancastrian lords who lay there kept a strong guard on the main roads, it was still possible to enter or depart unseen by any of the lesser streets or across the open country.

The lane which Sir Daniel had been following came to an abrupt end. Before him there was a stretch of rough down, and the noise of the sea-surf was audible upon one hand. There were no guards in the neighborhood nor any light in that quarter of the town.

Dick and his two outlaws drew a little closer to the object of their chase, and presently, as they came forth from between the houses and could see a little farther upon either hand, they were aware of another torch drawing near from another direction.

"Hey," said Dick, "I smell treason."

Meanwhile Sir Daniel had come to a full halt. The torches were stuck into the sand, and the men lay down, as if to await the arrival of the other party.

This drew near at a good rate. It consisted of four men only—a pair of archers, a varlet with a link, and a cloaked gentleman walking in their midst.

"Is it you, my lord?" cried Sir Daniel.

"It is I, indeed; and if ever true knight gave proof I am that man," replied the leader of the second troop; "for who would not rather face giants, sorcerers, or pagans than this pinching cold?"

"My lord," returned Sir Daniel, "beauty will be more beholden, misdoubt it not. But shall we forth? For the sooner ye have seen my merchandise, the sooner we shall both get home."

"But why keep ye her here, good knight?" inquired the other. "An she be so young, and so fair, and so wealthy, why do ye not bring her forth among her mates? Ye would soon make her a good marriage and no need to freeze your fingers and risk arrow-shots by going abroad at such unseemly seasons in the dark."

"I have told you, my lord," replied Sir Daniel, "the reason thereof concerneth me only. Neither do I purpose to explain it further. Suffice it that if ye be weary of your old gossip, Daniel Brackley, publish it abroad that y'are to wed Joanna Sedley, and I give you my word ye will be quit of him right soon. Ye will find him with an arrow in his back."

Meantime the two gentlemen were walking briskly forward over the down, the three torches going before them, stopping against the wind and scattering clouds of smoke and tufts of flame, and the rear brought up by the six archers.

Close upon the heels of these Dick followed. He had, of course, heard no word of this conversation; but he had recognized in the second of the speakers old Lord Shoreby himself, a man of an infamous reputation, whom even Sir Daniel affected in public to condemn.

Presently they came close down upon the beach. The air smelled salt; the noise of the surf increased; and here in a large walled garden there stood a small house of two stories with stables and other offices.

The foremost torch-bearer unlocked a door in the wall, and after the whole party had passed into the garden, again closed and locked it on the other side.

Dick and his men were thus excluded from any further following, unless they should scale the wall and thus put their necks in a trap.

They sat down in a tuft of furze and waited. The red glow of the torches moved up and down and to and fro within the inclosure, as if the link-bearers steadily patrolled the garden.

Twenty minutes passed, and then the whole party issued forth again upon the down; and Sir Daniel and the baron, after an elaborate salutation, separated and turned severally homeward, each with his own following of men and lights.

As soon as the sound of their steps had been swallowed by the wind, Dick got to his feet as briskly as he was able, for he was stiff and aching with the cold.

"Capper, ye will give me a back up," he said.

They advanced, all three, to the wall; Capper stooped, and Dick, getting upon his shoulders, clambered on to the cope-stone.

"Now, Greensheve," whispered Dick, "follow me up here; lie flat upon your face, that ye may be the less seen; and be ever ready to give me a hand if I fall foully on the other side."

And so saying he dropped into the garden.

It was all pitch dark; there was no light in the house. The wind whistled shrill among the poor shrubs, and the surf beat upon the beach; there was no other sound. Cautiously Dick footed it forth, stumbling among bushes and groping with his hands; and presently the crisp noise of gravel under foot told him that he had struck upon an alley.

Here he paused, and taking his cross-bow from where he kept it concealed under his long tabard, he prepared it for instant action and went forward once more with greater resolution and assurance. The path led him straight to the group of buildings.

All seemed to be sorely dilapidated: the windows of the house were secured by crazy shutters, the stables were open and empty; there was no hay in the hayloft; no corn in the corn-box. Anyone would have supposed the place to be deserted; but Dick had good reason to think otherwise. He continued his inspection, visiting the offices, trying all the windows. At length he came round to the sea-side of the house, and there, sure enough, there burned a pale light in one of the upper windows.

He stepped back a little way, till he thought he could see the movement of a shadow on the wall of the apartment. Then he remembered that in the stable his groping hand had rested for a moment on a ladder, and he returned with all dispatch to bring it. The ladder was very short, but yet, by standing on the topmost round, he could bring his hands as high as the iron bars of the windows; and seizing these he raised his body by main force until his eyes commanded the interior of the room.

Two persons were within: the first he readily knew to be Dame Hatch; the second, a tall and beautiful and grave young lady, in a long, embroidered dress—could that be Joanna Sedley? his old wood-companion, Jack, whom he had thought to punish with a belt?

He dropped back again to the top round of the ladder in a kind of amazement. He had never thought of his sweetheart as of so superior a being, and he was instantly taken with a feeling of diffidence. But he had little opportunity for thought. A low "Hist!" sounded from close by, and he hastened to descend the ladder.

"Who goes?" he whispered.

"Greensheve," came the reply, in tones similarly guarded.

"What want ye?" asked Dick.

"The house is watched, Master Shelton," returned the outlaw. "We are not alone to watch it; for even as I lay on my belly on the wall I saw men prowling in the dark and heard them whistle softly one to the other."

"By my sooth," said Dick, "but this is passing strange! Were they not men of Sir Daniel's?"

"Nay, sir, that they were not," returned Greensheve, "for if I have eyes in my head, every man-Jack of them weareth me a white badge in his bonnet, something checkered with dark."

"White, checkered with dark?" repeated Dick. "Faith, 'tis a badge I know not. It is none of this country's badges. Well, an that be so, let us slip as quietly forth from this garden as we may; for here we are in an evil posture for defense. Beyond all question there are men of Sir Daniel's in that house, and to be taken between two shots is a beggarman's position. Take me this ladder; I must leave it where I found it."

They returned the ladder to the stable and groped their way to the place where they had entered.

Capper had taken Greensheve's position on the cope, and now he leaned down his hand, and, first one and then the other, pulled them up.

Cautiously and silently they dropped again upon the other side; nor did they dare to speak until they had returned to their old ambush in the gorse.

"Now, John Capper," said Dick, "back with you to Shoreby, even as for your life. Bring me instantly what men ye can collect. Here shall be the rendezvous; or if the men be scattered and the day be near at hand before they muster, let the place be something farther back and by the entering in of the town. Greensheve and I lie here to watch. Speed ye, John Capper, and the saints aid you to dispatch! And now, Greensheve," he continued as soon as Capper had departed, "let thou and I go round about the garden in a wide circuit. I would fain see whether thine eyes betrayed thee."

Keeping well outward from the wall, and profiting by every height and hollow, they passed about two sides, beholding nothing. On the third side the garden wall was built close upon the beach, and to preserve the distance necessary to their purpose, they had to go some way down upon the sands. Although the tide was still pretty far out, the surf was so high and the sands so flat that at each breaker a great sheet of froth and water came careering over the expanse, and Dick and Greensheve made this part of their inspection wading now to the ankles and now as deep as to the knees in the salt and icy waters of the German Ocean.

Suddenly, against the comparative whiteness of the garden wall, the figure of a man was seen like a faint Chinese shadow violently signaling with both arms. As he dropped again to the earth, another arose a little farther on and repeated the same performance. And so, like a silent watchword, these gesticulations made the round of the beleaguered garden.

"They keep good watch," Dick whispered.

"Let us back to land, good master," answered Greensheve. "We stand here too open; for look ye, when the seas break heavy and white out there behind us, they shall see us plainly against the foam."

"Ye speak sooth," returned Dick. "Ashore with us, right speedily."

A Skirmish in the Dark

Thoroughly drenched and chilled, the two adventurers returned to their position in the gorse.

"I pray Heaven that Capper make good speed!" said Dick. "I vow a candle to Saint Mary of Shoreby if he come before the hour!"

"Y'are in a hurry, Master Dick?" asked Greensheve.

"Aye, good fellow," answered Dick; "for in that house lieth my lady, whom I love, and who should these be that lie about her secretly by night? Unfriends for sure!"

"Well," returned Greensheve, "an John come speedily, we shall give a good account of them. They are not two score at the outside—I judge so by the spacing of their sentries—and taken where they are, lying so widely, one score would scatter them like sparrows. And yet, Master Dick, an she be in Sir Daniel's power already, it will little hurt that she should change into another's. Who should these be?"

"I do suspect the Lord of Shoreby," Dick replied. "When came they?"

"They began to come, Master Dick," said Greensheve, "about the time ye crossed the wall. I had not lain there the space of a minute ere I marked the first of the knaves crawling round the corner."

The last light had been already extinguished in the little house when they were wading in the wash of the breakers, and it was impossible to predict at what moment the lurking men about the garden wall might make their onslaught. Of two evils, Dick preferred the least. He preferred that Joanna should remain under the guardianship of Sir Daniel rather than pass into the clutches of Lord Shoreby; and his mind was made up, if the house should be assaulted, to come at once to the relief of the besieged.

But the time passed, and still there was no movement. From quarter of an hour to quarter of an hour the same signal passed about the garden wall, as if the leader desired to assure himself of the vigilance of his scattered followers; but in every other particular the neighborhood of the little house lay undisturbed.

Presently Dick's reënforcements began to arrive. The night was not yet old before nearly a score of men crouched beside him in the gorse.

Separating these into two bodies, he took the command of the smaller himself and intrusted the large to the leadership of Greensheve.

"Now, Kit," said he to this last, "take me your men to the near angle of the garden wall upon the beach. Post them strongly and wait till that ye hear me falling on upon the other side. It is those upon the sea-front that I would fain make certain of, for there will be the leader. The rest will run; even let them. And now, lads, let no man draw an arrow; ye will but hurt friends. Take to the steel, and keep to the steel; and if we have the uppermost, I promise every man of you a gold noble when I come to mine estate."

Out of the odd collection of broken men, thieves, murderers, and ruined peasantry whom Duckworth had gathered together to serve the purposes of his revenge, some of the boldest and most experienced in war had volunteered to follow Richard Shelton. The service of watching Sir Daniel's movements in the town of Shoreby had from the first been irksome to their temper, and they had of late begun to grumble loudly and threaten to disperse. The prospect of a sharp encounter and possible spoils restored them to good humor, and they joyfully prepared for battle.

Their long tabards thrown aside, they appeared, some in plain green jerkins and some in stout leathern jacks; under their hoods many wore bonnets strengthened by iron plates; and for offensive armor, swords, daggers, a few stout boar-spears, and a dozen of bright bills put them in a posture to engage even regular feudal troops. The bows, quivers, and tabards were concealed among the gorse, and the two bands set resolutely forward.

Dick, when he had reached the other side of the house, posted his six men in a line about twenty yards from the garden wall and took position himself a few paces in front. Then they all shouted with one voice and closed upon the enemy.

These, lying widely scattered, stiff with cold and taken at unawares, sprang stupidly to their feet and stood undecided. Before they had time to get their courage about them or even to form an idea of the number and mettle of their assailants, a similar shout of onslaught sounded in their ears from the far side of the inclosure. Thereupon they gave themselves up for lost and ran.

In this way the two small troops of the men of the Black Arrow closed upon the sea-front of the garden wall and took a part of the strangers, as it were, between two fires; while the whole of the remainder ran for their lives in different directions and were soon scattered in the darkness.

For all that, the fight was but beginning. Dick's outlaws, although they had the advantage of the surprise, were still considerably outnumbered by the men they had surrounded. The tide had flowed in the meanwhile; the beach was narrowed to a strip; and on this wet field, between the surf and the garden wall, there began in the darkness a doubtful, furious, and deadly contest.

The strangers were well armed; they fell in silence upon their assailants; and the affray became a series of single combats. Dick, who had come first into the mellay, was engaged by three; the first he cut down at the first blow, but the other two coming upon him hotly he was fain to give ground before their onset. One of these two was a huge fellow, almost a giant for stature and armed with a two-handed sword which he brandished like a switch. Against this opponent with his reach of arm and the length and weight of his weapon Dick and his bill were quite defenseless; and had the other continued to join vigorously in the attack, the lad must have indubitably fallen. This second man, however, paused for a moment to peer about him in the darkness and to give ear to the sounds of the battle.

The giant still pursued his advantage, and still Dick fled before him, spying for his chance. Then the huge blade flashed and descended, and the lad, leaping on one side and running in, slashed sideways and upward with his bill. A roar of agony responded, and before the wounded man could raise his formidable weapon, Dick, twice repeating his blow, had brought him to the ground.

The next moment he was engaged upon more equal terms with his second pursuer. Here there was no great difference in size, and though the man, fighting with sword and dagger against a bill and being wary and quick of fence had a certain superiority of arms, Dick more than made it up by his greater agility on foot. Neither at first gained any obvious advantage; but the older man was still insensibly profiting by the ardor of the younger to lead him where he would; and presently Dick found that they had crossed the whole width of the beach and were now fighting above the knees in the spume and bubble of the breakers. Here his own superior activity was rendered useless; he found himself more or less at the discretion of his foe; yet a little and he had his back turned upon his own men and saw that this adroit and skillful adversary was bent upon drawing him farther and farther away.

Dick ground his teeth. He determined to decide the combat instantly; and when the wash of the next wave had ebbed and left them dry, he rushed in, caught a blow upon his bill, and leaped right at the throat of his opponent. The man went down backward with Dick still upon the top of him; and the next wave, speedily succeeding the last, buried him below a rush of water.

While he was still submerged, Dick forced his dagger from his grasp and rose to his feet victorious.

"Yield ye!" he said. "I give you life."

"I yield me," said the other, getting to his knees. "Ye fight like a young man, ignorantly and foolhardily; but, by the array of the saints, ye fight bravely!"

Dick turned to the beach. The combat was still raging doubtfully in the night; over the hoarse roar of the breakers steel clanged upon steel, and cries of pain and the shout of battle resounded.

"Lead me to your captain, youth," said the conquered knight. "It is fit this butchery should cease."

"Sir," replied Dick, "so far as these brave fellows have a captain, the poor gentleman who addresses you is he."

"Call off your dogs, then, and I will bid my villains hold," returned the other.

There was something noble both in the voice and manner of his late opponent, and Dick instantly dismissed all fears of treachery.

"Lay down your arms, men!" cried the stranger knight. "I have yielded me upon promise of life."

The tone of the stranger was one of absolute command, and almost instantly the din and confusion of the mellay ceased.

"Lawless," cried Dick, "are ye safe?"

"Aye," cried Lawless, "safe and hearty."

"Light me the lantern," said Dick.

"Is not Sir Daniel here?" inquired the knight.

"Sir Daniel?" echoed Dick. "Now, by the rood, I pray not. It would go ill with me if he were."

"Ill with you, fair sir?" inquired the other. "Nay, then, if ye be not of Sir Daniel's party, I profess I comprehend no longer. Wherefore, then, fell ye upon mine ambush? in what quarrel, my young and very fiery friend? to what earthly purpose? and to make a clear end of questioning to what good gentleman have I surrendered?"

But before Dick could answer, a voice spoke in the darkness from close by. Dick could see the speaker's black and white badge and the respectful salute which he addressed to his superior.

"My lord," said he, "if these gentlemen be unfriends to Sir Daniel, it is a pity, indeed, we should have been at blows with them; but it were tenfold greater that either they or we should linger here. The watchers in the house—unless they be all dead or deaf—have heard our hammering this quarter-hour agone; instantly they have signaled to the town; and unless we be the livelier in our departure, we are like to be taken, both of us, by a fresh foe."

"Hawksley is in the right," added the lord. "How please ye, sir? Whither shall we march?"

"Nay, my lord," said Dick, "go where you will for me. I do begin to suspect we have some ground of friendship, and if, indeed, I began our acquaintance somewhat ruggedly, I would not churlishly continue. Let us, then, separate, my lord, you laying your right hand in mine; and at the hour and place that ye shall name, let us encounter and agree."

"Y'are too trustful, boy," said the other; "but this time your trust is not misplaced. I will meet you at the point of day at Saint Bride's Cross. Come, lads, follow!"

The strangers disappeared from the scene with a rapidity that seemed suspicious; and while the outlaws fell to the congenial task of rifling the dead bodies Dick made once more the circuit of the garden wall to examine the front of the house. In a little upper loophole of the roof he beheld a light set; and as it would certainly be visible in town from the back windows of Sir Daniel's mansion, he doubted not that this was the signal feared by Hawksley, and that ere long the lances of the knight of Tunstall would arrive upon the scene.

He put his ear to the ground, and it seemed to him as if he heard a jarring and hollow noise from townward. Back to the beach he went hurrying. But the work was already done; the last body was disarmed and stripped to the skin, and four fellows were already wading seaward to commit it to the mercies of the deep.

A few minutes later, when there debouched out of the nearest lanes of Shoreby some two score horsemen, hastily arrayed and moving at the gallop of their steeds, the neighborhood of the house beside the sea was entirely silent and deserted.

Meanwhile, Dick and his men had returned to the ale-house of the Goat and Bagpipes to snatch some hours of sleep before the morning tryst.

Saint Bride's Cross

Saint Bride's Cross stood a little way from Shoreby on the skirts of Tunstall Forest. Two roads met: one from Holy-wood across the forest; one, that road from Risingham down which we saw the wrecks of a Lancastrian army flee-ing in disorder. Here the two joined issue and went on together down the hill to Shoreby; and a little back from the point of junction, the summit of a little knoll was crowned by the ancient and weather-beaten cross.

Here, then, about seven in the morning, Dick arrived. It was as cold as ever; the earth was all gray and silver with the hoar-frost, and the day began to break in the east with many colors of purple and orange.

Dick set him down upon the lowest step of the cross, wrapped himself well in his tabard and looked vigilantly upon all sides. He had not long to wait. Down the road from Holywood a gentleman in very rich and bright armor and wearing over that a surcoat of the rarest furs, came pacing on a splendid charger. Twenty yards behind him followed a clump of lancers; but these halted as soon as they came in view of the trysting-place, while the gentle-man in the fur surcoat continued to advance alone.

His visor was raised and showed a countenance of great command and dignity answerable to the richness of his attire and arms. And it was with some confusion of man-ner that Dick arose from the cross and stepped down the bank to meet his prisoner.

"I thank you, my lord, for your exactitude," he said, lout-ing* very low. "Will it please your lordship to set foot to earth?"

"Are ye here alone, young man?" inquired the other.

"I was not so simple," answered Dick; "and to be plain with your lordship the woods upon either hand of this cross lie full of mine honest fellows lying on their weapons."

"Y'ave done wisely," said the lord. "It pleaseth me the rather, since last night ye fought foolhardily and more like a savage Saracen lunatic than any Christian warrior. But it becomes not me to complain that had the undermost."

"Ye had the undermost indeed, my lord, since ye so fell," returned Dick; "but had the waves not holpen me, it was I that should have had the worst. Ye were pleased to make me yours with several dagger marks, which I still carry. And in fine, my lord, methinks I had all the danger, as well as all the profit, of that little blind-man's medley on the beach."

"Y'are shrewd enough to make light of it, I see," returned the stranger.

"Nay, my lord, not shrewd," replied Dick, "in that I shoot at no advantage to myself. But when, by the light of this new day, I see how stout a knight hath yielded, not to my arms alone but to fortune, and the darkness, and the surf—and how easily the battle had gone otherwise, with a soldier so untried and rustic as myself—think it not strange, my lord, if I feel confounded with my victory."

"Ye speak well," said the stranger. "Your name?"

"My name, an't like you, is Shelton," answered Dick.

"Men call me the Lord Foxham," added the other.

"Then my lord, and under your good favor, ye are guardian to the sweetest maid in England," replied Dick; "and for your ransom and the ransom of such as were taken with you on the beach there will be no uncertainty

*Bowing respectfully.

of terms. I pray you, my lord, of your good will and charity, yield me the hand of my mistress, Joan Sedley; and take ye, upon the other part, your liberty, the liberty of these your followers, and (if ye will have it) my gratitude and service till I die."

"But are ye not ward to Sir Daniel? Methought, if y'are Harry Shelton's son, that I had heard it so reported," said Lord Foxham.

"Will it please you, my lord, to alight? I would fain tell you fully who I am, how situate, and why so bold in my demands. Beseech you, my lord, take place upon these steps, hear me to a full end, and judge me with allowance."

And so saying, Dick lent a hand to Lord Foxham to dismount; led him up the knoll to the cross; installed him in the place where he had himself been sitting; and standing respectfully before his noble prisoner, related the story of his fortunes up to the events of the evening before.

Lord Foxham listened gravely, and, when Dick had done, "Master Shelton," he said, "ye are a most fortunate-unfortunate young gentleman; but what fortune y'ave had, that ye have amply merited; and what unfortune, ye have noways deserved. Be of good cheer; for ye have made a friend who is devoid neither of power nor favor. For yourself, although it fits not for a person of your birth to herd with outlaws, I must own ye are both brave and honorable; very dangerous in battle, right courteous in peace; a youth of excellent disposition and brave bearing. For your estates, ye will never see them till the world shall change again; so long as Lancaster hath the strong hand, so long shall Sir Daniel enjoy them for his own. For my ward, it is another matter; I had promised her before to a gentleman, a kinsman of my house, one Hamley; the promise is old——"

"Aye, my lord, and now Sir Daniel hath promised her to my Lord Shoreby," interrupted Dick. "And his promise, for all it is but young, is still the likelier to be made good."

"'Tis the plain truth," returned his lordship. "And

considering, moreover, that I am your prisoner, upon no better composition than my bare life, and over and above that, that the maiden is unhappily in other hands, I will so far consent. Aid me with your good fellows——"

"My lord," cried Dick, "they are these same outlaws that ye blame me for consorting with."

"Let them be what they will, they can fight," returned Lord Foxham. "Help me, then; and if between us we regain the maid, upon my knightly honor, she shall marry you!"

Dick bent his knee before his prisoner; but he, leaping up lightly from the cross, caught the lad up and embraced him like a son.

"Come," he said, "an y'are to marry Joan, we must be early friends."

The *Good Hope*

An hour thereafter, Dick was back at the Goat and Bag-pipes, breaking his fast and receiving the report of his messengers and sentries. Duckworth was still absent from Shoreby; and this was frequently the case, for he played many parts in the world, shared many different interests, and conducted many various affairs. He had founded that fellowship of the Black Arrow as a ruined man longing for vengeance and money; and yet among those who knew him best, he was thought to be the agent and emissary of the great king-maker of England, Richard, Earl of Warwick.

In his absence, at any rate, it fell upon Richard Shelton to command affairs in Shoreby; and as he sat at meat his mind was full of care and his face heavy with considera-tion. It had been determined between him and the Lord Foxham to make one bold stroke that evening and by brute force to set Joanna free. The obstacles, however, were many; and as one after another of his scouts arrived, each brought him more discomfortable news.

Sir Daniel was alarmed by the skirmish of the night

before. He had increased the garrison of the house in the garden; but not content with that, he had stationed horsemen in all the neighboring lanes, so that he might have instant word of any movement. Meanwhile, in the court of his mansion, steeds stood saddled, and the riders, armed at every point, awaited but the signal to ride.

The adventure of the night appeared more and more difficult of execution, till suddenly Dick's countenance lightened.

"Lawless!" he cried, "you that were a shipman, can ye steal me a ship?"

"Master Dick," replied Lawless, "if ye would back me, I would agree to steal York Minster."

Presently after, these two set forth and descended to the harbor. It was a considerable basin, lying among sandhills and surrounded with patches of down, ancient ruinous lumber, and tumble-down slums of the town. Many decked ships and many open boats either lay there at anchor or had been drawn up on the beach. A long duration of bad weather had driven them from the high seas into the shelter of the port; and the great trooping of black clouds and the cold squalls that followed one another, now with a sprinkling of dry snow, now in a mere swoop of wind, promised no improvement but rather threatened a more serious storm in the immediate future.

The seamen, in view of the cold and the wind, had for the most part slunk ashore and were now roaring and singing in the shoreside taverns. Many of the ships already rode unguarded at their anchors; and as the day wore on, and the weather offered no appearance of improvement, the number was continually being augmented. It was to these deserted ships, and above all to those of them that lay far out that Lawless directed his attention; while Dick, seated upon an anchor that was half embedded in the sand and giving ear now to the rude, potent, and boding voices of the gale and now to the hoarse singing of the shipmen in a neighboring tavern, soon forgot his immediate surroundings and concerns in the agreeable recollection of Lord Foxham's promise.

He was disturbed by a touch upon his shoulder. It was Lawless, pointing to a small ship that lay somewhat by itself and within but a little of the harbor mouth, where it heaved regularly and smoothly on the entering swell. A pale gleam of winter sunshine fell at that moment on the vessel's deck, relieving her against a bank of scowling cloud; and in this momentary glitter Dick could see a couple of men hauling the skiff alongside.

"There, sir," said Lawless, "mark ye it well! There is the ship for tonight."

Presently the skiff put out from the vessel's side, and the two men, keeping her head well to the wind, pulled lustily for shore. Lawless turned to a loiterer.

"How call ye her?" he asked, pointing to the little vessel.

"They call her the *Good Hope* of Dartmouth," replied the loiterer. "Her captain, Arblaster by name. He pulleth the bow oar in yon skiff."

This was all that Lawless wanted. Hurriedly thanking the man, he moved round the shore to a certain sandy creek for which the skiff was heading. There he took up his position, and as soon as they were within earshot, opened fire on the sailors of the *Good Hope*.

"What! Gossip Arblaster!" he cried. "Why, ye be well met; nay, gossip, ye be right well met, upon the rood! And is that the *Good Hope*? Aye, I would know her among ten thousand!—a sweet shear, a sweet boat! But marry come up, my gossip, will ye drink? I have come into mine estate, which doubtless ye remember to have heard on. I am now rich; I have left to sail upon the sea; I do sail now, for the most part, upon spiced ale. Come, fellow, thy hand upon't! Come, drink with an old shipfellow!"

Skipper Arblaster, a long-faced, elderly, weather-beaten man, with a knife hanging about his neck by a plaited cord and for all the world like any modern seaman in his gait and bearing, had hung back in obvious amazement and distrust. But the name of an estate and a certain air of tipsified simplicity and good-fellowship which Lawless very well affected, combined to conquer his suspicious jealousy; his countenance relaxed, and he at once extended his open hand and squeezed that of the outlaw in a formidable grasp.

"Nay," he said, "I cannot mind you. But what o' that? I would drink with any man, gossip, and so would my man Tom. Man Tom," he added, addressing his follower, "here is my gossip, whose name I cannot mind but no doubt a very good seaman. Let's go drink with him and his shore friend."

Lawless led the way, and they were soon seated in an alehouse, which, as it was very new and stood in an exposed and solitary station, was less crowded than those nearer to the center of the port. It was but a shed of timber, much like a block-house in the backwoods of today, and was coarsely furnished with a press or two, a number of naked benches, and boards set upon barrels to play the part of tables. In the middle and besieged by half a hundred violent drafts, a fire of wreckwood blazed and vomited thick smoke.

"Aye, now," said Lawless, "here is a shipman's joy—a good fire and a good stiff cup ashore, with foul weather without and an off-sea gale a-snoring in the roof! Here's to the *Good Hope*! May she ride easy!"

"Aye," said Skipper Arblaster, "'tis good weather to be ashore in, that is sooth. Man Tom, how say ye to that? Gossip, ye speak well, though I can never think upon your name; but ye speak very well. May the *Good Hope* ride easy! Amen."

"Friend Dickon," resumed Lawless, addressing his commander, "ye have certain matters on hand, unless I err? Well, prithee be about them incontinently. For here I be with the choice of all good company, two tough old shipmen; and till that ye return I will go warrant these brave fellows will bide here and drink me cup for cup. We are not like shoremen, we old, tough tarry-Johns!"

"It is well meant," returned the skipper. "Ye can go, boy; for I will keep your good friend and my good gossip company till curfew—aye, and by Saint Mary, till the sun get up again! For, look ye, when a man hath been long enough at sea, the salt getteth me into the clay upon his bones; and let him drink a draw-well, he will never be quenched."

Thus encouraged upon all hands, Dick rose, saluted his company, and going forth again into the gusty afternoon, got him as speedily as he might to the Goat and Bagpipes. Thence he sent word to my Lord Foxham that, so soon as ever the evening closed, they would have a stout boat to keep the sea in. And then leading along with him a couple of outlaws who had some experience, he returned himself to the harbor and the little sandy creek.

The skiff of the *Good Hope* lay among many others, from which it was easily distinguished by its extreme smallness and fragility. Indeed, when Dick and his two men had taken their places and begun to put forth out of the creek into the open harbor, the little cockle dipped into the swell and staggered under every gust of wind like a thing upon the point of sinking.

The *Good Hope*, as we have said, was anchored far out, where the swell was heaviest. No other vessel lay nearer than several cables' length; those that were the nearest were themselves entirely deserted; and as the skiff approached, a thick flurry of snow and a sudden darkening of the weather further concealed the movements of the outlaws from all possible espial. In a trice they had leaped upon the heaving deck, and the skiff was dancing at the stern. The *Good Hope* was captured.

She was a good stout boat, decked in the bows and amidships but open in the stern. She carried one mast and was rigged between a felucca and a lugger. It would seem that Skipper Arblaster had made an excellent venture, for the hold was full of pieces of French wine; and in the little cabin, besides the Virgin Mary in the bulkhead which proved the captain's piety, there were many lockfast chests and cupboards, which showed him to be rich and careful.

A dog, who was the sole occupant of the vessel, furiously barked and bit the heels of the boarders; but he was soon kicked into the cabin and the door shut upon his just resentment. A lamp was lit and fixed in the shrouds to mark the vessel clearly from the shore; one of the wine-pieces in the hold was broached, and a cup of excellent Gascony emptied to the adventure of the evening; and then, while one of the outlaws began to get ready his bow and arrows and prepare to hold the ship against all com-ers, the other hauled in the skiff and got overboard, where he held on, waiting for Dick.

"Well, Jack, keep me a good watch," said the young commander, preparing to follow his subordinate. "Ye will do right well."

"Why," returned Jack, "I shall do excellent well indeed, so long as we lie here; but once we put the nose of this poor ship outside the harbor—— See, there, she trem-bles! Nay, the poor shrew heard the words, and the heart misgave her in her oak-tree ribs. But look, Master Dick! how black the weather gathers!"

The darkness ahead was, indeed, astonishing. Great bil-lows heaved up out of the blackness one after another; and one after another the *Good Hope* buoyantly climbed and giddily plunged upon the farther side. A thin sprinkle of snow and thin flakes of foam came flying and powdered the deck; and the wind harped dismally among the rigging.

"In sooth, it looketh evilly," said Dick. "But what cheer! 'Tis but a squall, and presently it will blow over." But in spite of his words he was depressingly affected by the bleak disorder of the sky and the wailing and fluting of the wind; and as he got over the side of the *Good Hope* and made once more for the landing-creek with the best speed of oars, he crossed himself devoutly, and recommended to Heaven the lives of all who should adventure on the sea.

At the landing-creek there had already gathered about a dozen of the outlaws. To these the skiff was left, and they were bidden embark without delay.

A little farther up the beach Dick found Lord Foxham hurrying in quest of him, his face concealed with a dark hood, and his bright armor covered by a long russet mantle of a poor appearance.

"Young Shelton," he said, "are ye for the sea, then, truly?"

"My lord," replied Richard, "they lie about the house with horsemen; it may not be reached from the land side without alarum; and, Sir Daniel once advertised of our adventure, we can no more carry it to a good end than, saving your presence, we could ride upon the wind. Now, in going round by sea, we do run some peril by the elements; but, what much outweigheth all, we have a chance to make good our purpose and bear off the maid."

"Well," returned Lord Foxham, "lead on. I will, in some sort, follow you for shame's sake; but I own I would I were in bed."

"Here, then," said Dick. "Hither we go to fetch our pilot."

And he led the way to the rude alehouse where he had given rendezvous to a portion of his men. Some of these he found lingering round the door outside; others had pushed more boldly in, and choosing places as near as possible to where they saw their comrade, gathered close about Lawless and the two shipmen. These, to judge by the distempered countenance and cloudy eye, had long since gone beyond the boundaries of moderation; and as Richard entered, closely followed by Lord Foxham, they were all three tuning up an old, pitiful sea-ditty to the chorus of the wailing of the gale.

The young leader cast a rapid glance about the shed. The fire had just been replenished and gave forth volumes of black smoke, so that it was difficult to see clearly in the farther corners. It was plain, however, that the outlaws very largely outnumbered the remainder of the guests. Satisfied upon this point, in case of any failure in the operation of his plan, Dick strode up to the table and resumed his place upon the bench.

"Hey?" cried the skipper tipsily, "who are ye, hey?"

"I want a word with you without, Master Arblaster,"

returned Dick; "and here is what we shall talk of." And he showed him a gold noble in the glimmer of the firelight.

The shipman's eyes burned, although he still failed to recognize our hero.

"Aye, boy," he said, "I am with you. Gossip, I will be back anon. Drink fair, gossip"; and taking Dick's arm to steady his uneven steps, he walked to the door of the alehouse.

As soon as he was over the threshold, ten strong arms had seized and bound him; and in two minutes more, with his limbs trussed one to another and a good gag in his mouth, he had been tumbled neck and crop into a neighboring hay-barn. Presently, his man Tom, similarly secured, was tossed beside him, and the pair were left to their uncouth reflections for the night.

And now, as the time for concealment had gone by, Lord Foxham's followers were summoned by a preconcerted signal, and the party, boldly taking possession of as many boats as their numbers required, pulled in a flotilla for the light in the rigging of the ship. Long before the last man had climbed to the deck of the *Good Hope,* the sound of furious shouting from the shore showed that a part, at least, of the seamen had discovered the loss of their skiffs.

But it was now too late, whether for recovery or revenge. Out of some forty fighting men now mustered in the stolen ship, eight had been to sea and could play the part of mariners. With the aid of these, a slice of sail was got upon her. The cable was cut. Lawless, vacillating on his feet, and still shouting the chorus of sea-ballads, took the long tiller in his hands; and the *Good Hope* began to flit forward into the darkness of the night, and to face the great waves beyond the harbor-bar.

Richard took his place beside the weather rigging. Except for the ship's own lantern and for some lights in Shoreby town that were already fading to leeward, the whole world of air was as black as in a pit. Only from time to time, as the *Good Hope* swooped dizzily down into the valley of the rollers, a crest would break—a great cataract of snowy foam would leap in one instant into being—and in an instant more would stream into the wake and vanish.

Many of the men lay holding on and praying aloud; many more were sick and had crept into the bottom, where they sprawled among the cargo. And what with the extreme violence of the motion and the continual drunken bravado of Lawless, still shouting and singing at the helm, the stoutest heart on board may have nourished a shrewd misgiving as to the result.

But Lawless, as if guided by an instinct, steered the ship across the breakers, struck the lee of a great sandbank, where they sailed for a while in smooth water and presently after laid her alongside a rude, stone pier, where she was hastily made fast and lay ducking and grinding in the dark.

The *Good Hope*
(continued)

The pier was not far distant from the house in which Joanna lay; it now only remained to get the men on shore, to surround the house with a strong party, burst in the door, and carry off the captive. They might then regard themselves as done with the *Good Hope*; it had placed them on the rear of their enemies; and the retreat, whether they should succeed or fail in the main enterprise, would be directed with a greater measure of hope in the direction of the forest and my Lord Foxham's reserve.

To get the men on shore, however, was no easy task; many had been sick, all were pierced with cold; the promiscuity and disorder on board had shaken their discipline; the movement of the ship and the darkness of the night had cowed their spirits. They made a rush upon the pier; my lord, with his sword drawn on his own retainers, must throw himself in front; and this impulse of rabblement was not restrained without a certain clamor of voices, highly to be regretted in the case.

When some degree of order had been restored, Dick with a few chosen men set forth in advance. The darkness on shore, by contrast with the flashing of the surf, appeared before him like a solid body; and the howling and whistling of the gale drowned any lesser noise.

He had scarce reached the end of the pier, however, when there fell a lull of the wind; and in this he seemed to hear on shore the hollow footing of horses and the clash of arms. Checking his immediate followers, he passed forward a step or two alone, even setting foot upon the down; and here he made sure he could detect the shape of men and horses moving. A strong discouragement assailed him. If their enemies were really on the watch, if they had beleaguered the shoreward end of the pier, he and Lord Foxham were taken in a posture of very poor defense—the sea behind, the men jostled in the dark upon a narrow causeway. He gave a cautious whistle, the signal previously agreed upon.

It proved to be a signal for more than he desired. Instantly there fell, through the black night, a shower of arrows sent at a venture; and so close were the men huddled on the pier that more than one was hit, and the arrows were answered with cries of both fear and pain. In this first discharge, Lord Foxham was struck down; Hawksley had him carried on board again at once; and his men, during the brief remainder of the skirmish, fought (when they fought at all) without guidance. That was, perhaps, the chief cause of the disaster which made haste to follow.

At the shore end of the pier, for perhaps a minute, Dick held his own with a handful; one or two were wounded upon either side; steel crossed steel; nor had there been the least signal of advantage, when in the twinkling of an eye the tide turned against the party from the ship. Someone cried out that all was lost; the men were in the very humor to lend an ear to a discomfortable counsel; the cry was taken up. "On board, lads, for your lives!" cried another. A third, with the true instinct of the coward, raised that inevitable report on all retreats: "We are betrayed!" And in a moment the whole mass of men went surging and jostling backward down the pier, turning their defenseless backs on their pursuers and piercing the night with craven outcry.

One coward thrust off the ship's stern, while another still held her by the bows. The fugitives leaped, screaming, and were hauled on board or fell back and perished in the sea. Some were cut down upon the pier by the pursuers. Many were injured on the ship's deck in the blind haste and terror of the moment, one man leaping upon another, and a third on both. At last, whether by design or accident, the bows of the *Good Hope* were liberated; and the ever-ready Lawless, who had maintained his place at the helm through all the hurly-burly by sheer strength of body and a liberal use of the cold steel, instantly clapped her on the proper tack. The ship began to move once more forward on the stormy sea, its scuppers running blood, its deck heaped with fallen men, sprawling and struggling in the dark.

Thereupon, Lawless sheathed his dagger and, turning to his next neighbor, "I have left my mark on them, gossip," said he, "the yelping, coward hounds."

Now, while they were all leaping and struggling for their lives, the men had not appeared to observe the rough shoves and cutting stabs with which Lawless had held his post in the confusion. But perhaps they had already begun to understand somewhat more clearly, or perhaps another ear had overheard the helmsman's speech.

Panic-stricken troops recover slowly, and men who have just disgraced themselves by cowardice, as if to wipe out the memory of their fault, will sometimes run straight into the opposite extreme of insubordination. So it was now; and the same men who had thrown away their weapons and been hauled feet foremost into the *Good*

Hope began to cry out upon their leaders and demand that someone should be punished.

This growing ill-feeling turned upon Lawless.

In order to get a proper offing, the old outlaw had put the head of the *Good Hope* to seaward.

"What!" bawled one of the grumblers, "he carrieth us to seaward!"

"'Tis sooth," cried another. "Nay, we are betrayed for sure."

And they all began to cry out in chorus that they were betrayed, and in shrill tones and with abominable oaths bade Lawless go about-ship and bring them speedily ashore. Lawless, grinding his teeth, continued in silence to steer the true course, guiding the *Good Hope* among the formidable billows. To their empty terrors, as to their dishonorable threats, between drink and dignity he scorned to make reply. The malcontents drew together a little abaft the mast, and it was plain they were like barnyard cocks, "crowing for courage." Presently they would be fit for any extremity of injustice or ingratitude. Dick began to mount by the ladder, eager to interpose; but one of the outlaws, who was also something of a seaman, got beforehand.

"Lads," he began, "y'are right wooden heads, I think. For to get back, by the mass, we must have an offing, must we not? And this old Lawless——"

Someone struck the speaker on the mouth, and the next moment, as a fire springs among dry straw, he was felled upon the deck, trampled under the feet, and dispatched by the daggers of his cowardly companions. At this the wrath of Lawless rose and broke.

"Steer yourselves," he bellowed, with a curse; and, careless of the result, he left the helm.

The *Good Hope* was, at that moment, trembling on the summit of a swell. She subsided with sickening velocity upon the farther side. A wave, like a great black bulwark, hove immediately in front of her; and, with a staggering blow, she plunged headforemost through that liquid hill. The green water passed right over her from stem to stern as high as a man's knees; the sprays ran higher than the mast; and she rose again upon the other side with an appalling, tremulous indecision, like a beast that has been deadly wounded.

Six or seven of the malcontents had been carried bodily overboard; and as for the remainder, when they found their tongues again, it was to bellow to the saints and wail upon Lawless to come back and take the tiller.

Nor did Lawless wait to be twice bidden. The terrible result of his fling of just resentment sobered him completely. He knew better than anyone on board how nearly the *Good Hope* had gone bodily down below their feet; and he could tell by the laziness with which she met the sea that the peril was by no means over.

Dick, who had been thrown down by the concussion and half drowned, rose wading to his knees in the swamped well of the stern and crept to the old helmsman's side.

"Lawless," he said, "we do all depend on you; y'are a brave, steady man, indeed, and crafty in the management of ships; I shall put three sure men to watch upon your safety."

"Bootless, my master, bootless," said the steersman, peering forward through the dark. "We come every moment somewhat clearer of these sandbanks; with every moment, then, the sea packeth upon us heavier, and for all these whimperers, they will presently be on their backs. For, my master, 'tis a right mystery, but true, there never yet was a bad man that was a good shipman. None but the honest and the bold can endure me this tossing of a ship."

"Nay, Lawless," said Dick, laughing, "that is a right shipman's byword and hath no more of sense than the whistle of the wind. But, prithee, how go we? Do we lie well? Are we in good case?"

"Master Shelton," replied Lawless, "I have been a Gray Friar—I praise fortune—an archer, a thief, and a shipman. Of all these coats, I had the best fancy to die in the Gray Friar's, as ye may readily conceive, and the least fancy to die in John Shipman's tarry jacket; and that for two excellent good reasons: first, that the death might take a man suddenly; and second, for the horror of that great salt smother and welter under my foot here"—and Lawless stamped with his foot. "Howbeit," he went on, "an I die not a sailor's death, and that this night, I shall owe a tall candle to our Lady."

"Is it so?" asked Dick.

"It is right so," replied the outlaw. "Do ye not feel how heavy and dull she moves upon the waves? Do ye not hear the water washing in her hold? She will scarce mind the rudder even now. Bide till she has settled a bit lower; and she will either go down below your boots like a stone image or drive ashore here under our lee and come all to pieces like a twist of string."

"Ye speak with a good courage," returned Dick. "Ye are not then appalled?"

"Why, master," answered Lawless, "if ever a man had an ill crew to come to port with, it is I—a renegade friar, a thief, and all the rest on't. Well, ye may wonder, but I keep a good hope in my wallet; and if that I be to drown, I will drown with a bright eye, Master Shelton, and a steady hand."

Dick returned no answer, but he was surprised to find the old vagabond of so resolute a temper, and fearing some fresh violence or treachery, set forth upon his quest for three sure men. The great bulk of the men had now deserted the deck, which was continually wetted with the flying sprays and where they lay exposed to the shrewdness of the winter wind. They had gathered, instead, into the hold of the merchandise, among the butts of wine and lighted by two swinging lanterns.

Here a few kept up the form of revelry and toasted each other deep in Arblaster's Gascony wine. But as the *Good*

Hope continued to tear through the smoking waves and toss her stem and stern alternately high in air and deep into white foam, the number of these jolly companions diminished with every moment and with every lurch. Many sat apart, tending their hurts, but the majority were already prostrated with sickness and lay moaning in the bilge.

Greensheve, Cuckow, and a young fellow of Lord Foxham's whom Dick had already remarked for his intelligence and spirit, were still, however, both fit to understand and willing to obey. These Dick set as a bodyguard about the person of the steersman, and then, with a last look at the black sky and sea, he turned and went below into the cabin, whither Lord Foxham had been carried by his servants.

The *Good Hope*
(concluded)

The moans of the wounded baron blended with the wailing of the ship's dog. The poor animal, whether he was merely sick at heart to be separated from his friends, or whether he indeed recognized some peril in the laboring of the ship, raised his cries like minute-guns above the roar of wave and weather; and the more superstitious of the men heard in these sounds the knell of the *Good Hope*.

Lord Foxham had been laid in a berth upon a fur cloak. A little lamp burned dim before the Virgin in the bulkhead, and by its glimmer Dick could see the pale countenance and hollow eyes of the hurt man.

"I am sore hurt," said he. "Come near to my side, young Shelton; let there be one by me who, at least, is gentle born; for after having lived nobly and richly all the days of my life, this is a sad pass that I should get my hurt in a little ferreting skirmish and die here, in a foul, cold ship upon the sea among broken men and churls."

"Nay, my lord," said Dick, "I rather pray to the saints

that ye will recover you of your hurt and come soon and sound ashore."

"How?" demanded his lordship. "Come sound ashore? There is, then, a question of it?"

"The ship laboreth—the sea is grievous and contrary," replied the lad; "and by what I can learn of my fellow that steereth us, we shall do well, indeed, if we come dryshod to land."

"Ha!" said the baron gloomily, "thus shall every terror attend upon the passage of my soul! Sir, pray rather to live hard that ye may die easy than to be fooled and fluted all through life, as to the pipe and tabor, and in the last hour be plunged among misfortunes! Howbeit, I have that upon my mind that must not be delayed. We have no priest aboard?"

"None," replied Dick.

"Here, then, to my secular interests," resumed Lord Foxham; "ye must be as good a friend to me dead, as I found you a gallant enemy when I was living. I fall in an evil hour for me, for England, and for them that trusted me. My men are being brought by Hamley—he that was your rival; they will rendezvous in the long room at Holywood; this ring from off my finger will accredit you to represent mine orders; and I shall write, besides, two words upon this paper, bidding Hamley yield to you the damsel. Will ye obey? I know not."

"But, my lord, what orders?" inquired Dick.

"Aye," quoth the baron, "aye—the orders"; and he looked upon Dick with hesitation. "Are ye Lancaster or York?" he asked, at length.

"I shame to say it," answered Dick, "I can scarce clearly answer. But so much I think is certain: since I serve with Ellis Duckworth, I serve the House of York. Well, if that be so, I declare for York."

"It is well," returned the other; "it is exceedingly well. For, truly, had ye said Lancaster, I wot not for the world what I had done. But sith ye are for York, follow me. I came hither but to watch these lords at Shoreby, while mine excellent young lord, Richard of Gloucester,[1] prepareth a sufficient force to fall upon and scatter them. I have made me notes of their strength, what watch they keep, and how they lie; and these I was to deliver to my young lord on Sunday an hour before noon at St. Bride's Cross beside the forest. This tryst I am not like to keep, but I pray you, of courtesy, to keep it in my stead; and see that not pleasure, nor pain, tempest, wound, nor pestilence withhold you from the hour and place, for the welfare of England lieth upon this cast."

"I do soberly take this upon me," said Dick. "In so far as in me lieth, your purpose shall be done."

"It is good," said the wounded man. "My lord duke shall order you further, and if ye obey him with spirit and good will, then is your fortune made. Give me the lamp a little nearer to mine eyes, till I write these words for you."

He wrote a note "to his worshipful kinsman, Sir John Hamley"; and then a second, which he left without external superscription.

"This is for the duke," he said. "The word is 'England and Edward,' and the counter, 'England and York.'"

"And Joanna, my lord?" asked Dick.

"Nay, ye must get Joanna how ye can," replied the baron. "I have named ye for my choice in both these letters; but ye must get her for yourself, boy. I have tried, as ye see here before you, and have lost my life. More could no man do."

By this time the wounded man began to be very weary; and Dick, putting the precious papers in his bosom, bade him be of good cheer and left him to repose.

The day was beginning to break, cold and blue, with flying squalls of snow. Close under the lee of the *Good Hope,* the coast lay in alternate rocky headlands and sandy

---

[1] At the date of this story, Richard Crookback could not have been created Duke of Gloucester; but for clearness, with the reader's leave, he shall so be called.

bays; and farther inland the wooded hill-tops of Tunstall showed along the sky. Both the wind and the sea had gone down; but the vessel wallowed deep and scarce rose upon the waves.

Lawless was still fixed at the rudder; and by this time nearly all the men had crawled on deck and were now gazing with blank faces upon the inhospitable coast.

"Are we going ashore?" asked Dick.

"Aye," said Lawless, "unless we get first to the bottom."

And just then the ship rose so languidly to meet a sea, and the water weltered so loudly in her hold, that Dick involuntarily seized the steersman by the arm.

"By the mass!" cried Dick as the bows of the *Good Hope* reappeared above the foam, "I thought we had foundered, indeed; my heart was at my throat."

In the waist, Greensheve, Hawksley, and the better men of both companies were busy breaking up the deck to build a raft; and to these Dick joined himself, working the harder to drown the memory of his predicament. But even as he worked every sea that struck the poor ship, and every one of her dull lurches as she tumbled wallowing among the waves recalled him with a horrid pang to the immediate proximity of death.

Presently, looking up from his work, he saw that they were close in below a promontory; a piece of ruinous cliff, against the base of which the sea broke white and heavy, almost overplumbed the deck; and, above that again, a house appeared, crowning a down.

Inside the bay, the seas ran gayly, raised the *Good Hope* upon their foam-flecked shoulders, carried her beyond the control of the steersman, and in a moment dropped her with a great concussion on the sand and began to break over her half-mast high and roll her to and fro. Another great wave followed, raised her again, and carried her yet farther in; and then a third succeeded, and left her far inshore of the more dangerous breakers, wedged upon a bank.

"Now, boys," cried Lawless, "the saints have had a care of us, indeed. The tide ebbs; let us but sit down and drink a cup of wine, and before half an hour ye may all march me ashore as safe as on a bridge."

A barrel was broached, and sitting in what shelter they could find from the flying snow and spray, the ship-wrecked company handed the cup around and sought to warm their bodies and restore their spirits.

Dick, meanwhile, returned to Lord Foxham, who lay in great perplexity and fear, the floor of his cabin washing knee-deep in water, and the lamp, which had been his only light, broken and extinguished by the violence of the blow.

"My lord," said young Shelton, "fear not at all; the saints are plainly for us; the seas have cast us high upon a shoal, and as soon as the tide hath somewhat ebbed, we may walk ashore upon our feet."

It was nearly an hour before the vessel was sufficiently deserted by the ebbing sea, and they could set forth for the land, which appeared dimly before them through a veil of driving snow.

Upon a hillock on one side of their way a party of men lay huddled together, suspiciously observing the movements of the new arrivals.

"They might draw near and offer us some comfort," Dick remarked.

"Well, an they come not to us, let us even turn aside to them," said Hawksley. "The sooner we come to a good fire and a dry bed, the better for my poor lord."

But they had not moved far in the direction of the hillock before the men, with one consent, rose suddenly to their feet and poured a flight of well-directed arrows on the shipwrecked company.

"Back! back!" cried his lordship. "Beware in Heaven's name, that ye reply not!"

"Nay," cried Greensheve, pulling an arrow from his leather jack. "We are in no posture to fight, it is certain, being drenching wet, dog-weary, and three-parts frozen; but, for the love of old England, what aileth them to shoot thus cruelly on their poor country people in distress?"

"They take us to be French pirates," answered Lord Foxham. "In these most troublesome and degenerate days we cannot keep our own shores of England; but our old enemies whom we once chased on sea and land do now range at pleasure, robbing and slaughtering and burning. It is the pity and reproach of this poor land."

The men upon the hillock lay closely observing them while they trailed upward from the beach and wound inland among desolate sand-hills; for a mile or so they even hung upon the rear of the march, ready at a sign to pour another volley on the weary and dispirited fugitives; and it was only when, striking at length upon a firm highroad, Dick began to call his men to some more martial order, that these jealous guardians of the coast of England silently disappeared among the snow. They had done what they desired; they had protected their own homes and farms, their own families and cattle; and their private interest being thus secured, it mattered not the weight of a straw to any one of them, although the Frenchmen should carry blood and fire to every other parish in the realm of England.

BOOK IV: THE DISGUISE

The Den

THE PLACE where Dick had struck the line of a high-road was not far from Holywood and within nine or ten miles of Shoreby-on-the-Till; and here after making sure that they were pursued no longer, the two bodies separated. Lord Foxham's followers departed, carrying their wounded master toward the comfort and security of the great abbey; and Dick, as he saw them wind away and disappear in the thick curtain of the falling snow, was left alone with near upon a dozen outlaws, the last remainder of his troop of volunteers.

Some were wounded; one and all were furious at their ill-success and long exposure; and though they were now too cold and hungry to do more, they grumbled and cast sullen looks upon their leaders. Dick emptied his purse among them, leaving himself nothing; thanked them for the courage they had displayed, though he could have found it more readily in his heart to rate them for poltroonery; and having thus somewhat softened the effect of his prolonged misfortune, dispatched them to find their way either severally or in pairs to Shoreby and the Goat and Bagpipes.

For his own part, influenced by what he had seen on board of the *Good Hope*, he chose Lawless to be his companion on the walk. The snow was falling without pause or variation in one even, blinding cloud; the wind had been strangled and now blew no longer; and the whole world was blotted out and sheeted down below that silent inundation. There was great danger of wandering by the way and perishing in drifts; and Lawless, keeping half a step in front of his companion, and holding his head forward like a hunting dog upon the scent, inquired his way of every tree and studied out their path as though he were conning a ship among dangers.

About a mile into the forest they came to a place where several ways met under a grove of lofty and contorted oaks. Even in the narrow horizon of the falling snow, it was a spot that could not fail to be recognized; and Lawless evidently recognized it with particular delight.

"Now, Master Richard," said he, "an y'are not too proud to be the guest of a man who is neither a gentleman by birth nor so much as a good Christian, I can offer you a cup of wine and a good fire to melt the marrow in your frozen bones."

"Lead on, Will," answered Dick. "A cup of wine and a good fire! Nay, I would go a far way round to see them."

Lawless turned aside under the bare branches of the grove and walking resolutely forward for some time came to a steepish hollow or den that had now drifted a quarter full of snow. On the verge a great beech-tree hung, precariously rooted; and here the old outlaw, pulling aside some bushy underwood, bodily disappeared into the earth.

The beech had in some violent gale been half-uprooted and had torn up a considerable stretch of turf; and it was under this that old Lawless had dug out his forest hiding-place. The roots served him for rafters, the turf was his thatch, for walls and floor he had his mother the earth. Rude as it was, the hearth in one corner, blackened by fire, and the presence in another of a large oaken chest well fortified with iron showed it at one glance to be the den of a man and not the burrow of a digging beast.

Though the snow had drifted at the mouth and sifted in upon the floor of this earth-cavern, yet was the air much warmer than without; and when Lawless had struck a spark, and the dry furze bushes had begun to blaze and crackle on the hearth, the place assumed even to the eye an air of comfort and of home.

With a sigh of great contentment Lawless spread his broad hands before the fire and seemed to breathe the smoke.

"Here, then," he said, "is this old Lawless's rabbit-hole; pray Heaven there come no terrier! Far have I rolled hither and thither, and here and about, since that I was fourteen years of mine age and first ran away from mine abbey, with the sacrist's gold chain and a mass-book that I sold for four marks. I have been in England and France and Burgundy, and in Spain, too, on a pilgrimage for my poor soul; and upon the sea, which is no man's country. But here is my place, Master Shelton. This is my native land, this burrow in the earth. Come rain or wind—and whether it's April, and the birds all sing, and the blossoms fall about my bed, or whether it's winter, and I sit alone with my good gossip the fire, and robin redbreast twitters in the woods—here is my church and market, my wife and child. It's here I come back to, and it's here, so please the saints, that I would like to die."

"'Tis a warm corner, to be sure," replied Dick, "and a pleasant and a well hid."

"It had need to be," returned Lawless, "for an they found it, Master Shelton, it would break my heart. But here," he added, burrowing with his stout fingers in the sandy floor, "here is my wine cellar, and ye shall have a flask of excellent strong stingo."

Sure enough, after a little digging he produced a big bottle of about a gallon nearly three parts full of a very heady and sweet wine; and when they had drunk to each other comradely, and the fire had been replenished and blazed up again, the pair lay at full length thawing and steaming, and divinely warm.

"Master Shelton," observed the outlaw, "y'ave had two mischances this last while, and y'are like to lose the maid—do I take it aright?"

"Aright," returned Dick, nodding his head.

"Well, now," continued Lawless, "hear an old fool that hath been nigh-hand everything and seen nigh-hand all. Ye go too much on other people's errands, Master Dick. Ye go on Ellis's; but he desireth rather the death of Sir Daniel. Ye go on Lord Foxham's; well—the saints preserve him!—doubtless he meaneth well. But go ye upon your own, good Dick. Come right to the maid's side. Court her, lest that she forget you. Be ready; and when the chance shall come, off with her at the saddlebow."

"Aye, but, Lawless, beyond doubt she is now in Sir Daniel's own mansion," answered Dick.

"Thither, then, go we," replied the outlaw.

Dick stared at him.

"Nay, I mean it," nodded Lawless. "And if y'are of so little faith and stumble at a word, see here!"

And the outlaw, taking a key from about his neck, opened the oak chest and dipping and groping deep among its contents, produced first a friar's robe and next a girdle of rope; and then a huge rosary of wood heavy enough to be counted as a weapon.

"Here," he said, "is for you. On with them!"

And then, when Dick had clothed himself in this clerical disguise, Lawless produced some colors and a pencil and proceeded with the greatest cunning to disguise his face. The eyebrows he thickened and produced; to the mustache, which was yet hardly visible, he rendered a like service; while by a few lines around his eyes he changed the expression and increased the apparent age of this young monk.

"Now," he resumed, "when I have done the like, we shall make as bonny a pair of friars as the eye could wish. Boldly to Sir Daniel's we shall go and there be hospitably welcomed for the love of Mother Church."

"And how, dear Lawless," cried the lad, "shall I repay you?"

"Tut, brother," replied the outlaw, "I do naught but for my pleasure. Mind not for me. I am one, by the mass, that mindeth for himself. When that I lack, I have a long tongue and a voice like the monastery bell—I do ask, my son; and where asking faileth, I do most usually take."

The old rogue made a humorous grimace, and although Dick was displeased to lie under so great favors to so equivocal a personage, he was yet unable to restrain his mirth.

With that, Lawless returned to the big chest and was soon similarly disguised; but below his gown, Dick wondered to observe him conceal a sheaf of black arrows.

"Wherefore do ye that?" asked the lad. "Wherefore arrows, when ye take no bow?"

"Nay," replied Lawless, lightly, "'tis like there will be heads broke—not to say backs—ere you and I win sound from where we're going to; and if any fall, I would our fellowship should come by the credit on't. A black arrow, Master Dick, is the seal of our abbey; it showeth you who writ the bill."

"An ye prepare so carefully," said Dick, "I have here some papers that for mine own sake, and the interest of those that trusted me were better left behind than found upon my body. Where shall I conceal them, Will?"

"Nay," replied Lawless, "I will go forth into the wood and whistle me three verses of a song; meanwhile, do you bury them where ye please, and smooth the sand upon the place."

"Never!" cried Richard. "I trust you, man. I were base indeed if I not trusted you."

"Brother, y'are but a child," replied the old outlaw, pausing and turning his face upon Dick from the threshold of the den. "I am a kind old Christian, and no traitor to men's blood, and no sparer of mine own in a friend's jeopardy. But fool, child, I am a thief by trade and birth and habit. If my bottle were empty and my mouth dry, I would rob you, dear child, as sure as I love, honor, and admire your parts and person! Can it be clearer spoken? No."

And he stumped forth through the bushes with a snap of his big fingers.

Dick, thus left alone, after a wondering thought upon

the inconsistencies of his companion's character, hastily produced, reviewed, and buried his papers. One only he reserved to carry along with him, since it in nowise compromised his friends and yet might serve him, in a pinch, against Sir Daniel. That was the knight's own letter to Lord Wensleydale, sent by Throgmorton on the morrow of the defeat at Risingham and found next day by Dick upon the body of the messenger.

Then treading down the embers of the fire Dick left the den and rejoined the old outlaw, who stood awaiting him under the leafless oaks and was already beginning to be powdered by the falling snow. Each looked upon the other and each laughed, so thorough and so droll was the disguise.

"Yet I would it were but summer and a clear day," grumbled the outlaw, "that I might see myself in the mirror of a pool. There be many of Sir Daniel's men that know me; and if we fell to be recognized, there might be two words for you, my brother, but as for me, in a paternoster while, I should be kicking in a rope's-end."

Thus they set forth together along the road to Shoreby, which in this part of its course kept near the margin of a forest, coming forth from time to time in the open country and passing beside poor folk's houses and small farms.

Presently, at sight of one of these, Lawless pulled up.

"Brother Martin," he said in a voice capitally disguised, and suited to his monkish robe, "let us enter and seek alms from these poor sinners. 'Pax vobiscum!' Aye," he added, in his own voice, "'tis as I feared; I have somewhat lost the whine of it; and by your leave, good Master Shelton, ye must suffer me to practice in these country places before that I risk my fat neck by entering Sir Daniel's. But look ye a little, what an excellent thing it is to be a Jack-of-all-trades! An I had not been a shipman, ye had infallibly gone down in the *Good Hope*; an I had not been a thief, I could not have painted me your face! and but that I had been a Gray Friar and sung loud in the choir and ate hearty at the board, I could not have carried this disguise, but the very dogs would have spied us out and barked at us for shams."

He was by this time close to the window of the farm and he rose on his tip-toes and peeped in.

"Nay," he cried, "better and better. We shall here try our false faces with a vengeance and have a merry jest on Brother Capper to boot."

And so saying he opened the door and led the way into the house.

Three of their own company sat at the table, greedily eating. Their daggers, stuck beside them in the board, and the black and menacing looks which they continued to shower upon the people of the house proved that they owed their entertainment rather to force than favor. On the two monks, who now with a sort of humble dignity entered the kitchen of the farm, they seemed to turn with a particular resentment; and one—it was John Capper in person—who seemed to play the leading part, instantly and rudely ordered them away.

"We want no beggars here!" he cried.

But another—although he was far from recognizing Dick and Lawless—inclined to more moderate counsels.

"Not so," he cried. "We be strong men and take: these be weak and crave; but in the latter end these shall be uppermost and we below. Mind him not, my father; but come, drink of my cup and give me a benediction."

"Y'are men of a light mind, carnal and accursed," said the monk. "Now, may the saints forbid that ever I should drink with such companions! But here, for the pity I bear to sinners, here I do leave you a blessed relic, the which, for your soul's interest, I bid you kiss and cherish."

So far Lawless thundered upon them like a preaching friar; but with these words he drew from under his robe a black arrow, tossed it on the board in front of the three startled outlaws, turned in the same instant, and taking Dick along with him was out of the room and out of sight among the falling snow before they had time to utter a word or move a finger.

"So," he said, "we have proved our false faces, Master Shelton. I will now adventure my poor carcass where ye please."

"Good!" returned Richard. "It irks me to be doing. Set we on for Shoreby!"

"In Mine Enemies' House"

Sir Daniel's residence in Shoreby was a tall, commodious, plastered mansion, framed in carven oak, and covered by a low-pitched roof of thatch. To the back there stretched a garden, full of fruit-trees, alleys, and thick arbors, and overlooked from the far end by the tower of the abbey church.

The house might contain upon a pinch the retinue of a greater person than Sir Daniel; but even now it was filled with hubbub. The court rang with arms and horseshoe-iron; the kitchen roared with cookery like a bees'-hive; minstrels, and the players of instruments, and the cries of tumblers sounded from the hall. Sir Daniel, in his profusion, in the gayety and gallantry of his establishment, rivaled with Lord Shoreby and eclipsed Lord Risingham.

All guests were made welcome. Minstrels, tumblers, players of chess, sellers of relics, medicines, perfumes, and enchantments, and along with these every sort of priest, friar, or pilgrim were made welcome to the lower table and slept together in the ample lofts or on the bare boards of the long dining-hall.

On the afternoon following the wreck of the *Good Hope,* the buttery, the kitchens, the stables, the covered cart-shed that surrounded two sides of the court were all crowded by idle people, partly belonging to Sir Daniel's establishment and attired in his livery of murrey and blue, partly nondescript strangers, attracted to the town by greed and received by the knight through policy and because it was the fashion of the time.

The snow, which still fell without interruption, the

extreme chill of the air, and the approach of night, combined to keep them under shelter. Wine, ale, and money were all plentiful; many sprawled gambling in the straw of the barn, many were still drunken from the noontide meal. To the eye of a modern it would have looked like the sack of a city; to the eye of a contemporary it was like any other rich and noble household at a festive season.

Two monks—a young and an old—had arrived late and were now warming themselves at a bonfire in a corner of the shed. A mixed crowd surrounded them—jugglers, mountebanks, and soldiers; and with these the elder of the two had soon engaged so brisk a conversation and exchanged so many loud guffaws and country witticisms, that the group momentarily increased in number.

The younger companion, in whom the reader has already recognized Dick Shelton, sat from the first somewhat backward and gradually drew himself away. He listened, indeed, closely, but he opened not his mouth; and by the grave expression of his countenance, he made but little account of his companion's pleasantries.

At last his eye, which traveled continually to and fro and kept a guard upon all the entrances of the house, lit upon a little procession entering by the main gate and crossing the court in an oblique direction. Two ladies muffled in thick furs led the way and were followed by a pair of waiting-women and four stout men-at-arms. The next moment they had disappeared within the house; and Dick, slipping through the crowd of loiterers in the shed, was already giving hot pursuit.

"The taller of these twain was Lady Brackley," he thought; "and where Lady Brackley is, Joan will not be far."

At the door of the house the four men-at-arms had ceased to follow, and the ladies were now mounting the stairway of polished oak, under no better escort than that of the two waiting-women. Dick followed close behind. It was already the dusk of the day; and in the house the darkness of the night had almost come. On the stair-landings torches flared in iron holders; down the long tapestried corridors a lamp burned by every door. And where the door stood open, Dick could look in upon arras-covered walls and rush-bescattered floors glowing in the light of the wood-fires.

Two floors were passed, and at every landing the younger and shorter of the two ladies had looked back keenly at the monk. He, keeping his eyes lowered and affecting the demure manners that suited his disguise, had but seen her once and was unaware that he had attracted her attention. And now on the third floor the party separated, the younger lady continuing to ascend alone, the other, followed by the waiting-maids, descending the corridor to the right.

Dick mounted with a swift foot, and holding to the corner, thrust forth his head and followed the three women with his eyes. Without turning or looking behind them, they continued to descend the corridor.

"It is right well," thought Dick. "Let me but know my Lady Brackley's chamber, and it will go hard an I find not Dame Hatch upon an errand."

And just then a hand was laid upon his shoulder, and, with a bound and a choked cry, he turned to grapple his assailant.

He was somewhat abashed to find, in the person whom he had so roughly seized, the short young lady in the furs. She, on her part, was shocked and terrified beyond expression and hung trembling in his grasp.

"Madam," said Dick, releasing her, "I cry you a thousand pardons; but I have no eyes behind, and, by the mass, I could not tell ye were a maid."

The girl continued to look at him, but by this time terror began to be succeeded by surprise and surprise by suspicion. Dick, who could read these changes on her face, became alarmed for his own safety in that hostile house.

"Fair maid," he said, affecting easiness, "suffer me to kiss your hand, in token ye forgive my roughness, and I will even go."

"Y'are a strange monk, young sir," returned the young lady, looking him both boldly and shrewdly in the face; "and now that my first astonishment hath somewhat passed away, I can spy the layman in each word you utter. What do ye here? Why are ye thus sacrilegiously tricked out? Come ye in peace or war? And why spy ye after Lady Brackley like a thief?"

"Madam," quoth Dick, "of one thing I pray ye to be very sure: I am no thief. And even if I come here in war, as in some degree I do, I make no war upon fair maids, and I hereby entreat them to copy me so far and leave me be. For, indeed, fair mistress, cry out—if such be your pleasure—cry but once and say what ye have seen, and the poor gentleman before you is merely a dead man. I cannot think ye would be cruel," added Dick; and taking the girl's hand gently in both of his, he looked at her with courteous admiration.

"Are ye then a spy—a Yorkist?" asked the maid.

"Madam," he replied, "I am indeed a Yorkist, and in some sort, a spy. But that which bringeth me into this house, the same which will win for me the pity and interest of your kind heart, is neither of York nor Lancaster. I will wholly put my life in your discretion. I am a lover, and my name——"

But here the young lady clapped her hand suddenly upon Dick's mouth, looked hastily up and down and east and west, and seeing the coast clear began to drag the young man with great strength and vehemence upstairs.

"Hush!" she said, "and come. Shalt talk hereafter."

Somewhat bewildered, Dick suffered himself to be pulled upstairs, bustled along a corridor, and thrust suddenly into a chamber, lit like so many of the others by a blazing log upon the hearth.

"Now," said the young lady, forcing him down upon a stool, "sit ye there and attend my sovereign good pleasure. I have life and death over you, and I will not scruple to abuse my power. Look to yourself; y'ave cruelly mauled my arm. He knew not I was a maid, quoth he! Had he known I was a maid, he had ta'en his belt to me, forsooth!"

And with these words she whipped out of the room, and left Dick gaping with wonder and not very sure if he were dreaming or awake.

"Ta'en my belt to her!" he repeated. "Ta'en my belt to her!" And the recollection of that evening in the forest flowed back upon his mind, and he once more saw Matcham's wincing body and beseeching eyes.

And then he was recalled to the dangers of the present. In the next room he heard a stir as of a person moving; then followed a sigh, which sounded strangely near; and then the rustle of skirts and tap of feet once more began. As he stood hearkening, he saw the arras wave along the hall; there was the sound of a door being opened, the hangings divided, and lamp in hand Joanna Sedley entered the apartment.

She was attired in costly stuffs of deep and warm colors, such as befit the winter and the snow. Upon her head her hair had been gathered together and became her as a crown. And she, who had seemed so little and so awkward in the attire of Matcham, was now tall like a young willow and swam across the floor as though she scorned the drudgery of walking.

Without a start, without a tremor, she raised her lamp and looked at the young monk.

"What make ye here, good brother?" she inquired. "Ye are doubtless ill-directed. Whom do ye require?" And she set her lamp upon the bracket.

"Joanna," said Dick; and then his voice failed him. "Joanna," he began again, "ye said ye loved me; and the more fool I, but I believed it!"

"Dick!" she cried. "Dick!"

And then, to the wonder of the lad, this beautiful and tall young lady made but one step of it and threw her arms about his neck and gave him a hundred kisses all in one.

"Oh, the fool fellow!" she cried. "Oh, dear Dick! Oh, if ye could see yourself! Alack!" she added, pausing, "I have spoilt you, Dick! I have knocked some of the paint off. But that can be mended. What cannot be mended, Dick—or I much fear it cannot!—is my marriage with Lord Shoreby."

"Is it decided, then?" asked the lad.

"Tomorrow, before noon, Dick, in the abbey church," she answered, "John Matcham and Joanna Sedley both shall come to a right miserable end. There is no help in tears, or I could weep mine eyes out. I have not spared myself to pray, but Heaven frowns on my petition. And, dear Dick—good Dick—but that ye can get me forth of this house before the morning, we must even kiss and say good-by."

"Nay," said Dick, "not I; I will never say that word. 'Tis like despair; but while there's life, Joanna, there is hope. Yet will I hope. Aye, by the mass, and triumph! Look ye, now, when ye were but a name to me, did I not follow—did I not rouse good men—did I not stake my life upon the quarrel? And now that I have seen you for what ye are—the fairest maid and stateliest of England—think ye I would turn?—if the deep sea were there, I would straight through it; if the way were full of lions, I would scatter them like mice."

"Aye," she said dryly, "ye make a great ado about a sky-blue robe!"

"Nay, Joan," protested Dick, "'tis not alone the robe. But, lass, ye were disguised. Here am I disguised; and, to the proof, do I not cut a figure of fun—a right fool's figure?"

"Aye, Dick, an' that ye do!" she answered, smiling.

"Well, then!" he returned, triumphant. "So was it with you, poor Matcham, in the forest. In sooth, ye were a wench to laugh at. But now!"

So they ran on, holding each other by both hands, exchanging smiles and lovely looks and melting minutes into seconds; and so they might have continued all night long. But presently there was a noise behind them; and they were aware of the short young lady with her finger on her lips.

"Saints!" she cried, "but what a noise ye keep! Can ye not speak in compass? And now, Joanna, my fair maid of the woods, what will ye give your gossip for bringing you your sweetheart?"

Joanna ran to her by way of answer and embraced her fierily.

"And you, sir," added the young lady, "what do ye give me?"

"Madam," said Dick, "I would fain offer to pay you in the same money."

"Come then," said the lady, "it is permitted you."

But Dick, blushing like a peony, only kissed her hand.

"What ails ye at my face, fair sir?" she inquired, curtsying to the very ground; and then, when Dick had at length and most tepidly embraced her, "Joanna," she added, "your sweetheart is very backward under your eyes; but I warrant you, when first we met, he was more ready. I am all black and blue, wench; trust me never, if I be not black and blue! And now," she continued, "have ye said your sayings? for I must speedily dismiss the paladin."

But at this they both cried out that they had said nothing, that the night was still very young, and that they would not be separated so early.

"And supper?" asked the young lady. "Must we not go down to supper?"

"Nay, to be sure!" cried Joan. "I had forgotten."

"Hide me, then," said Dick, "put me behind the arras, shut me in a chest, or what ye will, so that I may be here on your return. Indeed, fair lady," he added, "bear this in mind, that we are sore bested, and may never look upon each other's face from this night forward till we die."

At this the young lady melted; and when a little after the bell summoned Sir Daniel's household to the board, Dick was planted very stiffly against the wall at a place where a division in the tapestry permitted him to breathe the more freely and even to see into the room.

He had not been long in this position when he was somewhat strangely disturbed. The silence in that upper story of the house was only broken by the flickering of the flames and the hissing of a green log in the chimney; but presently to Dick's strained hearing there came the sound of someone walking with extreme precaution; and soon after the door opened and a little black-faced, dwarfish fellow in Lord Shoreby's colors pushed first his head and then his crooked body into the chamber. His mouth was open as though to hear the better; and his eyes, which were very bright, flitted restlessly and swiftly to and fro. He went round and round the room, striking here and there upon the hangings: but Dick by a miracle escaped his notice. Then he looked below the furniture and examined the lamp; and at last, with an air of cruel disappointment, was preparing to go away as silently as he had come, when down he dropped upon his knees, picked up something from among the rushes on the floor, examined it and with every signal of delight concealed it in the wallet at his belt.

Dick's heart sank, for the object in question was a tassel from his own girdle; and it was plain to him that this dwarfish spy, who took a malign delight in his employment, would lose no time in bearing it to his master, the baron. He was half-tempted to throw aside the arras, fall upon the scoundrel, and at the risk of his life remove the tell-tale token. And while he was still hesitating, a new cause of concern was added. A voice, hoarse and broken by drink, began to be audible from the stair; and presently after, uneven, wandering, and heavy footsteps sounded without along the passage.

"What make ye here, my merry men, among the greenwood shaws?" sang the voice. "What make ye here? Hey! sots, what make ye here!" it added, with a rattle of drunken laughter; and then once more breaking into song:

> "If ye should drink the clary wine,
>   Fat Friar John, ye friend o' mine—
> If I should eat, and ye should drink,
>   Who shall sing the mass, d'ye think?"

Lawless, alas! rolling drunk, was wandering the house, seeking for a corner wherein to slumber off the effect of his potations. Dick inwardly raged. The spy, at first terrified, had grown reassured as he found he had to deal with an intoxicated man and now with a movement of cat-like rapidity slipped from the chamber and was gone from Richard's eyes.

What was to be done? If he lost touch of Lawless for the night he was left impotent, whether to plan or carry forth Joanna's rescue. If on the other hand he dared to address the drunken outlaw, the spy might still be lingering within sight and the most fatal consequences ensue.

It was, nevertheless, upon this last hazard that Dick decided. Slipping from behind the tapestry, he stood ready in the doorway of the chamber with a warning hand upraised. Lawless, flushed crimson, with his eyes injected, vacillating on his feet, drew still unsteadily nearer. At last he hazily caught sight of his commander, and in despite of Dick's imperious signals hailed him instantly and loudly by his name.

Dick leaped upon and shook the drunkard furiously.

"Beast!" he hissed, "beast, and no man! It is worse than treachery to be so witless. We may all be shent for thy sotting."

But Lawless only laughed and staggered and tried to clap young Shelton on the back.

And just then Dick's quick ear caught a rapid brushing in the arras. He leaped toward the sound, and the next moment a piece of the wall-hanging had been torn down, and Dick and the spy were sprawling together in its folds. Over and over they rolled, grappling for each other's throat, and still baffled by the arras, and still silent in their deadly fury. But Dick was by much the stronger, and soon the spy lay prostrate under his knee, and with a single stroke of the long poniard, ceased to breathe.

The Dead Spy

Throughout this furious and rapid passage, Lawless had looked on helplessly, and even when all was over, and Dick, already re-arisen to his feet, was listening with the most passionate attention to the distant bustle in the lower stories of the house, the old outlaw was still wavering on his legs like a shrub in a breeze of wind and still stupidly staring on the face of the dead man.

"It is well," said Dick, at length; "they have not heard us, praise the saints! But, now, what shall I do with this poor spy? At least, I will take my tassel from his wallet."

So saying, Dick opened the wallet; within he found a few pieces of money, the tassel, and a letter addressed to Lord Wensleydale and sealed with my Lord Shoreby's seal. The name awoke Dick's recollections; and he instantly broke the wax and read the contents of the letter. It was short, but, to Dick's delight, it gave evident proof that Lord Shoreby was treacherously corresponding with the House of York.

The young fellow usually carried his ink-horn and implements about him, and so now, bending a knee beside the body of the dead spy, he was able to write these words upon a corner of the paper:

My Lord of Shoreby, ye that writt the letter, wot ye why your man is ded! But let me rede you, marry not.

JON AMEND-ALL

He laid this paper on the breast of the corpse; and then Lawless, who had been looking on upon these last maneuvers with some flickering returns of intelligence, suddenly drew a black arrow from below his robe and therewith pinned the paper in its place. The sight of this disrespect, or, as it almost seemed, cruelty to the dead, drew a cry of horror from young Shelton; but the old outlaw only laughed.

"Nay, I will have the credit for mine order," he hiccuped. "My jolly boys must have the credit on't—the credit, brother"; and then, shutting his eyes tight and opening his mouth like a precentor, he began to thunder, in a formidable voice:

"If ye should drink the clary wine——"

"Peace, sot!" cried Dick, and thrust him hard against the wall. "In two words—if so be that such a man can understand me who hath more wine than wit in him—in two words, and a-Mary's name, begone out of this house, where, if ye continue to abide, ye will not only hang yourself but me also! Faith, then, up foot! be yare, or by the mass, I may forget that I am in some sort your captain and in some your debtor! Go!"

The sham monk was now in some degree recovering the use of his intelligence; and the ring in Dick's voice and the glitter in Dick's eye stamped home the meaning of his words.

"By the mass," cried Lawless, "an I be not wanted, I can go"; and he turned tipsily along the corridor and proceeded to flounder downstairs, lurching against the wall.

So soon as he was out of sight, Dick returned to his hiding-place, resolutely fixed to see the matter out. Wisdom, indeed, moved him to be gone; but love and curiosity were stronger.

Time passed slowly for the young man, bolt upright behind the arras. The fire in the room began to die down, and the lamp to burn low and to smoke. And still there was no word of the return of anyone to these upper quarters of the house; still the faint hum and clatter of the supper party sounded from far below; and still under the thick fall of the snow Shoreby town lay silent upon every side.

At length, however, feet and voices began to draw near upon the stair; and presently after several of Sir Daniel's guests arrived upon the landing, and turning down the corridor beheld the torn arras and the body of the spy.

Some ran forward and some back, and all together began to cry aloud.

At the sound of their cries, guests, men-at-arms, ladies, servants, and in a word all the inhabitants of that great house came flying from every direction, and began to join their voices to the tumult.

Soon a way was cleared, and Sir Daniel came forth in person, followed by the bridegroom of the morrow, my Lord Shoreby.

"My lord," said Sir Daniel, "have I not told you of this

knave black arrow? To the proof, behold it! There it
stands, and by the rood, my gossip, in a man of yours, or
one that stole your colors?"

"In good sooth, it was a man of mine," replied Lord
Shoreby, hanging back. "I would I had more such. He was
keen as a beagle and secret as a mole."

"Aye, gossip, truly?" asked Sir Daniel, keenly. "And what
came he smelling up so many stairs in my poor mansion?
But he will smell no more."

"An't please you, Sir Daniel," said one, "here is a paper
written upon with some matter pinned upon his breast."

"Give it me, arrow and all," said the knight. And when he
had taken into his hand the shaft, he continued for some
time to gaze upon it in a sullen musing. "Aye," he said,
addressing Lord Shoreby, "here is a hate that followeth
hard and close upon my heels. This black stick or its like-
ness shall yet bring me down. And, gossip, suffer a plain
knight to counsel you; and if these hounds begin to wind
you, flee! 'Tis like a sickness—it still hangeth, hangeth
upon the limbs. But let us see what they have written. It is
as I thought, my lord; y'are marked, like an old oak, by the
woodman; tomorrow or next day, by will come the ax. But
what wrote ye in a letter?"

Lord Shoreby snatched the paper from the arrow, read
it, crumpled it between his hands, and overcoming the
reluctance which had hitherto withheld him from
approaching, threw himself on his knees beside the body
and eagerly groped in the wallet.

He rose to his feet with a somewhat unsettled countenance.

"Gossip," he said, "I have indeed lost a letter here that
much imported; and could I lay my hand upon the knave
that took it, he should incontinently grace a halter. But let
us, first of all, secure the issues of the house. Here is
enough harm already, by Saint George!"

Sentinels were posted close around the house and garden; a sentinel on every landing of the stair, a whole troop
in the main entrance-hall; and yet another about the bonfire in the shed. Sir Daniel's followers were supplemented

by Lord Shoreby's; there was thus no lack of men or weapons to make the house secure, or to entrap a lurking enemy, should one be there.

Meanwhile, the body of the spy was carried out through the falling snow and deposited in the abbey church.

It was not until these dispositions had been taken, and all had returned to a decorous silence, that the two girls drew Richard Shelton from his place of concealment and made a full report to him of what had passed. He, upon his side, recounted the visit of the spy, his dangerous discovery, and speedy end.

Joanna leaned back very faint against the curtain wall.

"It will avail but little," she said. "I shall be wed tomorrow, in the morning, after all!"

"What!" cried her friend. "And here is our paladin that driveth lions like mice! Ye have little faith, of a surety. But come, friend lion-driver, give us some comfort; speak and let us hear bold counsels."

Dick was confounded to be thus outfaced with his own exaggerated words; but though he colored he still spoke stoutly.

"Truly," said he, "we are in straits. Yet, could I but win out of this house for half an hour, I do honestly tell myself that all might still go well; and for the marriage, it should be prevented."

"And for the lions," mimicked the girl, "they shall be driven."

"I crave your excuse," said Dick. "I speak not now in any boasting humor, but rather as one inquiring after help or counsel; for if I get not forth of this house through these sentinels, I can do less than naught. Take me, I pray you, rightly."

"Why said ye he was rustic, Joan?" the girl inquired. "I warrant he hath a tongue in his head; ready, soft, and bold is his speech at pleasure. What would ye more?"

"Nay," sighed Joanna, with a smile, "they have changed my friend Dick, 'tis sure enough. When I beheld him, he was rough indeed. But it matters little; there is no help for my hard case, and I must still be Lady Shoreby!"

"Nay, then," said Dick, "I will even make the adventure. A friar is not much regarded; and if I found a good fairy to lead me up, I may find another belike to carry me down. How call they the name of this spy?"

"Rutter," said the young lady; "and an excellent good name to call him by. But how mean ye, lion-driver? What is in your mind to do?"

"To offer boldly to go forth," returned Dick; "and, if any stop me, to keep an unchanged countenance and say I go to pray for Rutter. They will be praying over his poor clay even now."

"The device is somewhat simple," replied the girl, "yet it may hold."

"Nay," said young Shelton, "it is no device but mere boldness, which serveth often better in great straits."

"Ye say true," she said. "Well, go, a-Mary's name. And may Heaven speed you! Ye leave here a poor maid that loves you entirely and another that is most heartily your friend. Be wary, for their sakes, and make not shipwreck of your safety."

"Aye," added Joanna, "go, Dick. Ye run no more peril, whether ye go or stay. Go; ye take my heart with you; the saints defend you!"

Dick passed the first sentry with so assured a countenance that the fellow merely fidgeted and stared; but at the second landing the man carried his spear across and bade him name his business.

"Pax vobiscum," answered Dick. "I go to pray over the body of this poor Rutter."

"Like enough," returned the sentry; "but to go alone is not permitted you." He leaned over the oaken balusters and whistled shrill. "One cometh," he cried; and then motioned Dick to pass.

At the foot of the stairs he found the guard afoot and awaiting his arrival; and when he had once more repeated his story, the commander of the post ordered four men to accompany him to the church.

"Let him not slip, my lads," he said. "Bring him to Sir Oliver, on your lives!"

The door was then opened; one of the men took Dick by either arm, another marched ahead with a link, and the fourth with bent bow and the arrow on the string brought up the rear. In this order they proceeded through the garden, under the thick darkness of the night and the scattering snow, and drew near to the dimly illuminated windows of the abbey church.

At the western portal a picket of archers stood, taking what shelter they could find in the hollow of the arched doorways and all powdered with the snow; and it was not until Dick's conductors had exchanged a word with these, that they were suffered to pass forth and enter the nave of the sacred edifice.

The church was doubtfully lighted by the tapers upon the great altar and by a lamp or two that swung from the arched roof before the private chapels of illustrious families. In the midst of the choir the dead spy lay, his limbs piously composed, upon a bier.

A hurried mutter of prayer sounded along the arches; cowled figures knelt in the stalls of the choir, and on the steps of the high altar a priest in pontifical vestments celebrated mass.

Upon this fresh entrance, one of the cowled figures arose, and coming down the steps which elevated the level of the choir above that of the nave, demanded from the leader of the four men what business brought him to the church. Out of respect for the service and the dead, they spoke in guarded tones; but the echoes of that huge, empty building caught up their words and hollowly repeated and repeated them along the aisles.

"A monk!" returned Sir Oliver (for he it was), when he had heard the report of the archer. "My brother, I looked not for your coming," he added, turning to young Shelton. "In all civility, who are ye? and at whose instance do ye join your supplications to ours?"

Dick, keeping his cowl about his face, signed to Sir Oliver to move a pace or two aside from the archers; and, so soon as the priest had done so, "I cannot hope to deceive you, sir," he said. "My life is in your hands."

Sir Oliver violently started; his stout cheeks grew pale, and for a space he was silent.

"Richard," he said, "what brings you here, I know not; but I much misdoubt it to be evil. Nevertheless, for the kindness that was, I would not willingly deliver you to harm. Ye shall sit all night beside me in the stalls: ye shall sit there till my Lord of Shoreby be married and the party gone safe home; and if all goeth well, and ye have planned no evil, in the end ye shall go whither ye will. But if your purpose be bloody, it shall return upon your head. Amen!"

And the priest devoutly crossed himself and turned and louted to the altar.

With that, he spoke a few words more to the soldiers and taking Dick by the hand led him up to the choir and placed him in the stall beside his own, where for mere decency the lad had instantly to kneel and appear to be busy with his devotions.

His mind and his eyes, however, were continually wandering. Three of the soldiers, instead of returning to the house, had got them quietly into a point of vantage in the aisle; and he could not doubt that they had done so by Sir Oliver's command. Here, then, he was trapped. Here he must spend the night in the ghostly glimmer and shadow of the church and looking on the pale face of him he slew; and here, in the morning, he must see his sweetheart married to another man before his eyes.

But for all that he obtained a command upon his mind, and built himself up in patience to await the issue.

In the Abbey Church

In Shoreby Abbey Church the prayers were kept up all night without cessation, now with the singing of psalms, now with a note or two upon the bell.

Rutter, the spy, was nobly waked. There he lay, mean-while, as they had arranged him, his dead hands crossed upon his bosom, his dead eyes staring on the roof; and hard by, in the stall, the lad who had slain him waited in sore disquietude the coming of the morning.

Once only, in the course of the hours, Sir Oliver leaned across to his captive.

"Richard," he whispered, "my son, if ye mean me evil, I will certify, on my soul's welfare, ye design upon an inno-cent man. Sinful in the eye of Heaven I do declare myself! but sinful against you I am not, neither have been ever."

"My father," returned Dick, in the same tone of voice, "trust me, I design nothing; but as for your innocence, I may not forget that ye cleared yourself but lamely."

"A man may be innocently guilty," replied the priest. "He may be set blindfolded upon a mission, ignorant of its true scope. So it was with me. I did decoy your father to his death; but as Heaven sees us in this sacred place, I knew not what I did."

"It may be," returned Dick, "but see what a strange web ye have woven, that I should be at this hour at once your prisoner and your judge; that ye should both threaten my days and deprecate my anger. Methinks, if ye had been all your life a true man and a good priest, ye would neither thus fear nor thus detest me. And now to your prayers. I do obey you, since needs must; but I will not be bur-thened with your company."

The priest uttered a sigh so heavy that it had almost touched the lad into some sentiment of pity, and he bowed his head upon his hands like a man borne down below a weight of care. He joined no longer in the psalms; but Dick could hear the beads rattle through his fingers and the prayers a-pattering between his teeth.

Yet a little, and the gray of the morning began to strug-gle through the painted casements of the church and to put to shame the glimmer of the tapers. The light slowly broadened and brightened, and presently through the southeastern clerestories a flush of rosy sunlight flickered on the walls. The storm was over; the great clouds had disburdened their snow and fled farther on, and the new day was breaking on a merry winter landscape sheathed in white.

A bustle of church officers followed; the bier was carried forth to the dead-house, and the stains of blood were cleansed from off the tiles, that no such ill-omened spectacle should disgrace the marriage of Lord Shoreby. At the same time, the very ecclesiastics who had been so dismally engaged all night began to put on morning faces to do honor to the merrier ceremony which was about to follow. And further to announce the coming of the day, the pious of the town began to assemble and fall to prayer before their favorite shrines or wait their turn at the confessionals.

Favored by this stir, it was, of course, easily possible for any man to avoid the vigilance of Sir Daniel's sentries at the door; and presently Dick, looking about him warily, caught the eye of no less a person than Will Lawless, still in his monk's habit.

The outlaw, at the same moment, recognized his leader and privily signed to him with hand and eye.

Now, Dick was far from having forgiven the old rogue his most untimely drunkenness, but he had no desire to involve him in his own predicament; and he signaled back to him as plain as he was able to begone.

Lawless, as though he had understood, disappeared at once behind a pillar, and Dick breathed again.

What, then, was his dismay to feel himself plucked by the sleeve and to find the old robber installed beside him, upon the next seat and to all appearance plunged in his devotions!

Instantly Sir Oliver arose from his place, and gliding behind the stalls made for the soldiers in the aisle. If the priest's suspicions had been so lightly wakened, the harm was already done and Lawless a prisoner in the church.

"Move not," whispered Dick. "We are in the plaguiest pass, thanks, before all things, to thy swinishness of yestereven. When ye saw me here, so strangely seated, where I have neither right nor interest, what a murrain! could ye not smell harm and get ye gone from evil?"

"Nay," returned Lawless, "I thought ye had heard from Ellis and were here on duty."

"Ellis!" echoed Dick, "is Ellis then returned?"

"For sure," replied the outlaw. "He came last night and belted me sore for being in wine—so there ye are avenged, my master. A furious man is Ellis Duckworth! He hath ridden me hot-spur from Craven to prevent this marriage; and, Master Dick, ye know the way of him—do so he will!"

"Nay, then," returned Dick, with composure, "you and I, my poor brother, are dead men; for I sit here a prisoner upon suspicion, and my neck was to answer for this very marriage that he purposeth to mar. I had a fair choice, by the rood; to lose my sweetheart or else lose my life! Well, the cast is thrown—it is to be my life."

"By the mass," cried Lawless, half rising, "I am gone!"

But Dick had his hand at once upon his shoulder.

"Friend Lawless, sit ye still," he said. "An ye have eyes, look yonder at the corner by the chancel arch; see ye not that, even upon the motion of your rising, yon armed men are up and ready to intercept you? Yield ye, friend. Ye were bold aboard ship, when ye thought to die a sea-death; be bold again, now that y'are to die presently upon the gallows."

"Master Dick," gasped Lawless, "the thing hath come upon me somewhat of the suddenest. But give me a moment till I fetch my breath again; and, by the mass, I will be as stout-hearted as yourself."

"Here is my bold fellow!" returned Dick. "And yet, Lawless, it goes hard against the grain with me to die; but where whining mendeth nothing, wherefore whine?"

"Nay, that indeed!" chimed Lawless. "And a fig for death at worst! It has to be done, my master, soon or late. And hanging in a good quarrel is an easy death, they say, though I could never hear of any that came back to say so."

And so saying the stout old rascal leaned back in his stall, folded his arms, and began to look about him with the greatest air of insolence and unconcern.

"And for the matter of that," Dick added, "it is yet our best chance to keep quiet. We wot not yet what Duckworth purposes; and when all is said, and if the worst befall, we may yet clear our feet of it."

Now that they ceased talking, they were aware of a very distant and thin strain of mirthful music which steadily drew nearer, louder, and merrier. The bells in the tower began to break forth into a doubling peal, and a greater and greater concourse of people to crowd into the church, shuffling the snow from off their feet and clapping and blowing their hands. The western door was flung wide open, showing a glimpse of sunlit, snowy street, and admitting in a great gust the shrewd air of the morning; and in short, it became plain by every sign that Lord Shoreby desired to be married very early in the day, and that the wedding-train was drawing near.

Some of Lord Shoreby's men now cleared a passage down the middle aisle, forcing the people back with lance-stocks; and just then, outside the portal, the secular musicians could be descried drawing near over the frozen snow, the fifers and trumpeters scarlet in the face with lusty blowing, the drummers and the cymbalists beating as for a wager.

These, as they drew near the door of the sacred building, filed off on either side and marking time to their own vigorous music, stood stamping in the snow. As they thus opened their ranks, the leaders of this noble bridal train appeared behind and between them; and such was the variety and gayety of their attire, such the display of silks and velvet, fur and satin, embroidery and lace, that the procession showed forth upon the snow like a flower-bed in a path or a painted window in a wall.

First came the bride, a sorry sight, as pale as winter, clinging to Sir Daniel's arm and attended, as bridesmaid, by the short young lady who had befriended Dick the night before. Close behind, in the most radiant toilet, followed the bridegroom, halting on a gouty foot, and as he passed the threshold of the sacred building and doffed his hat, his bald head was seen to be rosy with emotion.

And now came the hour of Ellis Duckworth.

Dick, who sat stunned among contrary emotions, grasping the desk in front of him, beheld a movement in the crowd, people jostling backward and eyes and arms uplifted. Following these signs, he beheld three or four men with bent bows, leaning from the clerestory gallery. At the same instant they delivered their discharge, and before the clamor and cries of the astounded populace had time to swell fully upon the ear, they had flitted from their perch and disappeared.

The nave was full of swaying heads and voices screaming; the ecclesiastics thronged in terror from their places; the music ceased, and though the bells overhead continued for some seconds to clang upon the air, some wind of the disaster seemed to find its way at last even to the chamber where the ringers were leaping on their ropes, and they also desisted from their merry labors.

Right in the midst of the nave the bridegroom lay stonedead, pierced by two black arrows. The bride had fainted. Sir Daniel stood, towering above the crowd in his surprise and anger, a clothyard shaft quivering in his left forearm and his face streaming blood from another which had grazed his brow.

Long before any search could be made for them, the authors of this tragic interruption had clattered down a turnpike stair and decamped by a postern door.

But Dick and Lawless still remained in pawn; they had indeed arisen on the first alarm and pushed manfully to gain the door; but what with the narrowness of the stalls and the crowding of terrified priests and choristers, the attempt had been in vain and they had stoically resumed their places.

And now, pale with horror, Sir Oliver rose to his feet and called upon Sir Daniel, pointing with one hand to Dick.

"Here," he cried, "is Richard Shelton—alas the hour! blood guilty! Seize him!—bid him be seized! For all our lives' sakes, take him and bind him surely! He hath sworn our fall."

Sir Daniel was blinded by anger—blinded by the hot blood that still streamed across his face.

"Where?" he bellowed. "Hale him forth! By the cross of Holywood but he shall rue this hour."

The crowd fell back, and a party of archers invaded the choir, laid rough hands on Dick, dragged him headforemost from the stall, and thrust him by the shoulders down the chancel steps. Lawless, on his part, sat as still as a mouse.

Sir Daniel, brushing the blood out of his eyes, stared blinkingly upon his captive.

"Aye," he said, "treacherous and insolent, I have thee fast; and by all potent oaths, for every drop of blood that now trickles in mine eyes, I will wring a groan out of thy carcass. Away with him!" he added. "Here is no place. Off with him to my house. I will number every point of thy body with a torture."

But Dick, putting off his captors, uplifted his voice.

"Sanctuary!" he shouted. "Sanctuary! Ho, there, my fathers! They would drag me from the church!"

"From the church thou hast defiled with murder, boy," added a tall man, magnificently dressed.

"On what probation?" cried Dick. "They do accuse me, indeed, of some complicity, but have not proved one tittle. I was, in truth, a suitor for this damsel's hand; and she, I will be bold to say, repaid my suit with favor. But what then? To love a maid is no offense, I trow—nay, nor to gain her love. In all else, I stand here free from guiltiness."

There was a murmur of approval among the bystanders, so boldly Dick declared his innocence; but at the same time a throng of accusers arose upon the other side, crying how he had been found last night in Sir Daniel's house, how he wore a sacrilegious disguise; and in the midst of the babel, Sir Oliver indicated Lawless, both by voice and gesture, as accomplice to the fact. He in his turn was dragged from his seat and set beside his leader. The feelings of the crowd rose high on either side, and while some dragged the prisoners to and fro to favor their escape, others cursed and struck them with their fists. Dick's ears rang and his brain swam dizzily, like a man struggling in the eddies of a furious river.

But the tall man who had already answered Dick, by a prodigious exercise of voice restored silence and order in the mob.

"Search them," he said, "for arms. We may so judge of their intentions."

Upon Dick they found no weapon but his poniard, and this told in his favor, until one man officiously drew it from its sheath and found it still uncleansed of the blood of Rutter. At this there was a great shout among Sir Daniel's followers, which the tall man suppressed by a gesture and an imperious glance. But when it came to the turn of Lawless, there was found under his gown a sheaf of arrows identical with those that had been shot.

"How say ye now?" asked the tall man, frowningly, of Dick.

"Sir," replied Dick, "I am here in sanctuary, is it not so? Well, sir, I see by your bearing that ye are high in station, and I read in your countenance the marks of piety and justice. To you, then, I will yield me prisoner, and that blithely, forgoing the advantage of this holy place. But rather than to be yielded into the discretion of that man—whom I do here accuse with a loud voice to be the murderer of my natural father and the unjust detainer of my lands and revenues—rather than that, I would beseech you, under favor, with your own gentle hand, to dispatch me on the spot. Your own ears have heard him, how before that I was proven guilty he did threaten me with torments. It standeth not with your own honor to deliver me to my sworn enemy and old oppressor, but to try me fairly by the way of law, and, if that I be guilty indeed, to slay me mercifully."

"My lord," cried Sir Daniel, "ye will not hearken to this wolf? His bloody dagger reeks him the lie into his face."

"Nay, but suffer me, good knight," returned the tall stranger; "your own vehemence doth somewhat tell against yourself."

And here the bride, who had come to herself some minutes past and looked wildly on upon this scene, broke loose from those that held her and fell upon her knees before the last speaker.

"My Lord of Risingham," she cried, "hear me, in justice. I am here in this man's custody by mere force, reft from mine own people. Since that day I had never pity, countenance, nor comfort from the face of man—but from him only—Richard Shelton—whom they now accuse and labor to undo. My lord, if he was yesternight in Sir Daniel's mansion, it was I that brought him there; he came but at my prayer and thought to do no hurt. While yet Sir Daniel was a good lord to him, he fought with them of the Black Arrow loyally; but when this foul guardian sought his life by practices, and he fled by night for his soul's sake out of that bloody house, whither was he to turn—he, helpless and penniless? Or if he be fallen among ill company, whom should ye blame—the lad that was unjustly handled or the guardian that did abuse his trust?"

And then the short young lady fell on her knees by Joanna's side.

"And I, my good lord and natural uncle," she added, "I can bear testimony, on my conscience and before the face of all, that what this maiden saith is true. It was I, unworthy, that did lead the young man in."

Earl Risingham had heard in silence, and when the voices ceased, he still stood silent for a space. Then he gave Joanna his hand to arise, though it was to be observed that he did not offer the like courtesy to her who had called herself his niece.

"Sir Daniel," he said, "here is a right intricate affair, the which with your good leave it shall be mine to examine and adjust. Content ye, then; your business is in careful hands; justice shall be done you; and in the meanwhile, get ye incontinently home and have your hurts attended. The air is shrewd, and I would not ye took cold upon these scratches."

He made a sign with his hand; it was passed down the nave by obsequious servants who waited upon his smallest gesture. Instantly, without the church, a tucket sounded shrill, and through the open portal archers and men-at-arms, uniformly arrayed in the colors and wearing the badge of Lord Risingham, began to file into the church, took Dick and Lawless from those who still detained them, and closing their files about the prisoners marched forth again and disappeared.

As they were passing, Joanna held both her hands to Dick and cried him her farewell; and the bridesmaid, nothing downcast by her uncle's evident displeasure, blew him a kiss, with a "Keep your heart up, lion-driver!" that for the first time since the accident called up a smile to the faces of the crowd.

Earl Risingham

Earl Risingham, although by far the most important person then in Shoreby, was poorly lodged in the house of a private gentleman upon the extreme outskirts of the town. Nothing but the armed men at the doors and the mounted messengers that kept arriving and departing announced the temporary residence of a great lord.

Thus it was that, from lack of space, Dick and Lawless were clapped into the same apartment.

"Well spoken, Master Richard," said the outlaw; "it was exceedingly well spoken, and for my part I thank you cordially. Here we are in good hands; we shall be justly tried, and some time this evening decently hanged on the same tree."

"Indeed, my poor friend, I do believe it," answered Dick.

"Yet we have a string to our bow," returned Lawless. "Ellis Duckworth is a man out of ten thousand; he holdeth you right near his heart, both for your own and for your father's sake; and knowing you guiltless of this fact, he will stir earth and heaven to bear you clear."

"It may not be," said Dick. "What can he do? He hath but a handful. Alack, if it were but tomorrow—could I but keep a certain tryst an hour before noon tomorrow—all were, I think, otherwise. But now there is no help."

"Well," concluded Lawless, "an ye will stand to it for my innocence, I will stand to it for yours, and that stoutly. It shall naught avail us; but an I be to hang, it shall not be for lack of swearing."

And then, while Dick gave himself over to his reflections, the old rogue curled himself down into a corner, pulled his monkish hood about his face, and composed himself to sleep. Soon he was loudly snoring, so utterly had his long life of hardship and adventure blunted the sense of apprehension.

It was long after noon, and the day was already failing before the door was opened and Dick taken forth and led upstairs to where, in a warm cabinet, Earl Risingham sat musing over the fire.

On his captive's entrance he looked up.

"Sir," he said, "I knew your father, who was a man of honor, and this inclineth me to be the more lenient; but I may not hide from you that heavy charges lie against your character. Ye do consort with murderers and robbers; upon a clear probation ye have carried war against the king's peace; ye are suspected to have piratically seized upon a ship; ye are found skulking with a counterfeit presentment in your enemy's house; a man is slain that very evening——"

"An it like you, my lord," Dick interposed, "I will at once avow my guilt, such as it is. I slew this fellow Rutter; and to the proof"—searching in his bosom—"here is a letter from his wallet."

Lord Risingham took the letter and opened it and read it twice.

"Ye have read this?" he inquired.

"I have read it," answered Dick.

"Are ye for York or Lancaster?" the earl demanded.

"My lord, it was but a little while back that I was asked that question and knew not how to answer it," said Dick; "but having answered once, I will not vary. My lord, I am for York."

The earl nodded approvingly.

"Honestly replied," he said. "But wherefore, then, deliver me this letter?"

"Nay, but against traitors, my lord, are not all sides arrayed?" cried Dick.

"I would they were, young gentleman," returned the earl; "and I do at least approve your saying. There is more youth than guile in you, I do perceive; and were not Sir Daniel a mighty man upon our side, I were half tempted to espouse your quarrel. For I have inquired, and it appears you have been hardly dealt with and have much excuse. But look ye, sir, I am, before all else, a leader in the Queen's interest; and though by nature a just man, as I believe, and leaning even to the excess of mercy, yet must I order my goings for my party's interest, and to keep Sir Daniel I would go far about."

"My lord," returned Dick, "ye will think me very bold to counsel you; but do ye count upon Sir Daniel's faith? Methought he had changed sides intolerably often."

"Nay, it is the way of England. What would ye have?" the earl demanded. "But ye are unjust to the knight of Tunstall; and as faith goes, in this unfaithful generation, he hath of late been honorably true to us of Lancaster. Even in our last reverses he stood firm."

"An it please you, then," said Dick, "to cast your eye upon this letter, ye might somewhat change your thought of him," and he handed to the earl Sir Daniel's letter to Lord Wensleydale.

The effect upon the earl's countenance was instant; he

lowered like an angry lion, and his hand with a sudden movement clutched at his dagger.

"Ye have read this also?" he asked.

"Even so," said Dick. "It is your lordship's own estate he offers to Lord Wensleydale."

"It is my own estate, even as ye say!" returned the earl. "I am your bedesman* for this letter. It hath shown me a fox's hole. Command me, Master Shelton; I will not be backward in gratitude, and to begin with, York or Lancaster, true man or thief, I do now set you at freedom. Go, a-Mary's name! But judge it right that I retain and hang your fellow Lawless. The crime hath been most open, and it were fitting that some open punishments should follow."

"My lord, I make it my first suit to you to spare him also," pleaded Dick.

"It is an old condemned rogue, thief, and vagabond, Master Shelton," said the earl. "He hath been gallows-ripe this score of years. And, whether for one thing or another, whether tomorrow or the day after, where is the great choice?"

"Yet, my lord, it was through love to me that he came hither," answered Dick, "and I were churlish and thankless to desert him."

"Master Shelton, ye are troublesome," replied the earl, severely. "It is an evil way to prosper in this world. Howbeit, and to be quit of your importunity, I will once more humor you. Go, then, together; but go warily, and get swiftly out of Shoreby town. For this Sir Daniel (whom may the saints confound!) thirsteth most greedily to have your blood."

"My lord, I do now offer you in words my gratitude, trusting at some brief date to pay you some of it in service," replied Dick, as he turned from the apartment.

---

*"I am at your bidding." (In a different context, the word "bedesman" might have a different meaning.)

Arblaster Again

When Dick and Lawless were suffered to steal by a back way out of the house where Lord Risingham held his garrison, the evening had already come.

They paused in shelter of the garden wall to consult on their best course. The danger was extreme. If one of Sir Daniel's men caught sight of them and raised the view-hallo, they would be run down and butchered instantly. And not only was the town of Shoreby a mere net of peril for their lives, but to make for the open country was to run the risk of the patrols.

A little way off upon some open ground they spied a windmill standing; and hard by that a very large granary with open doors.

"How if we lay there until the night fall?" Dick proposed.

And Lawless having no better suggestion to offer they made a straight push for the granary at a run and concealed themselves behind the door among some straw. The daylight rapidly departed; and presently the moon was silvering the frozen snow. Now or never was their opportunity to gain the Goat and Bagpipes unobserved and change their tell-tale garments. Yet even then it was advisable to go round by the outskirts and not run the gauntlet of the market-place, where in the concourse of people they stood the more imminent peril to be recognized and slain.

This course was a long one. It took them not far from the house by the beach, now lying dark and silent, and brought them forth at last by the margin of the harbor. Many of the ships, as they could see by the clear moonshine, had weighed anchor and, profiting by the calm sky, proceeded for more distant parts; answerable to this, the rude alehouses along the beach (although, in defiance of the curfew law, they still shone with fire and candle) were no longer thronged with customers and no longer echoed to the chorus of sea songs.

Hastily, half running, with their monkish raiment kilted

to the knee, they plunged through the deep snow and threaded the labyrinth of marine lumber; and they were already more than half-way round the harbor when as they were passing close before an alehouse the door suddenly opened and let out a gush of light upon their fleeting figures.

Instantly they stopped and made believe to be engaged in earnest conversation.

Three men, one after another, came out of the alehouse and the last closed the door behind him. All three were unsteady upon their feet, as if they had passed the day in deep potations, and they now stood wavering in the moonlight like men who knew not what they would be after. The tallest of the three was talking in a loud, lamentable voice.

"Seven pieces of as good Gascony as ever a tapster broached," he was saying, "the best ship out o' the port o' Dartmouth, a Virgin Mary parcel-gilt, thirteen pounds of good gold money——"

"I have had losses, too," interrupted one of the others. "I have had losses of mine own, gossip Arblaster. I was robbed at Martinmas of five shillings and a leather wallet well worth ninepence farthing."

Dick's heart smote him at what he heard. Until that moment he had not perhaps thought twice of the poor skipper who had been ruined by the loss of the *Good Hope*; so careless in those days were men who wore arms of the goods and interests of their inferiors. But this sudden encounter reminded him sharply of the high-handed manner and ill ending of his enterprise; and both he and Lawless turned their heads the other way to avoid the chance of recognition.

The ship's dog had, however, made his escape from the wreck and found his way back again to Shoreby. He was now at Arblaster's heels, and suddenly sniffing and pricking his ears, he darted forward and began to bark furiously at the two sham friars.

His master unsteadily followed him.

"Hey, shipmates!" he cried. "Have ye ever a penny piece for a poor old shipman, clean destroyed by pirates? I am a man that would have paid for you both o' Thursday morning; and now here I be o' Saturday night, begging for a flagon of ale! Ask my man Tom, if ye misdoubt me. Seven pieces of good Gascon wine, a ship that was mine own, and was my father's before me, a Blessed Mary of plane-tree wood and parcel-gilt, and thirteen pounds in gold and silver. Hey! what say ye? A man that fought the French, too; for I have fought the French; I have cut more French throats upon the high seas than ever a man that sails out of Dartmouth. Come, a penny piece."

Neither Dick nor Lawless durst answer him a word, lest he should recognize their voices; and they stood as helpless as a ship ashore, not knowing where to turn nor what to hope.

"Are ye dumb, boy?" inquired the skipper. "Mates," he added, with a hiccup, "they be dumb. I like not this manner of discourtesy; for an a man be dumb, so be as he's courteous, he will still speak when he was spoken to, methinks."

By this time the sailor Tom, who was a man of great personal strength, seemed to have conceived some suspicion of these two speechless figures; and being soberer than his captain, stepped suddenly before him, took Lawless roughly by the shoulder and asked him with an oath what ailed him that he held his tongue. To this the outlaw, thinking all was over, made answer by a wrestling feint that stretched the sailor on the sand, and calling upon Dick to follow him, took to his heels among the lumber.

The affair passed in a second. Before Dick could run at all, Arblaster had him in his arms; Tom, crawling on his face, had caught him by one foot, and the third man had a drawn cutlass brandishing above his head.

It was not so much the danger, it was not so much the annoyance, that now bowed down the spirits of young Shelton; it was the profound humiliation to have escaped Sir Daniel, convinced Lord Risingham, and now fall helpless in the hands of this old drunken sailor; and not merely helpless, but as his conscience loudly told him when it was too late, actually guilty—actually the bank-rupt debtor of the man whose ship he had stolen and lost.

"Bring me him back into the alehouse, till I see his face," said Arblaster.

"Nay, nay," returned Tom; "but let us first unload his wallet, lest the other lads cry share."

But though he was searched from head to foot, not a penny was found upon him; nothing but Lord Foxham's signet, which they plucked savagely from his finger.

"Turn me him to the moon," said the skipper; and tak-ing Dick by the chin, he cruelly jerked his head into the air. "Blessed Virgin!" he cried, "it is the pirate."

"Hey!" cried Tom.

"By the Virgin of Bordeaux, it is the man himself!" repeated Arblaster. "What, sea-thief, do I hold you?" he cried. "Where is my ship? Where is my wine? Hey! have I you in my hands? Tom, give me one end of a cord here; I will so truss me this sea-thief, hand and foot together, like a basting turkey—marry, I will so bind him up—and there-after I will so beat—so beat him!"

And so he ran on, winding the cord meanwhile about Dick's limbs with the dexterity peculiar to seamen and at every turn and cross securing it with a knot, and tighten-ing the whole fabric with a savage pull.

When he had done, the lad was a mere package in his hands—as helpless as the dead. The skipper held him at arm's length and laughed aloud. Then he fetched him a stunning buffet on the ear; and then turned him about and furiously kicked and kicked him. Anger rose up in Dick's bosom like a storm; anger strangled him, and he thought to have died; but when the sailor, tired of this cruel play, dropped him all his length upon the sand and turned to consult with his companions, he instantly regained com-mand of his temper. Here was a momentary respite; ere they began again to torture him, he might have found some method to escape from this degrading and fatal mis-adventure.

Presently, sure enough, and while his captors were still discussing what to do with him, he took heart of grace and with a pretty steady voice addressed them.

"My masters," he began, "are ye gone clean foolish? Here hath Heaven put into your hand as pretty an occasion to grow rich as ever shipman had—such as ye might make thirty over-sea adventures and not find again—and, by the mass! what do ye? Beat me?—nay; so would an angry child. But for long-headed tarry-Johns, that fear not fire nor water, and that love gold as they love beef, methinks ye are not wise."

"Aye," said Tom, "now y'are trussed ye would cozen us."

"Cozen you!" repeated Dick. "Nay, if ye be fools, it would be easy. But if ye be shrewd fellows, as I trow ye are, ye can see plainly where your interest lies. When I took your ship from you, we were many, we were well clad and armed; but now, bethink you a little, who mustered that array? One incontestably that hath made much gold. And if he, being already rich, continueth to hunt after more even in the face of storms—bethink you once more—shall there not be a treasure somewhere hidden?"

"What meaneth he?" asked one of the men.

"Why, if ye have lost an old skiff and a few jugs of vinegary wine," continued Dick, "forget them, for the trash they are; and do ye rather buckle to an adventure worth the name that shall in twelve hours make or mar you forever. But take me up from where I lie, and let us go somewhere near at hand and talk across a flagon, for I am sore and frozen, and my mouth is half among the snow."

"He seeks to cozen us," said Tom, contemptuously.

"Cozen! cozen!" cried the third man. "I would I could see the man that could cozen me! He were a cozener indeed! Nay, I was not born yesterday. I can see a church when it hath a steeple on it; and for my part, gossip Arblaster, methinks there is some sense in this young man. Shall we go hear him indeed? Say, shall we go hear him?"

"I would look gladly on a pottle of strong ale, good

Master Pirret," returned Arblaster. "How say ye, Tom? But then the wallet is empty."

"I will pay," said the other, "I will pay. I would fain see this matter out; I do believe, upon my conscience, there is gold in it."

"Nay, if ye get again to drinking, all is lost!" cried Tom.

"Gossip Arblaster, ye suffer your fellow to have too much liberty," returned Master Pirret. "Would ye be led by a hired man? Fie, fie!"

"Peace, fellow!" said Arblaster, addressing Tom. "Will ye put your oar in! Truly a fine pass, when the crew is to correct the skipper!"

"Well, then, go your way," said Tom; "I wash my hands of you."

"Set him, then, upon his feet," said Master Pirret. "I know a privy place where we may drink and discourse."

"If I am to walk, my friends, ye must set my feet at liberty," said Dick, when he had been once more planted upright like a post.

"He saith true," laughed Pirret. "Truly, he could not walk accoutered as he is. Give it a slit—out with your knife and slit it, gossip."

Even Arblaster paused at this proposal; but as his companion continued to insist, and Dick had the sense to keep the merest wooden indifference of expression and only shrugged his shoulders over the delay, the skipper consented at last and cut the cords which tied his prisoner's feet and legs. Not only did this enable Dick to walk, but the whole network of his bonds being proportionately loosened, he felt the arm behind his back begin to move freely and could hope with time and trouble to entirely disengage it. So much he owed already to the owlish silliness and greed of Master Pirret.

That worthy now assumed the lead and conducted them to the very same rude alehouse where Lawless had taken Arblaster on the day of the gale. It was now quite deserted; the fire was a pile of red embers, radiating the most ardent heat; and when they had chosen their places, and the landlord had set before them a measure of mulled ale, both Pirret and Arblaster stretched forth their legs and squared their elbows like men bent upon a pleasant hour.

The table at which they sat, like all the others in the ale-house, consisted of a heavy, square board set on a pair of barrels; and each of the four curiously assorted cronies sat at one side of the square, Pirret facing Arblaster, and Dick opposite to the common sailor.

"And now, young man," said Pirret, "to your tale. It doth appear, indeed, that ye have somewhat abused our gossip Arblaster; but what then? Make it up to him—show him but this chance to become wealthy—and I will go pledge he will forgive you."

So far Dick had spoken pretty much at random; but it was now necessary, under the supervision of six eyes, to invent and tell some marvelous story and, if it were possible, get back into his hands the all-important signet. To squander time was the first necessity. The longer his stay lasted, the more would his captors drink, and the surer should he be when he attempted his escape.

Well, Dick was not much of an inventor, and what he told was pretty much the tale of Ali Baba, with Shoreby and Tunstall Forest substituted for the East and the treasures of the cavern rather exaggerated than diminished. As the reader is aware, it is an excellent story, and has but one drawback—that it is not true; and so as these three simple shipmen now heard it for the first time, their eyes stood out of their faces and their mouths gaped like cod-fish at a fishmonger's.

Pretty soon a second measure of mulled ale was called for; and while Dick was artfully spinning out the incidents a third followed the second.

Here was the position of the parties toward the end:

Arblaster, three-parts drunk and one-half asleep, hung helpless on his stool. Even Tom had been much delighted with the tale, and his vigilance had abated in proportion.

Meanwhile, Dick had gradually wormed his right arm clear of its bonds and was ready to risk all.

"And so," said Pirret, "y'are one of these?"

"I was made so," replied Dick, "against my will; but an I could but get a sack or two of gold coin to my share, I should be a fool indeed to continue dwelling in a filthy cave and standing shot and buffet like a soldier. Here be we four; good! Let us, then, go forth into the forest tomorrow ere the sun be up. Could we come honestly by a donkey, it were better; but an we cannot, we have our four strong backs and I warrant me we shall come home staggering."

Pirret licked his lips.

"And this magic," he said—"this password, whereby the cave is opened—how call ye it, friend?"

"Nay, none know the word but the three chiefs," returned Dick; "but here is your great good fortune, that on this very evening I should be the bearer of a spell to open it. It is a thing not trusted twice a year beyond the captain's wallet."

"A spell!" said Arblaster, half awakening, and squinting upon Dick with one eye. "Aroint thee! no spells! I be a good Christian. Ask my man Tom, else."

"Nay, but this is white magic," said Dick. "It doth naught with the devil; only the powers of numbers, herbs, and planets."

"Aye, aye," said Pirret; "'tis but white magic, gossip. There is no sin therein, I do assure you. But proceed, good youth. This spell—in what should it consist?"

"Nay, that I will incontinently show you," answered Dick. "Have ye there the ring ye took from my finger? Good! Now hold it forth before you by the extreme finger-ends, at the arm's length, and over against the shining of these embers. 'Tis so exactly. Thus, then, is the spell."

With a haggard glance, Dick saw the coast was clear between him and the door. He put up an internal prayer. Then whipping forth his arm, he made but one snatch of the ring, and at the same instant, levering up the table, he sent it bodily over upon the seaman Tom. He, poor soul, went down bawling under the ruins; and before Arblaster understood that anything was wrong, or Pirret could collect his dazzled wits, Dick had run to the door and escaped into the moonlit night.

The moon, which now rode in the mid-heavens, and the extreme whiteness of the snow made the open ground about the harbor bright as day; and young Shelton leaping, with kilted robe, among the lumber was a conspicuous figure from afar.

Tom and Pirret followed him with shouts; from every drinking-shop they were joined by others whom their cries aroused; and presently a whole fleet of sailors was in full pursuit. But Jack ashore was a bad runner even in the fifteenth century, and Dick, besides, had a start which he rapidly improved until as he drew near the entrance of a narrow lane he even paused and looked laughingly behind him.

Upon the white floor of snow, all the shipmen of Shoreby came clustering in an inky mass and tailing out rearward in isolated clumps. Every man was shouting and screaming; every man was gesticulating with both arms in air; someone was continually falling; and to complete the picture, when one fell, a dozen would fall upon the top of him.

The confused mass of sound which they rolled up as high as to the moon was partly comical and partly terrifying to the fugitive whom they were hunting. In itself, it was impotent, for he made sure no seaman in the port could run him down. But the mere volume of noise, in so far as it must awake all the sleepers in Shoreby and bring all the skulking sentries to the street, did really threaten him with danger in the front. So, spying a dark doorway at a corner, he whipped briskly into it and let the uncouth hunt go by him, still shouting and gesticulating, and all red with hurry, and white with tumbles in the snow.

It was a long while, indeed, before this great invasion of

the town by the harbor came to an end, and it was long
before silence was restored. For long, lost sailors were
still heard pounding and shouting through the streets in
all directions and in every quarter of the town. Quarrels
followed, sometimes among themselves, sometimes with
the men of the patrols; knives were drawn, blows given
and received, and more than one dead body remained
behind upon the snow.

When a full hour later the last seaman returned grumblingly to the harbor side and his particular tavern, it may
fairly be questioned if he had ever known what manner of
man he was pursuing, but it was absolutely sure that he
had now forgotten. By next morning there were many
strange stories flying; and a little while after, the legend of
the devil's nocturnal visit was an article of faith with all
the lads of Shoreby.

But the return of the last seaman did not even yet set
free young Shelton from his cold imprisonment in the
doorway.

For some time after there was a great activity of patrols;
and special parties came forth to make the round of the
place and report to one or other of the great lords, whose
slumbers had been thus unusually broken.

The night was already well spent before Dick ventured
from his hiding-place and came safe and sound but aching
with cold and bruises to the door of the Goat and Bagpipes. As the law required, there was neither fire nor candle in the house; but he groped his way into a corner of
the icy guest-room, found an end of the blanket, which he
hitched around his shoulders, and creeping close to the
nearest sleeper, was soon lost in slumber.

BOOK V: CROOKBACK

The Shrill Trumpet

VERY EARLY the next morning, before the first peep of the day, Dick arose, changed his garments, armed himself once more like a gentleman, and set forth for Lawless's den in the forest. There, it will be remembered, he had left Lord Foxham's papers; and to get these and be back in time for the tryst with the young Duke of Gloucester could only be managed by an early start and the most vigorous walking.

The frost was more rigorous than ever; the air windless and dry, and stinging to the nostril. The moon had gone down, but the stars were still bright and numerous, and the reflection from the snow was clear and cheerful. There was no need for a lamp to walk by; nor in that still but ringing air the least temptation to delay.

Dick had crossed the greater part of the open ground between Shoreby and the forest and had reached the bottom of the little hill, some hundred yards below the Cross of Saint Bride, when through the stillness of the black morn, there rang forth the note of a trumpet, so shrill, clear, and piercing that he thought he had never heard the match of it for audibility. It was blown once and then hurriedly a second time; and then the clash of steel succeeded.

At this young Shelton pricked his ears and, drawing his sword, ran forward up the hill.

Presently he came in sight of the cross and was aware

of a most fierce encounter raging on the road before it. There were seven or eight assailants, and but one to keep head against them; but so active and dexterous was this one, so desperately did he charge and scatter his opponents, so deftly keep his footing on the ice, that already, before Dick could intervene, he had slain one, wounded another, and kept the whole in check.

Still it was by a miracle that he continued his defense, and at any moment, any accident, the least slip of foot or error of hand, his life would be a forfeit.

"Hold ye well, sir! Here is help!" cried Richard; and forgetting that he was alone and that the cry was somewhat irregular, "To the Arrow! to the Arrow," he shouted as he fell upon the rear of the assailants.

These were stout fellows also, for they gave not an inch at his surprise, but faced about and fell with astonishing fury upon Dick. Four against one, the steel flashed about him in the starlight: the sparks flew fiercely; one of the men opposed to him fell—in the stir of the fight he hardly knew why; then he himself was struck across the head, and though the steel cap below his hood protected him, the blow beat him down upon one knee with a brain whirling like a windmill sail.

Meanwhile the man whom he had come to rescue, instead of joining in the conflict, had, on the first sign of intervention, leaped aback and blown again, and yet more urgently and loudly, on that same shrill-voiced trumpet that began the alarm. Next moment, indeed, his foes were on him, and he was once more charging and fleeing, leaping, stabbing, dropping to his knee, and using indifferently sword and dagger, foot and hand, with the same unshaken courage and feverish energy and speed.

But that ear-piercing summons had been heard at last. There was a muffled rushing in the snow; and in a good hour for Dick, who saw the sword-points glitter already at his throat, there poured forth out of the wood upon both sides a disorderly torrent of mounted men-at-arms, each cased in iron and with visor lowered, each bearing his lance in rest or his sword bared and raised, and each carrying, so to speak, a passenger, in the shape of an archer or page, who leaped one after another from their perches and had presently doubled the array.

The original assailants seeing themselves outnumbered and surrounded, threw down their arms without a word.

"Seize me these fellows!" said the hero of the trumpet; and when his order had been obeyed, he drew near to Dick and looked him in the face.

Dick, returning this scrutiny, was surprised to find in one who had displayed such strength, skill, and energy, a lad no older than himself[1]—slightly deformed, with one shoulder higher than the other, and of a pale, painful, and distorted countenance. The eyes, however, were very clear and bold.

"Sir," said this lad, "ye come in good time for me and none too early."

"My lord," returned Dick, with a faint sense that he was in the presence of a great personage, "ye are yourself so marvelous a good swordsman that I believe ye had managed them single-handed. Howbeit, it was certainly well for me that your men delayed no longer than they did."

"How knew ye who I was?" demanded the stranger.

"Even now, my lord," Dick answered, "I am ignorant of whom I speak with."

"Is it so?" asked the other. "And yet ye threw yourself head first into this unequal battle."

"I saw one man valiantly contending against many," replied Dick, "and I had thought myself dishonored not to bear him aid."

A singular sneer played about the young nobleman's mouth as he made answer:

"These are very brave words. But to the more essential—are ye Lancaster or York?"

---

[1] Richard Crookback would have been really far younger at this date.

"My lord, I make no secret; I am clear for York," Dick answered.

"By the mass!" replied the other, "it is well for you."

And so saying, he turned toward one of his followers.

"Let me see," he continued, in the same sneering and cruel tones—"let me see a clean end of these brave gentlemen. Truss me them up."

There were but five survivors of the attacking party. Archers seized them by the arms; they were hurried to the borders of the wood and each placed below a tree of suitable dimensions; the rope was adjusted; an archer, carrying the end of it, hastily clambered overhead and before a minute was over and without a word passing upon either hand, the five men were swinging by the neck.

"And now," cried the deformed leader, "back to your posts, and when I summon you next, be readier to attend."

"My lord duke," said one man, "beseech you, tarry not here alone. Keep but a handful of lances at your hand."

"Fellow," said the duke, "I have forborne to chide you for your slowness. Cross me not, therefore. I trust my hand and arm, for all that I be crooked. Ye were backward when the trumpet sounded: and ye are now too forward with your counsels. But it is ever so; last with the lance and first with tongue. Let it be reversed."

And with a gesture that was not without a sort of dangerous nobility, he waved them off.

The footmen climbed again to their seats behind the men-at-arms, and the whole party moved slowly away and disappeared in twenty different directions under the cover of the forest.

The day was by this time beginning to break and the stars to fade. The first gray glimmer of dawn shone upon the countenances of the two young men, who now turned once more to face each other.

"Here," said the duke, "ye have seen my vengeance, which is, like my blade, both sharp and ready. But I would not have you, for all Christendom, suppose me thankless.

You that came to my aid with a good sword and a better courage—unless that ye recoil from my misshapenness—come to my heart."

And so saying the young leader held out his arms for an embrace.

In the bottom of his heart Dick already entertained a great terror and some hatred for the man whom he had rescued; but the invitation was so worded that it would not have been merely discourteous but cruel to refuse or hesitate, and he hastened to comply.

"And now, my lord duke," he said, when he had regained his freedom, "do I suppose aright? Are ye my Lord Duke of Gloucester?"

"I am Richard of Gloucester," returned the other. "And you—how call they you?"

Dick told him his name and presented Lord Foxham's signet, which the duke immediately recognized.

"Ye come too soon," he said; "but why should I complain? Ye are like me, that was here at watch two hours before the day. But this is the first sally of mine arms; upon this adventure, Master Shelton, shall I make or mar the quality of my renown. There lie mine enemies, under two old, skilled captains, Risingham and Brackley, well posted for strength, I do believe, but yet upon two sides without retreat, inclosed betwixt the sea, the harbor, and the river. Methinks, Shelton, here were a great blow to be stricken, an we could strike it silently and suddenly."

"I do think so, indeed," cried Dick, warming.

"Have ye my Lord Foxham's notes?" inquired the duke.

And then Dick, having explained how he was without them for the moment, made himself bold to offer information every jot as good, of his own knowledge.

"And for mine own part, my lord duke," he added, "an ye had men enough, I would fall on even at this present. For, look ye, at the peep of day the watches of the night are over; but by day they keep neither watch nor ward—only scour the outskirts with horsemen. Now, then, when the night-watch is already unarmed and the rest are at their morning cup—now were the time to break them."

"How many do ye count?" asked Gloucester.

"They number not two thousand," Dick replied.

"I have seven hundred in the woods behind us," said the duke; "seven hundred follow from Kettley and will be here anon; behind these, and farther, are four hundred more; and my Lord Foxham hath five hundred half a day from here at Holywood. Shall we attend their coming, or fall on?"

"My lord," said Dick, "when ye hanged these five poor rogues ye did decide the question. Churls although they were, in these uneasy times they will be lacked and looked for and the alarm be given. Therefore, my lord, if ye do count upon the advantage of a surprise, ye have not, in my poor opinion, one whole hour in front of you."

"I do think so indeed," returned Crookback. "Well, before an hour, ye shall be in the thick on't winning spurs. A swift man to Holywood, carrying Lord Foxham's signet; another along the road to speed my laggards! Nay, Shelton, by the rood, it may be done!"

Therewith he once more set his trumpet to his lips and blew.

This time he was not long kept waiting. In a moment the open space about the cross was filled with horse and foot. Richard of Gloucester took his place upon the steps and dispatched messenger after messenger to hasten the concentration of the seven hundred men that lay hidden in the immediate neighborhood among the woods; and before a quarter of an hour had passed, all his dispositions being taken, he put himself at their head and began to move down the hill toward Shoreby.

His plan was simple. He was to seize a quarter of the town of Shoreby lying on the right hand of the high-road and make his position good there in the narrow lanes until his reënforcements followed.

If Lord Risingham chose to retreat, Richard would

follow upon his rear and take him between two fires; or if he preferred to hold the town, he would be shut in a trap, there to be gradually overwhelmed by force of numbers.

There was but one danger, but that was imminent and great—Gloucester's seven hundred might be rolled up and cut to pieces in the first encounter, and to avoid this, it was needful to make the surprise of their arrival as complete as possible.

The footmen, therefore, were all once more taken up behind the riders, and Dick had the signal honor meted out to him of mounting behind Gloucester himself. For as far as there was any cover the troops moved slowly and when they came near the end of the trees that lined the highway, stopped to breathe and reconnoiter.

The sun was now well up, shining with a frosty brightness out of a yellow halo and right over against the luminary, Shoreby, a field of snowy roofs and ruddy gables, was rolling up its columns of morning smoke.

Gloucester turned round to Dick.

"In that poor place," he said, "where people are cooking breakfast, either you shall gain your spurs and I begin a life of mighty honor and glory in the world's eye, or both of us, as I conceive it, shall fall dead and be unheard of. Two Richards are we. Well then, Richard Shelton, they shall be heard about, these two! Their swords shall not ring more loudly on men's helmets than their names shall ring in people's ears."

Dick was astonished at so great a hunger after fame, expressed with so great vehemence of voice and language; and he answered very sensibly and quietly that for his part he promised he would do his duty and doubted not of victory if everyone did the like.

By this time the horses were well breathed, and the leader holding up his sword and giving rein, the whole troop of chargers broke into the gallop and thundered with their double load of fighting men down the remainder of the hill and across the snow-covered plain that still divided them from Shoreby.

The Battle of Shoreby

The whole distance to be crossed was not above a quarter of a mile. But they had no sooner debouched beyond the cover of the trees than they were aware of people fleeing and screaming in the snowy meadows upon either hand. Almost at the same moment a great rumor began to arise and spread and grow continually louder in the town; and they were not yet half-way to the nearest house before the bells began to ring backward from the steeple.

The young duke ground his teeth together. By these so early signals of alarm he feared to find his enemies prepared; and if he failed to gain a footing in the town, he knew that his small party would soon be broken and exterminated in the open.

In the town, however, the Lancastrians were far from being in so good a posture. It was as Dick had said. The night-guard had already doffed their harness; the rest were still hanging—unlatched, unbraced, all unprepared for battle—about their quarters; and in the whole of Shoreby there were not, perhaps, fifty men fully armed or fifty chargers ready to be mounted.

The beating of the bells, the terrifying summons of men who ran about the streets crying and beating upon the doors aroused in an incredibly short space at least two score out of that half hundred. These got speedily to horse, and the alarm still flying wild and contrary, galloped in different directions.

Thus it befell that when Richard of Gloucester reached the first house of Shoreby, he was met in the mouth of the street by a mere handful of lances, whom he swept before his onset as the storm chases the lark.

A hundred paces into the town, Dick Shelton touched

the duke's arm; the duke in answer gathered his reins, put the shrill trumpet to his mouth and blowing a concerted point turned to the right hand out of the direct advance. Swerving like a single rider, his whole command turned after him and still at the full gallop of the chargers, swept up the narrow by-street. Only the last score of riders drew rein and faced about in the entrance; the footmen, whom they carried behind them, leaped at the same instant to the earth and began, some to bend their bows and others to break into and secure the houses upon either hand.

Surprised at this sudden change of direction and daunted by the firm front of the rear-guard, the few Lancastrians after a momentary consultation turned and rode farther into town to seek for reënforcements.

The quarter of the town upon which, by the advice of Dick, Richard of Gloucester had now seized, consisted of five small streets of poor and ill-inhabited houses occupying a very gentle eminence and lying open toward the back.

The five streets being each secured by a good guard, the reserve would thus occupy the center, out of shot and yet ready to carry aid wherever it was needed.

Such was the poorness of the neighborhood that none of the Lancastrian lords and but few of their retainers had been lodged therein; and the inhabitants with one accord deserted their houses and fled squalling along the streets or over garden walls.

In the center where the five ways all met, a somewhat ill-favored alehouse displayed the sign of the Chequers; and here the Duke of Gloucester chose his headquarters for the day.

To Dick he assigned the guard of one of the five streets.

"Go," he said, "win your spurs. Win glory for me; one Richard for another. I tell you, if I rise, ye shall rise by the same ladder. Go," he added, shaking him by the hand.

But, as soon as Dick was gone, he turned to a little shabby archer at his elbow.

"Go, Dutton, and that right speedily," he added. "Follow

that lad. If ye find him faithful, ye answer for his safety, a head for a head. Woe unto you, if ye return without him! But if he be faithless—or for one instant ye misdoubt him—stab him from behind."

In the meanwhile Dick hastened to secure his post. The street he had to guard was very narrow and closely lined with houses which projected and overhung the roadway; but narrow and dark as it was, since it opened upon the market-place of the town, the main issue of the battle would probably fall to be decided on that spot.

The market-place was full of townspeople fleeing in disorder; but there was as yet no sign of any foeman ready to attack, and Dick judged he had some time before him to make ready his defense.

The two houses at the end stood deserted with open doors, as the inhabitants had left them in their flight, and from these he had the furniture hastily tossed forth and piled into a barrier in the entry of the lane. A hundred men were placed at his disposal, and of these he threw the more part into the houses where they might lie in shelter and deliver their arrows from the windows. With the rest, under his own immediate eye, he lined the barricade.

Meanwhile the utmost uproar and confusion had continued to prevail throughout the town; and what with the hurried clashing of bells, the sounding of trumpets, the swift movement of bodies of horse, the cries of the commanders, and the shrieks of women, the noise was almost deafening to the ear. Presently, little by little, the tumult began to subside; and soon after, files of men in armor and bodies of archers began to assemble and form in line for battle in the market-place.

A large portion of this body were in murrey and blue, and in the mounted knight who ordered their array Dick recognized Sir Daniel Brackley.

Then there befell a long pause, which was followed by the almost simultaneous sounding of four trumpets from four different quarters of the town. A fifth rang in answer from the market-place, and at the same moment the files began to move and a shower of arrows rattled about the barricade and sounded like blows upon the walls of the two flanking houses.

The attack had begun by a common signal on all the five issues of the quarter. Gloucester was beleaguered upon every side; and Dick judged, if he would make good his post, he must rely entirely on the hundred men of his command.

Seven volleys of arrows followed one upon the other, and in the very thick of the discharges Dick was touched from behind upon the arm and found a page holding out to him a leathern jack, strengthened with bright plates of mail.

"It is from my Lord of Gloucester," said the page. "He hath observed, Sir Richard, that ye went unarmed."

Dick, with a glow at his heart at being so addressed, got to his feet and with the assistance of the page donned the defensive coat. Even as he did so, two arrows rattled harmlessly upon the plates, and a third struck down the page mortally wounded at his feet.

Meanwhile the whole body of the enemy had been steadily drawing nearer across the market-place; and by this time were so close at hand that Dick gave the order to return their shot. Immediately, from behind the barrier and from the windows of the houses, a counterblast of arrows sped carrying death. But the Lancastrians, as if they had but waited for a signal, shouted loudly in answer, and began to close at a run upon the barrier, the horsemen still hanging back, with visors lowered.

Then followed an obstinate and deadly struggle, hand to hand. The assailants, wielding their falchions with one hand, strove with the other to drag down the structure of the barricade. On the other side, the parts were reversed, and the defenders exposed themselves like madmen to protect their rampart. So for some minutes the contest raged almost in silence, friend and foe falling one upon another. But it is always the easier to destroy; and when a single note upon the tucket recalled the attacking party from this desperate service, much of the barricade had been removed piecemeal and the whole fabric had sunk to half its height and tottered to a general fall.

And now the footmen in the market-place fell back at a run on every side. The horsemen, who had been standing in a line two deep, wheeled suddenly and made their flank into their front; and as swift as a striking adder, the long, steel-clad column was launched upon the ruinous barricade.

Of the first two horsemen, one fell, rider and steed, and was ridden down by his companions. The second leaped clean upon the summit of the rampart, transpiercing an archer with his lance. Almost in the same instant he was dragged from the saddle and his horse dispatched.

And then the full weight and impetus of the charge burst upon and scattered the defenders. The men-at-arms, surmounting their fallen comrades and carried onward by the fury of their onslaught, dashed through Dick's broken line and poured thundering up the lane beyond as a stream bestrides and pours across a broken dam.

Yet was the fight not over. Still, in the narrow jaws of the entrance, Dick and a few survivors plied their bills like woodmen; and already, across the width of the passage, there had been formed a second, a higher, and a more effectual rampart of fallen men and disemboweled horses lashing in the agonies of death.

Baffled by this fresh obstacle, the remainder of the cavalry fell back; and as, at the sight of this movement, the flight of arrows redoubled from the casements of the houses, their retreat had for a moment almost degenerated into flight.

Almost at the same time, those who had crossed the barricade and charged farther up the street, being met before the door of the Chequers by the formidable hunchback and the whole reserve of the Yorkists, began to come scattering backward in the excess of disarray and terror.

Dick and his fellows faced about, fresh men poured out

of the houses; a cruel blast of arrows met the fugitives full in the face, while Gloucester was already riding down their rear; in the inside of a minute and a half there was no living Lancastrian in the street.

Then and not till then did Dick hold up his reeking blade and give the word to cheer.

Meanwhile Gloucester dismounted from his horse and came forward to inspect the post. His face was as pale as linen; but his eyes shone in his head like some strange jewel, and his voice when he spoke was hoarse and broken with the exultation of battle and success. He looked at the rampart, which neither friend nor foe could now approach without precaution, so fiercely did the horses struggle in the throes of death, and at the sight of that great carnage he smiled upon one side.

"Dispatch these horses," he said; "they keep you from your vantage. Richard Shelton," he added, "ye have pleased me. Kneel."

The Lancastrians had already resumed their archery, and the shafts fell thick in the mouth of the street; but the duke, minding them not at all, deliberately drew his sword and dubbed Richard a knight upon the spot.

"And now, Sir Richard," he continued, "if that ye see Lord Risingham, send me an express upon the instant. Were it your last man, let me hear of it incontinently. I had rather venture the post than lose my stroke at him. For mark me, all of ye," he added, raising his voice, "if Earl Risingham fall by another hand than mine, I shall count this victory a defeat."

"My lord duke," said one of his attendants, "is your grace not weary of exposing his dear life unneedfully? Why tarry we here?"

"Catesby," returned the duke, "here is the battle, not elsewhere. The rest are but feigned onslaughts. Here must we vanquish. And for the exposure—if ye were an ugly hunchback, and the children gecked at you upon the street, ye would count your body cheaper and an hour of glory worth a life. Howbeit, if ye will, let us ride on and visit the other posts. Sir Richard here, my namesake, he shall still hold this entry, where he wadeth to the ankles in hot blood. Him can we trust. But mark it, Sir Richard, ye are not yet done. The worst is yet to ward. Sleep not."

He came right up to young Shelton, looking him hard in the eyes, and taking his hand in both of his, gave it so extreme a squeeze that the blood had nearly spurted. Dick quailed before his eyes. The insane excitement, the courage, and the cruelty that he read therein filled him with dismay about the future. This young duke's was indeed a gallant spirit, to ride foremost in the ranks of war; but after the battle, in the days of peace and in the circle of his trusted friends, that mind, it was to be dreaded, would continue to bring forth the fruits of death.

The Battle of Shoreby
(concluded)

Dick, once more left to his own counsels, began to look about him. The arrow-shot had somewhat slackened. On all sides the enemy were falling back, and the greater part of the market-place was now left empty, the snow here trampled into orange mud, there splashed with gore, scattered all over with dead men and horses and bristling thick with feathered arrows.

On his own side the loss had been cruel. The jaws of the little street and the ruins of the barricade were heaped with the dead and dying; and out of the hundred men with whom he had begun the battle, there were not seventy left who could still stand to arms.

At the same time the day was passing. The first reën-forcements might be looked for to arrive at any moment; and the Lancastrians, already shaken by the result of their desperate but unsuccessful onslaught, were in an ill temper to support a fresh invader.

There was a dial in the wall of one of the two flanking

houses; and this, in the frosty wintry sunshine, indicated ten of the forenoon.

Dick turned to the man who was at his elbow, a little insignificant archer, binding a cut in his arm.

"It was well fought," he said, "and, by my sooth, they will not charge us twice."

"Sir," said the little archer, "ye have fought right well for York and better for yourself. Never hath man in so brief space prevailed so greatly on the duke's affections. That he should have intrusted such a post to one he knew not is a marvel. But look to your head, Sir Richard! If ye be vanquished—aye, if ye give way one foot's breadth—ax or cord shall punish it; and I am set if ye do aught doubtful, I will tell you honestly, here to stab you from behind!"

Dick looked at the little man in amaze.

"You!" he cried. "And from behind!"

"It is right so," returned the archer; "and because I like not the affair I tell it you. Ye must make the post good, Sir Richard, at your peril. Oh, our Crookback is a bold blade and a good warrior; but whether in cold blood or in hot, he will have all things done exact to his commandment. If any fail or hinder, they shall die the death."

"Now, by the saints!" cried Richard, "is this so? And will men follow such a leader?"

"Nay, they follow him gleefully," replied the other; "for if he be exact to punish, he is most open-handed to reward. And if he spare not the blood and sweat of others, he is ever liberal of his own, still in the first front of battle, still the last to sleep. He will go far, will Crookback Dick o' Gloucester!"

The young knight, if he had before been brave and vigilant, was now all the more inclined to watchfulness and courage. His sudden favor, he began to perceive, had brought perils in its train. And he turned from the archer and once more scanned anxiously the market-place. It lay empty as before.

"I like not this quietude," he said. "Doubtless they prepare us some surprise."

And as if in answer to his remark, the archers began once more to advance against the barricade and the arrows to fall thick. But there was something hesitating in the attack. They came not on roundly, but seemed rather to await a further signal.

Dick looked uneasily about him spying for a hidden danger. And sure enough, about half-way up the little street a door was suddenly opened from within, and the house continued for some seconds and both by door and window to disgorge a torrent of Lancastrian archers. These, as they leaped down, hurriedly stood to their ranks, bent their bows, and proceeded to pour upon Dick's rear a flight of arrows.

At the same time, the assailants in the market-place redoubled their shot and began to close in stoutly upon the barricade.

Dick called down his whole command out of the houses, and facing them both ways, and encouraging their valor both by word and gesture, returned as best he could the double shower of shafts that fell about his post.

Meanwhile house after house was opened in the street, and the Lancastrians continued to pour out of the doors and leap down from the windows, shouting victory, until the number of enemies upon Dick's rear was almost equal to the number in his face. It was plain that he could hold the post no longer; what was worse, even if he could have held it, it had now become useless; and the whole Yorkist army lay in a posture of helplessness upon the brink of a complete disaster.

The men behind him formed the vital flaw in the general defense; and it was upon these that Dick turned, charging at the head of his men. So vigorous was the attack that the Lancastrian archers gave ground and staggered and at last, breaking their ranks, began to crowd back into the houses from which they had so recently and so vaingloriously sallied.

Meanwhile the men from the market-place had swarmed across the undefended barricade and fell on hotly upon the other side; and Dick must once again face about and proceed to drive them back. Once again the spirit of his men prevailed; they cleared the street in a triumphant style, but even as they did so the others issued again out of the houses and took them a third time upon the rear.

The Yorkists began to be scattered; several times Dick found himself alone among his foes and plying his bright sword for life; several times he was conscious of a hurt. And meanwhile the fight swayed to and fro in the street without determinate result.

Suddenly Dick was aware of a great trumpeting about the outskirts of the town. The war cry of York began to be rolled up to heaven as by many and triumphant voices. And at the same time the men in front of him began to give ground rapidly, streaming out of the street and back upon the market-place. Someone gave the word to fly. Trumpets were blown distractedly, some for a rally, some to charge. It was plain that a great blow had been struck, and the Lancastrians were thrown, at least for the moment, into full disorder and some degree of panic.

And then like a theater trick there followed the last act of Shoreby battle. The men in front of Richard turned tail like a dog that has been whistled home and fled like the wind. At the same moment there came through the market-place a storm of horsemen, fleeing and pursuing, the Lancastrians turning back to strike with the sword, the Yorkists riding them down at the point of the lance.

Conspicuous in the mellay, Dick beheld the Crookback. He was already giving a foretaste of that furious valor and skill to cut his way across the ranks of war, which years afterwards upon the field of Bosworth and when he was stained with crimes, almost sufficed to change the fortunes of the day and the destiny of the English throne. Evading, striking, riding down, he so forced and so maneuvered his strong horse, so aptly defended himself, and so liberally scattered death to his opponents, that he was now far ahead of the foremost of his knights, hewing his way with the truncheon of a bloody sword to where Lord Risingham was rallying the bravest. A moment more and they had just met; the tall, splendid, and famous warrior against the deformed and sickly boy.

Yet Shelton had never a doubt as to the result; and when the fight next opened for a moment the figure of the earl had disappeared; but still in the first of the danger Crookback Dick was launching his big horse and plying the truncheon of his sword.

Thus, by Shelton's courage in holding the mouth of the street against the first attack, and by the opportune arrival of his seven hundred reënforcements, the lad who was afterwards to be handed down to the execration of posterity under the name of Richard III had won his first considerable fight.

The Sack of Shoreby

There was not a foe left within striking distance; and Dick as he looked ruefully about him on the remainder of his gallant force began to count the cost of victory. He was himself, now that the danger was ended, so stiff and sore, so bruised and cut and broken, and above all so utterly exhausted by his desperate and unremitting labors in the fight that he seemed incapable of any fresh exertion.

But this was not yet the hour for repose. Shoreby had been taken by assault; and though an open town, and not in any manner to be charged with the resistance, it was plain that these rough fighters would be not less rough now that the fight was over and that the more horrid part of war would fall to be enacted. Richard of Gloucester was not the captain to protect the citizens from his infuriated soldiery; and even if he had the will, it might be questioned if he had the power.

It was therefore Dick's business to find and to protect Joanna; and with that end he looked about him at the faces of his men. The three or four who seemed likeliest to be obedient and to keep sober he drew aside; and promising them a rich reward and a special recommendation to the duke, led them across the market-place, now empty of horsemen, and into the streets upon the farther side.

Every here and there small combats of from two to a dozen still raged upon the open street; here and there a house was being besieged, the defenders throwing out stools and tables on the heads of the assailants. The snow was strewn with arms and corpses; but except for these partial combats the streets were deserted, and the houses, some standing open and some shuttered and barricaded, had for the most part ceased to give out smoke.

Dick, threading the skirts of these skirmishes, led his followers briskly in the direction of the abbey church; but when he came the length of the main street, a cry of horror broke from his lips. Sir Daniel's great house had been carried by assault. The gates hung in splinters from the hinges, and a double throng kept pouring in and out through the entrance, seeking and carrying booty. Meanwhile, in the upper stories, some resistance was still being offered to the pillagers; for just as Dick came within eyeshot of the building, a casement was burst open from within, and a poor wretch in murrey and blue, screaming and resisting, was forced through the embrasure, and tossed into the street below.

The most sickening apprehension fell upon Dick. He ran forward like one possessed, forced his way into the house among the foremost and mounted without pause to the chamber on the third floor where he had last parted from Joanna. It was a mere wreck; the furniture had been overthrown, the cupboards broken open, and in one place a trailing corner of the arras lay smoldering on the embers of the fire.

Dick, almost without thinking, trod out the incipient conflagration and then stood bewildered. Sir Daniel, Sir

Oliver, Joanna, all were gone; but whether butchered in the rout or safe escaped from Shoreby, who should say?

He caught a passing archer by the tabard.

"Fellow," he asked, "were ye here when this house was taken?"

"Let be," said the archer. "A murrain! let be, or I strike."

"Hark ye," returned Richard, "two can play at that. Stand and be plain."

But the man, flushed with drink and battle, struck Dick upon the shoulder with one hand, while with the other he twitched away his garment. Thereupon the full wrath of the young leader burst from his control. He seized the fellow in his strong embrace and crushed him on the plates of his mailed bosom like a child; then, holding him at arm's length, he bid him speak as he valued life.

"I pray you mercy!" gasped the archer. "An I had thought ye were so angry I would 'a' been charier of crossing you. I was here indeed."

"Know ye Sir Daniel?" pursued Dick.

"Well do I know him," returned the man.

"Was he in the mansion?"

"Aye, sir, he was," answered the archer; "but even as we entered by the yard gate he rode forth by the garden."

"Alone?" cried Dick.

"He may 'a' had a score of lances with him," said the man.

"Lances! No women, then?" asked Shelton.

"Troth, I saw not," said the archer. "But there were none in the house, if that be your quest."

"I thank you," said Dick. "Here is a piece for your pains." But groping in his wallet, Dick found nothing. "Inquire for me tomorrow," he added—"Richard Shel—Sir Richard Shelton," he corrected, "and I will see you handsomely rewarded."

And then an idea struck Dick. He hastily descended to the courtyard, ran with all his might across the garden, and came to the great door of the church. It stood wide open; within, every corner of the pavement was crowded with fugitive burghers, surrounded by their families and laden with the most precious of their possessions, while at the high altar priests in full canonicals were imploring the mercy of God. Even as Dick entered, the chorus began to thunder in the vaulted roofs.

He hurried through the groups of refugees and came to the door of the stair that led into the steeple. And here a tall churchman stepped before him and arrested his advance.

"Whither, my son?" he asked severely.

"My father," answered Dick, "I am here upon an errand of expedition. Stay me not. I command here for my Lord of Gloucester."

"For my Lord of Gloucester?" repeated the priest. "Hath, then, the battle gone so sore?"

"The battle, father, is at an end, Lancaster clean sped, my Lord of Risingham—Heaven rest him!—left upon the field. And now, with your good leave, I follow mine affairs." And thrusting on one side the priest, who seemed stupefied at the news, Dick pushed open the door and rattled up the stairs four at a bound and without pause or stumble till he stepped upon the open platform at the top.

Shoreby Church tower not only commanded the town as in a map but looked far on both sides over sea and land. It was now near upon noon, the day exceeding bright, the snow dazzling. And as Dick looked around him, he could measure the consequences of the battle.

A confused, growling uproar reached him from the streets and now and then, but very rarely, the clash of steel. Not a ship, not so much as a skiff remained in the harbor; but the sea was dotted with sails and rowboats laden with fugitives. On shore, too, the surface of the snowy meadows was broken up with bands of horsemen, some cutting their way toward the borders of the forest, others, who were doubtless of the Yorkist side, stoutly interposing and beating them back upon the town. Over all the open ground there lay a prodigious quantity of fallen men and horses clearly defined upon the snow.

To complete the picture, those of the foot soldiers as had not found place upon a ship still kept up an archery combat on the borders of the port and from the cover of the shoreside taverns. In that quarter, also, one or two houses had been fired, and the smoke towered high in the frosty sunlight and blew off to sea in voluminous folds.

Already close upon the margin of the woods and somewhat in the line of Holywood, one particular clump of fleeing horsemen riveted the attention of the young watcher on the tower. It was fairly numerous; in no other quarter of the field did so many Lancastrians still hold together; thus they had left a wide, discolored wake upon the snow, and Dick was able to trace them step by step from where they had left the town.

While Dick stood watching them, they had gained unopposed the first fringe of the leafless forest and turning a little from their direction, the sun fell for a moment full on their array as it was relieved against the dusky wood.

"Murrey and blue!" cried Dick. "I swear it—murrey and blue!"

The next moment he was descending the stairway.

It was now his business to seek out the Duke of Gloucester, who alone in the disorder of the forces might be able to supply him with a sufficiency of men. The fighting in the main town was now practically at an end; and as Dick ran hither and thither seeking the commander, the streets were thick with wandering soldiers, some laden with more booty than they could well stagger under, others shouting drunk. None of them, when questioned, had the least notion of the duke's whereabouts; and at last it was by sheer good fortune that Dick found him, where he sat in the saddle, directing operations to dislodge the archers from the harbor side.

"Sir Richard Shelton, ye are well found," he said. "I owe you one thing that I value little, my life; and one that I can never pay you for, this victory. Catesby, if I had ten such captains as Sir Richard Shelton, I would march forthright on London. But now, sir, claim your reward."

"Freely, my lord," said Dick, "freely and loudly. One hath escaped to whom I owe some grudges and taken with him one whom I owe love and service. Give me, then, fifty lances, that I may pursue; and for any obligation that your graciousness is pleased to allow, it shall be clean discharged."

"How call ye him?" inquired the duke.

"Sir Daniel Brackley," answered Richard.

"Out upon him, double-face!" cried Gloucester. "Here is no reward, Sir Richard; here is fresh service offered, and, if that ye bring his head to me, a fresh debt upon my conscience. Catesby, get him these lances; and you, sir, bethink ye, in the meanwhile, what pleasure, honor, or profit it shall be mine to give you."

Just then the Yorkist skirmishers carried one of the shoreside taverns, swarming in upon it on three sides and driving out or taking its defenders. Crookback Dick was pleased to cheer the exploit, and pushing his horse a little nearer, called to see the prisoners.

There were four or five of them—two men of my Lord Shoreby's and one of Lord Risingham's among the number, and last, but in Dick's eyes not least, a tall, shambling, grizzled old shipman, between drunk and sober and with a dog whimpering and jumping at his heels.

The young duke passed them for a moment under a severe review.

"Good," he said. "Hang them."

And he turned the other way to watch the progress of the fight.

"My lord," said Dick, "so please you, I have found my reward. Grant me the life and liberty of yon old shipman."

Gloucester turned and looked the speaker in the face.

"Sir Richard," he said, "I make not war with peacock's feathers but steel shafts. Those that are mine enemies I slay and that without excuse or favor. For, bethink ye, in this realm of England, that is so torn in pieces, there is not a man of mine but hath a brother or a friend upon the other party. If, then, I did begin to grant these pardons, I might sheathe my sword."

"It may be so, my lord; and yet I will be over bold and at the risk of your disfavor recall your lordship's promise," replied Dick.

Richard of Gloucester flushed.

"Mark it right well," he said harshly. "I love not mercy nor yet mercy-mongers. Ye have this day laid the foundations of high fortune. If ye oppose to me my word, which I have plighted, I will yield. But, by the glory of heaven, there your favor dies!"

"Mine is the loss," said Dick.

"Give him his sailor," said the duke; and wheeling his horse, he turned his back upon young Shelton.

Dick was nor glad nor sorry. He had seen too much of the young duke to set great store on his affection; and the origin and growth of his own favor had been too flimsy and too rapid to inspire much confidence. One thing alone he feared—that the vindictive leader might revoke the offer of the lances. But there he did justice neither to Gloucester's honor (such as it was) nor above all to his decision. If he had once judged Dick to be the right man to pursue Sir Daniel, he was not one to change; and he soon proved it by shouting after Catesby to be speedy, for the paladin was waiting.

In the meanwhile, Dick turned to the old shipman, who had seemed equally indifferent to his condemnation and to his subsequent release.

"Arblaster," said Dick, "I have done you ill; but now, by the rood, I think I have cleared the score."

But the old skipper only looked upon him dully and held his peace.

"Come," continued Dick, "a life is a life, old shrew, and it is more than ships or liquor. Say ye forgive me; for if your life is worth nothing to you, it hath cost me the beginnings of my fortune. Come, I have paid for it dearly; be not so churlish."

"An I had had my ship," said Arblaster, "I would 'a' been forth and safe on the high seas—I and my man Tom. But ye took my ship, gossip, and I'm a beggar; and for my man Tom, a knave fellow in russet shot him down. 'Murrain!' quoth he and spake never again. 'Murrain' was the last of his words, and the poor spirit of him passed. 'A will never sail no more, will my Tom."

Dick was seized with unavailing penitence and pity; he sought to take the skipper's hand, but Arblaster avoided his touch.

"Nay," said he, "let be. Y'have played the devil with me and let that content you."

The words died in Richard's throat. He saw through tears the poor old man bemused with liquor and sorrow go shambling away with bowed head across the snow and the unnoticed dog whimpering at his heels; and for the first time began to understand the desperate game that we play in life and how a thing once done is not to be changed or remedied by any penitence.

But there was no time left to him for vain regret. Catesby had now collected the horsemen, and riding up to Dick he dismounted and offered him his own horse.

"This morning," he said, "I was somewhat jealous of your favor; it hath not been of a long growth; and now, Sir Richard, it is with a very good heart that I offer you this horse—to ride away with."

"Suffer me yet a moment," replied Dick. "This favor of mine—whereupon was it founded?"

"Upon your name," answered Catesby. "It is my lord's chief superstition. Were my name Richard, I should be an earl tomorrow."

"Well, sir, I thank you," returned Dick; "and since I am little likely to follow these great fortunes, I will even say farewell. I will not pretend I was displeased to think myself upon the road to fortune; but I will not pretend, neither, that I am over sorry to be done with it. Command and riches, they are brave things to be sure; but a word in your ear—yon duke of yours, he is a fearsome lad."

Catesby laughed.

"Nay," said he, "of a verity he that rides with Crooked Dick will ride deep. Well, God keep us all from evil! Speed ye well."

Thereupon Dick put himself at the head of his men and giving the word of command rode off.

He made straight across the town, following what he supposed to be the route of Sir Daniel and spying around for any signs that might decide if he were right.

The streets were strewn with the dead and the wounded, whose fate in the bitter frost was far the more pitiable. Gangs of the victors went from house to house pillaging and stabbing and sometimes singing together as they went.

From different quarters as he rode on the sounds of violence and outrage came to young Shelton's ears; now the blows of the sledge-hammer on some barricaded door and now the miserable shrieks of women.

Dick's heart had just been awakened. He had just seen the cruel consequences of his own behavior; and the thought of the sum of misery that was now acting in the whole of Shoreby filled him with despair.

At length he reached the outskirts and there, sure enough, he saw straight before him the same broad, beaten track across the snow that he had marked from the summit of the church. Here, then, he went the faster on; but still as he rode he kept a bright eye upon the fallen men and horses that lay beside the track. Many of these, he was relieved to see, wore Sir Daniel's colors, and the faces of some who lay upon their backs he even recognized.

About half-way between the town and the forest, those whom he was following had plainly been assailed by archers; for the corpses lay pretty closely scattered, each pierced by an arrow. And here Dick spied among the rest the body of a very young lad, whose face was somehow hauntingly familiar to him.

He halted his troop, dismounted, and raised the lad's head. As he did so the hood fell back, and a profusion of

long brown hair unrolled itself. At the same time the eyes
opened.

"Ah, lion-driver!" said the feeble voice. "She is farther
on. Ride—ride fast!"

And then the poor young lady fainted once again.

One of Dick's men carried a flask of some strong cordial,
and with this Dick succeeded in reviving consciousness.
Then he took Joanna's friend upon his saddle-bow and
once more pushed toward the forest.

"Why do ye take me?" said the girl. "Ye but delay your
speed."

"Nay, Mistress Risingham," replied Dick. "Shoreby is full
of blood and drunkenness and riot. Here ye are safe; content ye."

"I will not be beholden to any of your faction," she
cried; "set me down."

"Madam, ye know not what ye say," returned Dick.
"Y'are hurt——"

"I am not," she said. "It was my horse was slain."

"It matters not one jot," replied Richard. "Ye are here in
the midst of open snow and compassed about with enemies. Whether ye will or not, I carry you with me. Glad am
I to have the occasion; for thus shall I repay some portion
of our debt."

For a little while she was silent. Then, very suddenly,
she asked:

"My uncle?"

"My Lord Risingham?" returned Dick. "I would I had
good news to give you, madam; but I have none. I saw him
once in the battle and once only. Let us hope the best."

Night in the Woods—
Alicia Risingham

It was almost certain that Sir Daniel had made for the
Moat House; but considering the heavy snow, the lateness
of the hour, and the necessity under which he would lie of

avoiding the few roads and striking across the wood, it was equally certain that he could not hope to reach it ere the morrow.

There were two courses open to Dick: either to continue to follow in the knight's trail and, if he were able, to fall upon him that very night in camp; or to strike out a path of his own and seek to place himself between Sir Daniel and his destination.

Either scheme was open to serious objection, and Dick, who feared to expose Joanna to the hazards of a fight, had not yet decided between them when he reached the borders of the wood.

At this point Sir Daniel had turned a little to his left and then plunged straight under a grove of very lofty timber. His party had then formed to a narrower front in order to pass between the trees, and the track was trod proportionately deeper in the snow. The eye followed it under the leafless tracery of the oaks running direct and narrow; the trees stood over it with knotty joints and the great, uplifted forest of their boughs; there was no sound whether of man or beast—not so much as the stirring of a robin; and over the field of snow the winter sun lay golden among netted shadows.

"How say ye," asked Dick of one of the men, "to follow straight on or strike across for Tunstall?"

"Sir Richard," replied the man-at-arms, "I would follow the line until they scatter."

"Ye are doubtless right," returned Dick; "but we came right hastily upon the errand even as the time commanded. Here are no houses, neither food nor shelter, and by the morrow's dawn we shall know both cold fingers and an empty belly. How say ye, lads? Will ye stand a pinch for expedition's sake, or shall we turn by Holywood and sup with Mother Church? The case being somewhat doubtful, I will drive no man; yet if ye would suffer me to lead you, ye would choose the first."

The men answered almost with one voice that they would follow Sir Richard where he would.

And Dick, setting spur to his horse, began once more to go forward.

The snow in the trail had been trodden very hard, and the pursuers had thus a great advantage over the pursued. They pushed on, indeed, at a round trot, two hundred hoofs beating alternately on the dull pavement of the snow and the jingle of weapons and the snorting of horses raising a warlike noise along the arches of the silent wood.

Presently, the wide slot of the pursued came out upon the high-road from Holywood; it was there for a moment indistinguishable; and where it once more plunged into the unbeaten snow upon the farther side, Dick was surprised to see it narrower and lighter trod. Plainly, profiting by the road, Sir Daniel had begun already to scatter his command.

At all hazards, one chance being equal to another, Dick continued to pursue the straight trail; and that, after an hour's riding, in which it led into the very depths of the forest, suddenly split like a bursting shell, into two dozen others leading to every point of the compass.

Dick drew bridle in despair. The short winter's day was near an end; the sun, a dull red orange, shorn of rays, swam low among the leafless thickets; the shadows were a mile long upon the snow; the frost bit cruelly at the finger-nails; and the breath and steam of the horses mounted in a cloud.

"Well, we are outwitted," Dick confessed. "Strike we for Holywood, after all. It is still nearer us than Tunstall—or should be by the station of the sun."

So they wheeled to their left, turning their backs on the red shield of sun and made across country for the abbey. But now times were changed with them; they could no longer spank forth briskly on a path beaten firm by the passage of their foes and for a goal to which that path itself conducted them. Now they must plow at a dull pace through the encumbering snow, continually pausing to decide their course, continually floundering in drifts. The sun soon left them; the glow of the west decayed; and presently they were wandering in a shadow of blackness, under frosty stars.

Presently, indeed, the moon would clear the hilltops, and they might resume their march. But till then, every random step might carry them wider of their march. There was nothing for it but to camp and wait.

Sentries were posted; a spot of ground was cleared of snow and after some failures a good fire blazed in the midst. The men-at-arms sat close about this forest hearth, sharing such provisions as they had and passing about the flask; and Dick, having collected the most delicate of this rough and scanty fare, brought it to Lord Risingham's niece where she sat apart from the soldiery against a tree.

She sat upon one horse-cloth, wrapped in another, and stared straight before her at the firelit scene. At the offer of food she started like one wakened from a dream and then silently refused.

"Madam," said Dick, "let me beseech you, punish me not so cruelly. Wherein I have offended you, I know not; I have, indeed, carried you away but with a friendly violence; I have, indeed, exposed you to the inclemency of night, but the hurry that lies upon me hath for its end the preservation of another, who is no less frail and no less unfriended than yourself. At least, madam, punish not yourself; and eat, if not for hunger, then for strength."

"I will eat nothing at the hands that slew my kinsman," she replied.

"Dear madam," Dick cried, "I swear to you upon the rood I touched him not."

"Swear to me that he still lives," she returned.

"I will not palter with you," answered Dick. "Pity bids me to wound you. In my heart I do believe him dead."

"And ye ask me to eat!" she cried. "Aye, and they call you 'sir'! Y'have won your spurs by my good kinsman's murder. And had I not been fool and traitor both and saved you in your enemy's house, ye should have died the death, and he—he that was worth twelve of you— were living."

"I did but my man's best, even as your kinsman did upon the other party," answered Dick. "Were he still living—as I vow to Heaven I wish it!—he would praise not blame me."

"Sir Daniel hath told me," she replied. "He marked you at the barricade. Upon you, he saith, their party foundered; it was you that won the battle. Well, then, it was you that killed my good Lord Risingham as sure as though ye had strangled him. And ye would have me eat with you—and your hands not washed from killing? But Sir Daniel hath sworn your downfall. He 'tis that will avenge me!"

The unfortunate Dick was plunged in gloom. Old Arblaster returned upon his mind, and he groaned aloud.

"Do ye hold me so guilty?" he said; "you that defended me—you that are Joanna's friend?"

"What made ye in the battle?" she retorted. "Y'are of no party; y'are but a lad—but legs and body without government of wit or counsel! Wherefore did ye fight? For the love of hurt, pardy!"

"Nay," cried Dick, "I know not. But as the realm of England goes, if that a poor gentleman fight not upon the one side, perforce he must fight upon the other. He may not stand alone, 'tis not in nature."

"They that have no judgment should not draw the sword," replied the young lady. "Ye that fight but for a hazard, what are ye but a butcher? War is but noble by the cause, and y'have disgraced it."

"Madam," said the miserable Dick, "I do partly see mine error. I have made too much haste; I have been busy before my time. Already I stole a ship—thinking, I do swear it, to do well—and thereby brought about the death of many innocent and the grief and ruin of a poor old man whose face this very day hath stabbed me like a dagger. And for this morning, I did but design to do myself credit and get fame to marry with and behold! I have brought about the death of your dear kinsman that was good to me. And what besides, I know not. For, alas! I may have set

York upon the throne, and that may be the worser cause
and may do hurt to England. Oh! madam, I do see my sin.
I am unfit for life. I will, for penance' sake and to avoid
worse evil, once I have finished this adventure, get me to
a cloister. I will forswear Joanna and the trade of arms. I
will be a friar, and pray for your good kinsman's spirit all
my days."

It appeared to Dick in this extremity of his humiliation
and repentance that the young lady had laughed.

Raising his countenance, he found her looking down
upon him in the firelight with a somewhat peculiar but not
unkind expression.

"Madam," he cried, thinking the laughter to have been
an illusion of his hearing but still from her changed looks
hoping to have touched her heart—"madam, will not this
content you? I give up all to undo what I have done amiss;
I make heaven certain for Lord Risingham. And all this
upon the very day that I have won my spurs and thought
myself the happiest young gentleman on ground."

"Oh, boy," she said, "good boy!"

And then to the extreme surprise of Dick she first very
tenderly wiped the tears away from his cheeks and then
as if yielding to a sudden impulse threw both her arms
about his neck, drew up his face, and kissed him. A pitiful
bewilderment came over simple-minded Dick.

"But come," she said, with great cheerfulness, "you that
are a captain, ye must eat. Why sup ye not?"

"Dear Mistress Risingham," replied Dick, "I did but wait
first upon my prisoner; but to say truth penitence will no
longer suffer me to endure the sight of food. I were better
to fast, dear lady, and to pray."

"Call me Alicia," she said; "are we not old friends? And
now, come, I will eat with you, bit for bit and sup for sup;
so if ye eat not, neither will I; but if ye eat hearty, I will
dine like a plowman."

So there and then she fell to; and Dick, who had an
excellent stomach, proceeded to bear her company, at
first with great reluctance but gradually as he entered into

the spirit with more and more vigor and devotion; until at last he forgot even to watch his model, and most heartily repaired the expenses of his day of labor and excitement.

"Lion-driver," she said, at length, "ye do not admire a maid in a man's jerkin?"

The moon was now up; and they were only waiting to repose the wearied horses. By the moon's light, the still penitent but now well-fed Richard beheld her looking somewhat coquettishly down upon him.

"Madam——" he stammered, surprised at this new turn in her manners.

"Nay," she interrupted, "it skills not to deny; Joanna hath told me, but come, Sir Lion-driver, look at me—am I so homely?—come!"

And she made bright eyes at him.

"Ye are something smallish, indeed——" began Dick.

And here again she interrupted him, this time with a ringing peal of laughter that completed his confusion and surprise.

"Smallish!" she cried. "Nay, now, be honest as ye are bold; I am a dwarf, or little better; but for all that—come, tell me!—for all that, passably fair to look upon; is't not so?"

"Nay, madam, exceedingly fair," said the distressed knight, pitifully trying to seem easy.

"And a man would be right glad to wed me?" she pursued.

"Oh, madam, right glad!" agreed Dick.

"Call me Alicia," said she.

"Alicia," quoth Sir Richard.

"Well, then, lion-driver," she continued, "sith that ye slew my kinsman and left me without stay, ye owe me, in honor, every reparation; do ye not?"

"I do, madam," said Dick. "Although upon my heart, I do hold me but partially guilty of that brave knight's blood."

"Would ye evade me?" she cried.

"Madam, not so. I have told you; at your bidding, I will even turn me a monk," said Richard.

"Then, in honor, ye belong to me?" she concluded.

"In honor, madam, I suppose——" began the young man.

"Go to!" she interrupted; "ye are too full of catches. In honor do ye belong to me, till ye have paid the evil?"

"In honor I do," said Dick.

"Hear, then," she continued. "Ye would make but a sad friar, methinks; and since I am to dispose of you at pleasure, I will even take you for my husband. Nay, now, no words!" cried she. "They will avail you nothing. For see how just it is, that ye who deprived me of one home should supply me with another. And as for Joanna, she will be the first, believe me, to commend the change; for, after all, as we be dear friends, what matters it with which of us ye wed? Not one whit!"

"Madam," said Dick, "I will go into a cloister, an ye please to bid me; but to wed with anyone in this big world besides Joanna Sedley is what I will consent to neither for man's force nor yet for lady's pleasure. Pardon me if I speak my plain thoughts plainly; but where a maid is very bold a poor man must even be the bolder."

"Dick," she said, "ye sweet boy, ye must come and kiss me for that word. Nay, fear not, ye shall kiss me for Joanna, and when we meet I shall give it back to her and say I stole it. And as for what ye owe me, why, dear simpleton, methinks ye were not alone in that great battle; and even if York be on the throne, it was not you that set him there. But for a good, sweet, honest heart, Dick, y'are all that; and if I could find it in my soul to envy your Joanna anything, I would envy her your love."

Night in the Woods (concluded)—
Dick and Joan

The horses had by this time finished the small store of provender and fully breathed from their fatigues. At Dick's command the fire was smothered in snow; and while his men got once more wearily to saddle, he himself, remembering, somewhat late, true woodland caution, chose a tall oak and nimbly clambered to the topmost fork. Hence he could look far abroad on the moonlit and snow-paved forest. On the southwest, dark against the horizon, stood those upland heathy quarters where he and Joanna had met with the terrifying misadventure of the leper. And there his eye was caught by a spot of ruddy brightness no bigger than a needle's eye.

He blamed himself sharply for his previous neglect. Were that, as it appeared to be, the shining of Sir Daniel's camp-fire he should long ago have seen and marched for it; above all, he should, for no consideration, have announced his neighborhood by lighting a fire of his own. But now he must no longer squander valuable hours. The direct way to the uplands was about two miles in length; but it crossed by a very deep, precipitous dingle, impassable to mounted men; and for the sake of speed, it seemed to Dick advisable to desert the horses and attempt the adventure on foot.

Ten men were left to guard the horses; signals were agreed upon by which they could communicate in case of need; and Dick set forth at the head of the remainder, Alicia Risingham walking stoutly by his side.

The men had freed themselves of heavy armor and left behind their lances; and they now marched with a very good spirit in the frozen snow and under the exhilarating luster of the moon. The descent into the dingle, where a stream strained sobbing through the snow and ice, was effected with silence and order; and on the farther side, being then within a short half-mile of where Dick had seen the glimmer of the fire, the party halted to breathe before the attack.

In the vast silence of the wood, the lightest sounds were audible from far; and Alicia, who was keen of hearing, held up her finger warningly and stooped to listen. All followed her example; but besides the groans of the choked brook in the dingle close behind, and the barking of a fox at a distance of many miles among the forest, to Dick's acutest hearkening not a breath was audible.

"But yet, for sure, I heard the clash of harness," whispered Alicia.

"Madam," returned Dick, who was more afraid of that young lady than of ten stout warriors, "I would not hint ye were mistaken; but it might well have come from either of the camps."

"It came not thence. It came from westward," she declared.

"It may be what it will," returned Dick; "and it must be as heaven please. Reck we not a jot, but push on the livelier and put it to the touch. Up, friends—enough breathed."

As they advanced, the snow became more and more trampled with hoof-marks, and it was plain that they were drawing near to the encampment of a considerable force of mounted men. Presently they could see the smoke pouring from among the trees, ruddily colored on its lower edge and scattering bright sparks.

And here, pursuant to Dick's orders, his men began to open out, creeping stealthily in the covert to surround on every side the camp of their opponents. He himself, placing Alicia in the shelter of a bulky oak, stole straight forth in the direction of the fire.

At last through an opening of the wood his eye embraced the scene of the encampment. The fire had been built upon a heathy hummock of the ground, surrounded on three sides by thicket, and it now burned very strong, roaring aloud and brandishing flames. Around it there sat not quite a dozen people, warmly cloaked; but though the neighboring snow was trampled down as by a regiment, Dick looked in vain for any horse. He began to have a terrible misgiving that he was out-maneuvered. At the same time, in a tall man with steel salet, who was spreading his hands before the blaze, he recognized his old friend and still kindly enemy, Bennet Hatch; and in two others, sitting a little back, he made out even in their male disguise Joanna Sedley and Sir Daniel's wife.

"Well," thought he to himself, "even if I lose my horses, let me get my Joanna, and why should I complain?"

And then from the farther side of the encampment, there came a little whistle announcing that his men had joined, and the investment was complete.

Bennet at the sound started to his feet; but ere he had time to spring upon his arms, Dick hailed him.

"Bennet," he said—"Bennet, old friend, yield ye. Ye will but spill the men's lives in vain if ye resist."

"'Tis Master Shelton, by Saint Barbary!" cried Hatch. "Yield me? Ye ask much. What force have ye?"

"I tell you, Bennet, ye are both outnumbered and begirt," said Dick. "Cæsar and Charlemagne would cry for quarter. I have two score men at my whistle, and with one shot of arrows I could answer for you all."

"Master Dick," said Bennet, "it goes against my heart; but I must do my duty. The saints help you!" And therewith he raised a little tucket to his mouth and wound a rousing call.

Then followed a moment of confusion; for while Dick, fearing for the ladies, still hesitated to give the word to shoot, Hatch's little band sprang to their weapons and formed back to back as for a fierce resistance. In the hurry of their change of place, Joanna sprang from her seat and ran like an arrow to her lover's side.

"Here, Dick!" she cried as she clasped his hand in hers.

But Dick still stood irresolute; he was yet young to the more deplorable necessities of war, and the thought of old Lady Brackley checked the command upon his tongue. His own men became restive. Some of them cried on him by name; others, of their own accord, began to shoot; and at the first discharge poor Bennet bit the dust. Then Dick awoke.

"On!" he cried. "Shoot, boys, and keep to cover. England and York!"

But just then the dull beat of many horses on the snow

suddenly arose in the hollow ear of the night and with incredible swiftness drew nearer and swelled louder. At the same time, answering tuckets repeated and repeated Hatch's call.

"Rally, rally!" cried Dick. "Rally upon me! Rally for your lives!"

But his men—afoot, scattered, taken in the hour when they counted on an easy triumph—began, instead, to give ground severally and either stood wavering or dispersed into the thickets. And when the first of the horsemen came charging through the open avenues and fiercely riding their steeds into the underwood, a few stragglers were overthrown or speared among the brush, but the bulk of Dick's command had simply melted at the rumor of their coming.

Dick stood for a moment, bitterly recognizing the fruits of his precipitate and unwise valor. Sir Daniel had seen the fire; he had moved out with his main force, whether to attack his pursuers or to take them in the rear if they should venture the assault. His had been throughout the part of a sagacious captain; Dick's the conduct of an eager boy. And here was the young knight, his sweetheart, indeed, holding him tightly by the hand, but otherwise alone, his whole command of men and horses dispersed in the night and the wide forest, like a paper of pins in a hay barn.

"The saints enlighten me!" he thought. "It is well I was knighted for this morning's matter; this doth me little honor."

And thereupon, still holding Joanna, he began to run.

The silence of the night was now shattered by the shouts of the men of Tunstall as they galloped hither and thither hunting fugitives; and Dick broke boldly through the underwood and ran straight before him like a deer. The silver clearness of the moon upon the open snow increased by contrast the obscurity of the thickets; and the extreme dispersion of the vanquished led the pursuers into widely divergent paths. Hence, in but a little while, Dick and Joanna paused in a close covert and heard the sounds of the pursuit scattering abroad, indeed, in all directions, but yet fainting already in the distance.

"An I had but kept a reserve of them together," Dick cried, bitterly, "I could have turned the tables yet! Well, we live and learn; next time it shall go better, by the rood."

"Nay, Dick," said Joanna, "what matters it? Here we are together once again."

He looked at her, and there she was—John Matcham, as of yore, in hose and doublet. But now he knew her; now even in that ungainly dress she smiled upon him, bright with love; and his heart was transported with joy.

"Sweetheart," he said, "if ye forgive this blunderer, what care I? Make we direct for Holywood; there lieth your good guardian and my friend, Lord Foxham. There shall we be wed; and whether poor or wealthy, famous or unknown, what matters it? This day, dear love, I won my spurs; I was commended by great men for my valor; I thought myself the goodliest man of war in all broad England. Then, first, I fell out of my favor with the great; and now have I been well thrashed and clean lost my soldiers. There was a downfall for conceit! But, dear, I care not—dear, if ye still love me and will wed, I would have my knighthood done away and mind it not a jot."

"My Dick!" she cried. "And did they knight you?"

"Aye, dear, ye are my lady now," he answered, fondly; "or ye shall, ere noon tomorrow—will ye not?"

"That will I, Dick, with a glad heart," she answered.

"Aye, sir? Methought ye were to be a monk!" said a voice in their ears.

"Alicia!" cried Joanna.

"Even so," replied the young lady, coming forward. "Alicia, whom ye left for dead, and whom your lion-driver found and brought to life again and, by my sooth, made love to if ye want to know."

"I'll not believe it," cried Joanna. "Dick!"

"Dick!" mimicked Alicia. "Dick, indeed! Aye, fair sir, and ye desert poor damsels in distress," she continued, turning to the young knight. "Ye leave them planted behind oaks. But they say true, the age of chivalry is dead."

"Madam," cried Dick in despair, "upon my soul I had forgotten you outright. Madam, ye must try to pardon me. Ye see, I had new found Joanna!"

"I did not suppose that ye had done it o' purpose," she retorted. "But I will be cruelly avenged. I will tell a secret to my Lady Shelton—she that is to be," she added, curt-sying. "Joanna," she continued, "I believe, upon my soul, your sweetheart is a bold fellow in a fight, but he is, let me tell you plainly, the softest-hearted simpleton in England. Go to—ye may do your pleasure with him! And now, fool children, first kiss me, either one of you, for luck and kindness; and then kiss each other just one minute by the glass and not one second longer; and then let us all three set forth for Holywood as fast as we can stir; for these woods, methinks, are full of peril and exceeding cold."

"But did my Dick make love to you?" asked Joanna, clinging to her sweetheart's side.

"Nay, fool girl," returned Alicia; "it was I made love to him. I offered to marry him, indeed; but he bade me go marry with my likes. These were his words. Nay, that I will say: he is more plain than pleasant. But now, children, for the sake of sense, set forward. Shall we go once more over the dingle or push straight for Holywood?"

"Why," said Dick, "I would like dearly to get upon a horse; for I have been sore mauled and beaten one way and another these last days, and my poor body is one bruise. But how think ye? If the men, upon the alarm of the fighting, had fled away, we should have gone about for nothing. 'Tis but some three short miles to Holywood direct; the bell hath not beat nine; the snow is pretty firm to walk upon, the moon clear; how if we went even as we are?"

Forth, then, they went, through open leafless groves and down snow-clad alleys, under the white face of the winter moon; Dick and Joanna walking hand in hand and in a heaven of pleasure; and their light-minded companion, her own bereavements heartily forgotten, followed a pace or two behind, now rallying them upon their silence and now drawing happy pictures of their future and united lives.

Still, indeed, in the distance of the wood, the riders of Tunstall might be heard urging their pursuit; and from time to time cries or the clash of steel announced the shock of enemies. But in these young folk, bred among the alarms of war and fresh from such a multiplicity of dangers, neither fear nor pity could be lightly wakened. Content to find the sounds still drawing farther and farther away, they gave up their hearts to the enjoyment of the hour, walking already, as Alicia put it, in a wedding procession; and neither the rude solitude of the forest nor the cold of the freezing night had any force to shadow or distract their happiness.

At length from a rising hill they looked below them on the dell of Holywood. The great windows of the forest abbey shone with torch and candle; its high pinnacles and spires arose very clear and silent, and the gold rood upon the topmost summit glittered brightly in the moon. All about it in the open glade camp-fires were burning, and the ground was thick with huts; and across the midst of the picture the frozen river curved.

"By the mass," said Richard, "there are Lord Foxham's fellows still encamped. The messenger hath certainly miscarried. Well, then, so better. We have power at hand to face Sir Daniel."

But if Lord Foxham's men still lay encamped in the long holm at Holywood, it was from a different reason from the one supposed by Dick. They had marched, indeed, for Shoreby; but ere they were half-way thither, a second messenger met them and bade them return to their morning's camp to bar the road against Lancastrian fugitives and to be so much nearer to the main army of York. For Richard of Gloucester, having finished the battle and stamped out his foes in that district, was already on the march to rejoin his brother;* and not long after the return of my Lord Foxham's retainers, Crookback himself drew rein before the abbey door. It was in honor of this august visitor that the windows shone with lights; and at the hour of Dick's arrival with his sweetheart and her friend, the whole ducal party was being entertained in the refectory with the splendor of that powerful and luxurious monastery.

Dick, not quite with his good will, was brought before them. Gloucester, sick with fatigue, sat leaning upon one hand his white and terrifying countenance; Lord Foxham, half recovered from his wound, was in a place of honor on his left.

"How, sir?" asked Richard. "Have ye brought me Sir Daniel's head?"

"My lord duke," replied Dick stoutly enough but with a qualm at heart, "I have not even the good fortune to return with my command. I have been, so please your grace, well beaten."

Gloucester looked upon him with a formidable frown.

"I gave you fifty lances,[1] sir," he said.

"My lord duke, I had but fifty men-at-arms," replied the young knight.

"How is this?" said Gloucester. "He did ask me fifty lances."

"May it please your grace," replied Catesby, smoothly, "for a pursuit we gave him but the horsemen."

"It is well," replied Richard, adding, "Shelton, ye may go."

"Stay!" said Lord Foxham. "This young man likewise had a charge from me. It may be he hath better sped. Say, Master Shelton, have ye found the maid?"

---

* Richard's eldest brother, Edward of York, deposed King Henry VI in 1461 and became king as Edward IV. However, in reality, Richard, born in 1452, was not made Duke of Gloucester until 1471. (See Stevenson's notes on pages 137 and 188.)

[1] Technically, the term "lance" included a not quite certain number of foot soldiers attached to the man-at-arms.

"I praise the saints, my lord," said Dick, "she is in this house."

"Is it even so? Well, then, my lord the duke," resumed Lord Foxham, "with your good will, tomorrow, before the army march, I do propose a marriage. This young squire——"

"Young knight," interrupted Catesby.

"Say ye so, Sir William?" cried Lord Foxham.

"I did myself, and for good service, dub him knight," said Gloucester. "He hath twice manfully served me. It is not valor of hands, it is a man's mind of iron that he lacks. He will not rise, Lord Foxham. 'Tis a fellow that will fight indeed bravely in a mellay but hath a capon's heart. Howbeit, if he is to marry, marry him in the name of Mary and be done!"

"Nay, he is a brave lad—I know it," said Lord Foxham. "Content ye, then, Sir Richard. I have compounded this affair with Master Hamley, and tomorrow ye shall wed."

Whereupon Dick judged it prudent to withdraw; but he was not yet clear of the refectory, when a man, but newly alighted at the gate, came running four stairs at a bound and brushing through the abbey servants threw himself on one knee before the duke.

"Victory, my lord," he cried.

And before Dick had got to the chamber set apart for him as Lord Foxham's guest, the troops in the holm were cheering around their fires; for upon that same day, not twenty miles away, a second crushing blow had been dealt to the power of Lancaster.

Dick's Revenge

The next morning Dick was afoot before the sun, and having dressed himself to the best advantage with the aid of Lord Foxham's baggage and got good reports of Joan, he set forth on foot to walk away his impatience.

For some while he made rounds among the soldiery,

who were getting to arms in the wintry twilight of the dawn and by the red glow of torches; but gradually he strolled farther afield and at length passed clean beyond the outpost and walked alone in the frozen forest waiting for the sun.

His thoughts were both quiet and happy. His brief favor with the duke he could not find it in his heart to mourn; with Joan to wife and my Lord Foxham for a faithful patron, he looked most happily upon the future; and in the past he found but little to regret.

As he thus strolled and pondered, the solemn light of the morning grew more clear, the east was already colored by the sun, and a little scathing wind blew up the frozen snow. He turned to go home; but even as he turned, his eye lit upon a figure behind a tree.

"Stand!" he cried. "Who goes?"

The figure stepped forth and waved its hand like a dumb person. It was arrayed like a pilgrim, the hood lowered over the face, but Dick in an instant recognized Sir Daniel.

He strode up to him, drawing his sword; and the knight, putting his hand in his bosom, as if to seize a hidden weapon, steadfastly awaited his approach.

"Well, Dickon," said Sir Daniel, "how is it to be? Do ye make war upon the fallen?"

"I made no war upon your life," replied the lad; "I was your true friend until ye sought for mine; but ye have sought for it greedily."

"Nay—self-defense," replied the knight. "And now, boy, the news of this battle and the presence of yon crooked devil in mine own wood have broken me beyond all help. I go to Holywood for sanctuary; thence over seas with what I can carry, and to begin life again in Burgundy or France."

"Ye may not go to Holywood," said Dick.

"How! May not?" asked the knight.

"Look ye, Sir Daniel, this is my marriage morn," said Dick; "and yon sun that is to rise will make the brightest day that ever shone for me. Your life is forfeit—doubly forfeit, for my father's death and your own practices to meward. But I myself have done amiss; I have brought about men's deaths; and upon this glad day I will be neither judge nor hangman. An ye were the devil, I would not lay a hand on you. An ye were the devil, ye might go where ye will for me. Seek God's forgiveness; mine ye have freely. But to go on to Holywood is different. I carry arms for York, and I will suffer no spy within their lines. Hold it, then, for certain, if ye set one foot before another, I will uplift my voice and call the nearest post to seize you."

"Ye mock me," said Sir Daniel. "I have no safety out of Holywood."

"I care no more," returned Richard. "I let you go east, west, or south; north I will not. Holywood is shut against you. Go, and seek not to return. For, once ye are gone, I will warn every post about this army, and there will be so shrewd a watch upon all pilgrims that, once again, were ye the very devil, ye would find it ruin to make the essay."

"Ye doom me," said Sir Daniel, gloomily.

"I doom you not," returned Richard. "If it so please you to set your valor against mine, come on; and though I fear it be disloyal to my party, I will take the challenge openly and fully, fight you with mine own single strength and call for none to help me. So shall I avenge my father with a perfect conscience."

"Aye," said Sir Daniel, "y'have a long sword against my dagger."

"I rely upon Heaven only," answered Dick, casting his sword some way behind him on the snow. "Now, if your ill fate bids you, come; and, under the pleasure of the Almighty, I make myself bold to feed your bones to foxes."

"I did but try you, Dickon," returned the knight, with an uneasy semblance of a laugh. "I would not spill your blood."

"Go then, ere it be too late," replied Shelton. "In five minutes I will call the post. I do perceive that I am long-suffering. Had but our places been reversed, I should have been bound hand and foot some minutes past."

"Well, Dickon, I will go," replied Sir Daniel. "When we next meet, it shall repent you that ye were so harsh."

And with these words, the knight turned and began to move off under the trees. Dick watched him with strangely mingled feelings as he went swiftly and warily and ever and again turning a wicked eye upon the lad who had spared him and whom he still suspected.

There was upon one side of where he went a thicket, strongly matted with green ivy and even in its winter state impervious to the eye. Herein, all of a sudden a bow sounded like a note of music. An arrow flew and with a great choked cry of agony and anger, the knight of Tunstall threw up his hands and fell forward in the snow.

Dick bounded to his side and raised him. His face desperately worked; his whole body was shaken by contorting spasms.

"Is the arrow black?" he gasped.

"It is black," replied Dick gravely.

And then, before he could add one word, a desperate seizure of pain shook the wounded man from head to foot, so that his body leaped in Dick's supporting arms, and with the extremity of that pang his spirit fled in silence.

The young man laid him back gently on the snow and prayed for that unprepared and guilty spirit, and as he prayed the sun came up at a bound, and the robins began chirping in the ivy.

When he rose to his feet, he found another man upon his knees but a few steps behind him and, still with uncovered head, he waited until the prayer also should be over. It took long; the man with his head bowed and his face covered with his hands, prayed like one in a great disorder or distress of mind; and by the bow that lay beside him, Dick judged that he was no other than the archer who had laid Sir Daniel low.

At length he also rose and showed the countenance of Ellis Duckworth.

"Richard," he said, very gravely, "I heard you. Ye took the better part and pardoned; I took the worse and there lies the clay of mine enemy. Pray for me."

And he wrung him by the hand.

"Sir," said Richard, "I will pray for you indeed; though how I may prevail I wot not. But if ye have so long pursued revenge and find it now of such a sorry flavor, bethink ye, were it not well to pardon others? Hatch—he is dead, poor shrew! I would have spared a better; and for Sir Daniel, here lies his body. But for the priest, if I might any-wise prevail, I would have you let him go."

A flash came into the eyes of Ellis Duckworth.

"Nay," he said, "the devil is still strong within me. But be at rest; the black arrow flieth nevermore—the fellowship is broken. They that still live shall come to their quiet and ripe end, in Heaven's good time, for me; and for yourself, go where your better fortune calls you, and think no more of Ellis."

Conclusion

About nine in the morning, Lord Foxham was leading his ward, once more dressed as befitted her sex and followed by Alicia Risingham, to the church of Holywood, when Richard Crookback, his brow already heavy with cares, crossed their path and paused.

"Is this the maid?" he asked; and when Lord Foxham had replied in the affirmative, "Minion," he added, "hold up your face until I see its favor."

He looked upon her sourly for a little.

"Ye are fair," he said at last, "and as they tell me, dow-ered. How if I offered you a brave marriage, as became your face and parentage?"

"My lord duke," replied Joanna, "may it please your grace, I had rather wed with Sir Richard."

"How so?" he asked harshly. "Marry but the man I name to you, and he shall be my lord, and you my lady, before night. For Sir Richard, let me tell you plainly, he will die Sir Richard."

"I ask no more of heaven, my lord, than but to die Sir Richard's wife," returned Joanna.

"Look ye at that, my lord," said Gloucester, turning to Lord Foxham. "Here be a pair for you. The lad, when for good services I gave him his choice of my favor, chose but the grace of an old, drunken shipman. I did warn him freely, but he was stout in his besottedness. 'Here dieth your favor,' said I; and he, my lord, with a most assured impertinence, 'Mine be the loss,' quoth he. It shall be so, by the rood!"

"Said he so?" cried Alicia. "Then well said, lion-driver!"

"Who is this?" asked the duke.

"A prisoner of Sir Richard's," answered Lord Foxham; "Mistress Alicia Risingham."

"See that she be married to a sure man," said the duke.

"I had thought of my kinsman, Hamley, an it like your grace," returned Lord Foxham. "He hath well served the cause."

"It likes me well," said Richard. "Let them be wedded speedily. Say, fair maid, will you wed?"

"My lord duke," said Alicia, "so as the man is straight ——" And there, in a perfect consternation, the voice died on her tongue.

"He is straight, my mistress," replied Richard, calmly. "I am the only crookback of my party; we are else passably well shapen. Ladies and you, my lord," he added, with a sudden change to grave courtesy, "judge me not too churlish if I leave you. A captain in the time of war hath not the ordering of his hours."

And with a very handsome salutation he passed on, followed by his officers.

"Alack," cried Alicia, "I am shent!"

"Ye know him not," replied Lord Foxham. "It is but a trifle; he hath already clean forgot your words."

"He is, then, the very flower of knighthood," said Alicia.

"Nay, he but mindeth other things," returned Lord Foxham. "Tarry we no more."

In the chancel they found Dick waiting, attended by a few young men; and there were he and Joan united. When they came forth again happy and yet serious into the frosty air and sunlight, the long files of the army were already winding forward up the road; already the Duke of Gloucester's banner was unfolded and began to move from before the abbey in a clump of spears; and behind it, girt by steel-clad knights, the bold, black-hearted, and ambitious hunchback moved on toward his brief kingdom and his lasting infamy. But the wedding party turned upon the other side and sat down with sober merriment to breakfast. The father cellarer attended on their wants and sat with them at table. Hamley, all jealousy forgotten, began to ply the nowise loath Alicia with courtship. And there, amid the sounding of tuckets and the clash of armored soldiery and horses continually moving forth, Dick and Joan sat side by side, tenderly held hands, and looked with ever-growing affection in each other's eyes.

Thenceforth the dust and blood of that unruly epoch passed them by. They dwelt apart from alarms in the green forest where their love began.

Two old men in the meanwhile enjoyed pensions in great prosperity and peace and with perhaps a superfluity of ale and wine in Tunstall hamlet. One had been all his life a shipman and continued to the last to lament his man Tom. The other, who had been a bit of everything, turned in the end toward piety and made a most religious death under the name of brother Honestus in the neighboring abbey. So Lawless had his will and died a friar.